The floor wa
boards starting to creak

Mack Bolan was running out of time. He grabbed the nearest MAT-49. The gunmen had emptied the magazines, but they had to have spares on their bodies.

As the soldier pressed forward, the double doors opposite were thrown open. He dived to the floor, rolling away from the bullets that pursued him. The shooters wore the standard ES camouflage BDUs, and they were trying to acquire their target with AK-type assault rifles. Bolan was a sitting duck.

He did the only thing he could. He stayed prone and fired his weapons with calm deliberation, despite the fury of the bullets striking all around him and the nearness of death.

In minutes it was over. When the smoke cleared, the Executioner was the only survivor.

Other titles available in this series:

Retaliation	Mission: Apocalypse
Pressure Point	Altered State
Silent Running	Killing Game
Stolen Arrows	Diplomacy Directive
Zero Option	Betrayed
Predator Paradise	Sabotage
Circle of Deception	Conflict Zone
Devil's Bargain	Blood Play
False Front	Desert Fallout
Lethal Tribute	Extraordinary Rendition
Season of Slaughter	Devil's Mark
Point of Betrayal	Savage Rule
Ballistic Force	Infiltration
Renegade	Resurgence
Survival Reflex	Kill Shot
Path to War	Stealth Sweep
Blood Dynasty	Grave Mercy
Ultimate Stakes	Treason Play
State of Evil	Assassin's Code
Force Lines	Shadow Strike
Contagion Option	Decision Point
Hellfire Code	Road of Bones
War Drums	Radical Edge
Ripple Effect	Fireburst
Devil's Playground	Oblivion Pact
The Killing Rule	Enemy Arsenal
Patriot Play	State of War
Appointment in Baghdad	Ballistic
Havana Five	Escalation Tactic
The Judas Project	Crisis Diplomacy
Plains of Fire	Apocalypse Ark
Colony of Evil	Lethal Stakes
Hard Passage	Illicit Supply
Interception	Explosive Demand
Cold War Reprise	Jungle Firestorm

Don Pendleton's Mack Bolan®

Terror Ballot

A GOLD EAGLE BOOK FROM

WORLDWIDE®

TORONTO • NEW YORK • LONDON
AMSTERDAM • PARIS • SYDNEY • HAMBURG
STOCKHOLM • ATHENS • TOKYO • MILAN
MADRID • WARSAW • BUDAPEST • AUCKLAND

Recycling programs
for this product may
not exist in your area.

First edition March 2014

ISBN-13: 978-0-373-61567-4

Special thanks and acknowledgment to
Phil Elmore for his contribution to this work.

TERROR BALLOT

Printed in U.S.A.

Success is not final, failure is not fatal: it is the courage to continue that counts.

—Winston Churchill,
1874–1965

Fear is a powerful emotion, but there are limits even to fear. You can't be afraid of evil if you're too busy fighting it. There just isn't time.

—Mack Bolan

CHAPTER ONE

Paris, France

The terrorist's arm snapped between Mack Bolan's palms as the Executioner described a circle with his hands. The thug screamed through his black ski mask, and the Browning Hi Power he'd been holding fell to the marble floor of the opulent Banque de France.

The blackened clip-point blade of the big American's fighting knife slipped silently from the inverted sheath mounted to his shoulder holster, where it had been hidden under his three-quarter-length leather jacket. The knife's false top edge was sharpened.

As the terrorist turned to face Bolan, the weapon bit deeply into his opponent's flesh. A spray of crimson jetted from a severed artery. Bolan took him down with a sweep of his front leg, ramming the sole of his combat boot into the back of the enemy's calf. The terrorist toppled in a puddle of his own blood.

Bolan sheathed his knife. He was counting in his head.

When he got to *zero* he hit the floor, sliding across it as automatic gunfire burned the air where he had been standing.

Bolan rolled over, twisted and put his feet between him and the gunmen behind the ornate bank counter. The sights of Bolan's Beretta 93R machine pistol lined up in the gap. He flicked the selector to 3-round-burst mode, a motion as simple and fluid as the leap of a single, practiced impulse across its corresponding synapse.

The Beretta spit flame through its custom-built sound suppressor.

The trio of 9 mm hollowpoint rounds skipped across the surface of the bank counter and sheared off pieces of a ski mask. Beneath the acrylic fabric was skin, flesh, muscle and bone. The gunman—believed to be part of the ES—squawked something wet and surprised before he dropped his Kalashnikov assault rifle.

LES ÉTRANGERS SUPPRIMENT—known to INTERPOL as ES—was "Foreigners Remove" loosely translated. This was the first fact Hal Brognola had related to Mack Bolan when the big Fed, director of the Special Operations Group, had placed a scrambled call through Bolan's secure satellite smartphone.

Brognola was one of the few human beings alive who knew that the man now carrying Justice Department identification declaring him to be Matthew Cooper was, in fact, Mack Samuel Bolan. The SOG counterterrorist professionals based at the Stony Man Farm in Virginia answered to Brognola, who answered only to the President.

As for Bolan, he answered only to himself…but when Brognola asked for his help, Bolan would agree to undertake the mission—as long as it was something that he thought needed to be taken care of.

"This ES is one of several antiforeigner terrorism groups active in France," Brognola had explained through the scrambled link. "It's often difficult to tell the rabble-rousers, the street gangs and the ethnic enclave enforcers from the terrorist and paramilitary groups, but our friends in INTERPOL and on the ground in France have been working up a dossier on ES for some time.

"They've stayed in the background for the last several years, building their base and recruiting street muscle, but there have been some high-profile attacks lately, tied to the election. That's what has the President concerned.

"France is electing their new president," Brognola stated. "That president will in turn appoint a prime minister."

"And the National Assembly and the Senate of France make up Parliament," Bolan had told him. "Why the French civics lesson?"

"Sorry, Striker," Brognola said. "I've spent all morning working behind the scenes to influence congressmen and senators. The usual politicking here in Wonderland. Talking down becomes an occupational hazard."

"I get that."

"The national election for France's president is a major power-position," Brognola explained. "As you can imagine, whoever wins is endowed with a great deal of influence on foreign policy. Right now the election boils down to a two-way call. It's either going to be Leslie Deparmond, an ultraradical nationalist, or Henri Gaston."

"Which one is the Man rooting for?" Bolan asked.

"Gaston has the nominal support of the United States," Brognola said. "He's a moderate who those in the halls of power believe will play ball with us. Deparmond, on the other hand, is a radical. He's vowed to rid France of foreign influence and, given the serious problems the French have with immigration pressures, anti-immigrant sentiment is running high.

"You remember the Paris riots a few years back in which hundreds of cars were burned. That was the first hint the rest of the world really had that some areas of France's major cities had become no-go zones for the French authorities. Their citizens are screaming for something to be done to contain the influence of non-French groups moving into the country. They're ripe for a leader who caters to that sentiment."

"'*Ausländer raus,*'" Bolan said in German. "'Foreigners out.' A rallying cry for skinheads and other neo-Nazi gangs in Germany and elsewhere."

"It does smack of that," Brognola agreed. "And the election has been complicated by a series of high-profile terrorist attacks by the ES, half of them targeting public places, the other half specifically going after rallies in support of Gaston."

"The folks in international intelligence figure ES is acting as street muscle for Deparmond?" Bolan asked.

"It looks that way."

"Are you saying I should pay Deparmond a visit to cut the head off the snake?"

"Absolutely not," Brognola stated. "The French won't hear of it, and even INTERPOL doesn't want to risk overplaying its hand. There are no links between ES and Deparmond. Not that we can establish with actual evidence. If there are shadows, we haven't found them yet.

"If we go after Deparmond directly, we'll cause an international incident, which will produce the opposite of what the Man wants in France, that being a government friendly to us and our interests, or at least willing to work with us to a mutual benefit."

"Nothing?" Bolan asked. "No thread at all? That's unusual, isn't it?"

"It is. Aaron—" Aaron "the Bear" Kurtzman, head of the cyberteam at Stony Man Farm "—and his team usually dig up at least some backdoor links. Nothing that will hold up in the legal arena but enough to paint the targets for us. So far we haven't found any.

"There are two possibilities. One is that Deparmond is very smart or very cautious. He has conducted himself in a way that has prevented any connection between ES and himself, perhaps operating exclusively through a personal intermediary somewhere near the top of the terrorist power structure."

"Or he's not linked at all," Bolan said. "The ES could simply be attacking Gaston because they want Deparmond to make good on his promises."

"We've considered that," Brognola said. "Striker, the ES is a large, powerful, well-equipped and well-trained organization. Clearly they've been laying their plans for a long time before finally going active. Half of the actions that haven't targeted Gaston have been made to look like the work of foreign gangs.

"Spray-painted anti-French slogans, or mottoes associated with immigrant street factions, have been found at the scene of the crimes. The French media is going berserk. They're not sure who to blame, and they're spinning bizarre conspiracy theories left and right. This is muddying everything."

"What do we have on the ES hierarchy specifically?"

"Their leader is a guy named Gerard Levesque," Brognola said. "He spent years with the Basques and half a dozen other splinter groups. He's more mercenary than terrorist, and while he's probably no fan of foreign competition, we have no reason to believe he cares about Deparmond's cause specifically.

"Chances are that Deparmond's people, if in fact he *is* involved, have put together a financial package for Levesque. Money is all the reason he needs to put his people into the fight. Some of them may be true believers, of course. We don't know. But their strikes in Paris and other French cities make the Basques look cute and cuddly. Levesque has learned well from his time in the political terror trenches. He sends his men in armed to the gills, and kills without hesitation."

"And the play?"

"We've put together a priority list of targets," Brognola told him. "It's a safehouse network used by the ES and Levesque. You need to hit them in order of priority. Aaron and his team will feed you real-time intel as they get it concerning any more terrorist operations initiated after you arrive. You're going to hit them full force, as fast as you can."

"And if the presidential election is disrupted in the process?"

"Then it will be."

"So we're fighting for the future impact on American interests and the United States' allied status with France. Not for justice in French politics."

"Correct," Brognola replied. "Is that a problem?"

"No. But if I uncover a snake pit, I'm not going to let it lie. I'll do what I can to safeguard the Man's interests in France, but if stopping the terrorists means I have to upset the French authorities, I'm going to do it. And if their election process is rigged or otherwise corrupted, that's going to expose that, too."

"The Man trusts your judgment, Striker. As I always do."

"Is Jack available?" "Jack" was Jack Grimaldi, Stony Man's ace pilot and Bolan's close friend.

"He's in North Africa on another mission. You're flying commercial this time around. Good hunting, Striker."

THAT HAD BEEN less than twenty-four hours earlier. Brognola, through the Farm's mission controller, Barbara Price, had arranged for Bolan's equipment, weapons and a rental car to be waiting for him at a Paris warehouse.

More important, Brognola had immediately begun running interference for Bolan with the French government, essentially clearing the way for an armed counterterror operative not under their control to work on their soil.

This type of arrangement never went over well. Bolan was prepared to meet significant resistance, up to and including naked opposition. He trusted the big Fed to smooth it over after the fact, even if Bolan had to break a few things along the way. It wouldn't be the first time.

No sooner had the Executioner gotten his bearings in Paris—a city he had visited before—than the call had come in on his satellite smartphone. A terrorist contingent declaring itself to be with the ES had taken over the Banque de France in downtown Paris. They had taken hostages but made no demands other than to order all police away from the building. They had subsequently released an order that Henri Gaston, the moderate presidential candidate, be delivered to them for "crimes against France."

Bolan had simply parked his rental car beyond the police cordon, flashed his counterfeit Justice Department credentials to the outraged cops at the barricades and strolled toward the bank. He was wearing his black combat BDUs under his leather jacket, but they would pass for civilian clothing as long as no one looked at him hard or noticed his predatory gait.

A quick visual survey was all he had required to determine that there were no guards outside the building. He had gambled then on speed and decisiveness.

He had walked in the door, crept up on the first enemy sentry he could find and dug his fingers into the man's right clavicle from behind, spinning him. As the terrorist brought his hand up reflexively, Bolan had broken his arm. The rest was a messy smear already behind him.

The terrorists opened up on full auto from where they hid behind the counter.

Bolan rolled, his motion not particularly hurried, into the shelter of an alcove. There were two to choose from on either side of the entryway. Again he counted in his head.

Brognola had said that the terrorists were disciplined and well trained. Their initial fusillade had lasted long enough to exhaust the 30-round magazines in their AK-type rifles. But smart shooters would have held back at least a man or two, preparing to aim and fire at the resistance they were sure was coming.

Bolan snapped up his pistol and leaned out from the shelter of the alcove, adjusting the selector switch to single shot.

He did not fire. In the fraction of a second he waited, he observed a pair of security mirrors facing the cameras set high in the walls behind the counter. That made it too easy. He could see what was coming even before they got to him.

The enemy was a half beat off, probably thrown by the lack of return fire. When the two terrorists popped up at either end of the bank counter, Bolan could hear the distinctive sound of Kalashnikov magazines being dropped and swapped by the other shooters. He would have to deal with those in turn.

He put a single bullet through the eye of the terrorist on his left, then swiveled and shot the one on the right through the bridge of the nose. Only then did Bolan dart back under cover. He had seen what he needed to see, however.

There were no hostages secured near the front of the bank.

"Fire!" came the command in French, screamed by someone behind the counter. A hail of 7.62 mm gunfire chipped away at the alcove, raising a cloud of plaster dust and pelting Bolan with debris.

Bolan wore a green canvas war bag under his leather jacket. He holstered his Beretta, then plucked a pair of M61 fragmentation grenades from the bag. Each bomb had an effective killing radius of five yards, with casualties virtually assured within fifteen yards. Some fragments might disperse as far away, Bolan knew, as two hundred yards or more.

He armed the bombs, tossed them and ducked back into cover. Almost casually the soldier put his middle fingers over his ear canals.

The twin explosions ripped through the counter, driving fragments of it and other shrapnel from the fragmentation grenades through the bodies of the men sheltered there. The screams of agony sounded inhuman.

The Executioner was up and moving in a crouch, tracking right and left for targets. To the rear of the counter area was an arched and fluted doorway, as overbuilt as everything else in the building. Bolan knew that archway was a choke point and that more ES forces would be staged behind it.

Aaron Kurtzman had transmitted the layout of the bank directly to Bolan's secure smartphone. If Bolan were in charge of holding hostages in the bank, he would have done just what the ES had done—establish a perimeter of shooters in the main foyer of the bank while guarding the hostages deeper within the building. That way they were secure from any grandstand plays—such as driving an armored vehicle through the front—the purpose of which was to deploy a tactical team.

He imagined the French authorities were still debating what to do, if they weren't spending their time screaming for official intervention through government and international channels. Bolan did not envy Brognola his job.

Bolan took another grenade from his war bag. He did not pull the pin. Instead he simply rolled the lethal egg across the marble floor through the archway. It *thunked* heavily before skittering through the opening.

The ploy worked perfectly. Bolan would no more throw a grenade in the vicinity of hostages than he would shoot them himself, but the terrorists couldn't know that. When the first ES gunman broke from cover to scramble for what he thought was a live grenade—no doubt thinking to throw it back the way it had come—Bolan pumped two rounds from his Beretta through the shooter's neck.

The second man was cagier. He tried to check the arch by exposing only one eye and the barrel of his gun. That was all the target Bolan needed. A single shot blew away the back of the terrorist's skull after tunneling through the eye socket.

The soldier pushed through the archway low and fast. The corridor beyond led to offices and the bank's safe-deposit box area. At the end of the corridor, the hallway made a hard right turn, which led to the vault area. If he had to guess, Bolan would put the hostages in the vault, guarded by reserves.

He shifted left as gunfire tore up the wall behind him. They were shooting from within at two levels, high and low. That would be a man standing and another crouching, from the same angle. They were shooting blind, or they would have corrected their fire by now. Bolan knelt and scooped up the grenade he had rolled in earlier, careful to watch the corridor beyond him.

Bolan waited for the lull in the shooting that he knew had to come. Then he leaned forward just enough to assess the deposit box room. There were two gunmen inside, each wearing military surplus camouflage fatigues and black ski masks. This was the standard uniform of the ES.

No hostages.

The Executioner pulled the pin on the grenade, let the spoon fly free and counted. Then he lobbed the grenade through the doorway.

"Merde!" one of the gunmen shouted, before the frag grenade blew both men to hell.

Bolan dropped the 20-round box magazine from his Beretta. It clattered to the floor, but not before he was already slamming a fresh magazine into the butt of the gun. He let the weapon lead him down the corridor.

The door at the end of the corridor, which fronted an anteroom to the vault, was closed. Bolan planted the sole of his combat boot against it and smashed it open. The gilded wood splintered under Bolan's assault. The flimsy frame was not meant to provide a significant barrier; it was for decoration only, shielding the vault room with its heavy safe from eyes that might be offended by its functional form.

He dropped to one knee as soon as he cleared the opening.

One of the skills Bolan had developed through years of combat was the ability to observe the threats before him and burn a flash picture of the scene in his mind. It was much like a popular memory game played by children and adults: given only a moment to record the details, the player had to act on his or her memories in choosing sectors of the game board.

Bolan, on seeing the tableau spread in front of the vault, instantly memorized the positions of each of the hostages in the room. He noted one discrepancy while fixing the relative locations of the ski-masked shooters in the room. Two of them held human shields as targets, their arms wrapped around the necks of a man and a woman, respectively.

Bolan dealt with those first. The gunmen had left large portions of their heads exposed behind their shields. The Executioner snapped a 9 mm bullet into the eyeball of one and the forehead of the other. He was still moving, still shooting, when return fire erupted, but as he pushed off laterally and fell to his side, he was already extending the Beretta and tracking to the right.

The sound of the suppressed Beretta was like the muted clapping of hands. The echoes of the Kalashnikovs were still ringing in Bolan's ears when the last of the terrorists collapsed. That left only the anomaly.

The ES gunmen were smart; Bolan could give them that, despite their tactical mistakes. One of the shooters had removed his mask and the camouflage jacket of his fatigues. He was sitting behind the other hostages with

a borrowed suit jacket on his lap to cover his camouflage pants.

But Bolan had seen the man's combat boots and
noted his disheveled, sweat-plastered hair. Before the
holdout shooter could bring up the pistol in his hand,
Bolan sat him back down with a 9 mm round to the
chin. The bullet dug a furrow through the man's jaw
and continued through, exiting the base of his skull.

One of the female hostages started to scream.

Mack Bolan couldn't blame her. Things were going
to get a lot bloodier before they got better.

He was only getting started.

CHAPTER TWO

The street gangs of Paris had a long history. Bolan considered his briefing with Brognola as he observed the activities on the street. He was trying to get the lay of the land around the first of the ES safehouses on his priority list. The neighborhood in which he found himself mirrored decaying neighborhoods the world over. He could practically smell the unemployment, the predation, the corruption, the social dynamics that spilled across the pavement and radiated from the doorways of the shops and flats he passed.

It was no coincidence that the ES would choose to place its safehouse network in the midst of the worst areas of Paris. The no-go areas—all but forbidden to police intervention—were well-known to the international media. Certain ethnic enclaves were firmly in control of the various immigrant groups that had flooded France in the past several years. The street gangs were an outgrowth, an extension of these, as many and varied as those who made up their ranks.

Bolan had read up on the factions. The Blousons Noirs, or "Black Jackets" of the 1950s and 1960s, had been ersatz greasers, an imitation of the motorcycle youth culture of the United States at the time. These biker gangs had long ago been supplanted by much more vicious, much more businesslike gangs. Their goals were power, money and gratification, not always in that order.

Zulu gangs, composed of Black Africans and their allies, were among the fiercest. Posses of Antilleans and Africans had started to take over the streets in the 1990s. They were not well organized, but street brawls among opposing gangs had become a fixture of life in Paris's worst sectors in the ensuing decades.

Into this mix had been added the neo-Nazi skin-head gangs, as well as other violent factions and pressure groups. Every faction that rejected the status quo and the "establishment," every antisocial mob of violent would-be predators, had a gang to back them up. The lawlessness, and the culture of "don't get involved" that this would breed, would appeal to the ES, allowing them to function with relatively little interference.

It also made the prospect of going in and rooting out the entrenched ES gunners that much more intimidating to the local authorities. It would take a force the size of an army to go into a neighborhood like this and challenge the ES on its own turf, where the citizens would look the other way.

France simply did not have those types of resources available, not with its government suffering the financial woes occurring in every nation during a difficult global economy, and not with its available law enforcement already dealing with the often pressure-cooker scenarios at the neighborhood level. These issues had spread from the cities proper, including Paris, to the outskirts or suburbs.

The riots that had ripped through Paris and then spread across the nation in 2005 were a prime example. Gangs consisting mostly of North African youths had created a state of emergency for months, burning cars and public buildings as the violence spread to low-income-housing projects across France. Almost three thousand people were arrested, and nine thousand cars burned. Nearly 130 police and firefighters were injured or wounded during the unrest.

The problems weren't confined to Paris, Bolan knew. In Marseille in southern France, drug-running gangs had become so great a problem that politicians were calling for military intervention. Gunmen equipped with automatic weapons were regularly dueling in the streets, taking lives from among their opposing numbers and from the ranks of innocent bystanders.

Poverty and ethnic discrimination had created a thriving black market in France, which operated hand-in-glove with the gangs and their criminal activities. Drugs flowed freely. The most popular of these were the staples: heroin, cocaine, ecstasy. There was plenty of marijuana to be had, as well, although in Bolan's experience, its traffic was rarely as violent as that for coke and heroin.

The address of the safehouse put it on the third floor of a squalid flat wedged into a block of crumbling concrete buildings, most likely another public housing project. The streets were narrow and cluttered with cars that appeared to be barely mobile. Two were burned-out shells that would never drive again—playground equipment now to the street children climbing over the blackened frames. Bolan brought his rental car to a stop, leaned out the driver's window and beckoned to a group of teenagers.

"Does anyone want to make some money?" he asked in French.

One of the youths stepped forward. "What for?" the kid asked.

Bolan waved a pair of twenty-euro notes in front of the youth's face, then took one back and tucked it in the pocket of his jacket. "One now," he said. "One if I come back and my car is still here. With all its parts still attached."

"Yes. We will watch it."

Bolan nodded. He stepped out of the vehicle and the teens immediately made themselves at home, sitting on the hood and climbing over the roof. He waved one of them away from the trunk and popped it, removing his M16 with its attached grenade launcher. He expected that to raise some comment, perhaps even alarm, but the teenagers simply took it in and looked away.

The street people were more inured to the constant violence here than even Bolan would have guessed. He filed that for future reference and pulled the weapon's single-point sling over his body.

He brought up the rifle, tugged on the magazine and slammed the plunger back with the side of his hand. The Farm's armorer, John "Cowboy" Kissinger, had fitted the charging handle with an extended L-shaped bolt that mimicked the bolt on a Ruger or Kalashnikov rifle.

That made it possible to operate comfortably with one hand, compared to using two fingers to claw it back. Kissinger had also fitted a smooth ergonomic pistol grip to the weapon, which was a nice touch. It reduced fatigue over long periods of carrying and operating the weapon.

The soldier made his way to the tiny alley between the nearest buildings. The flat he wanted was the one on the left. It was a gray graffiti-covered structure that reminded him of a cinder block on one end. Public housing, most likely, or something that had started that way. It did not take long for a decent neighborhood to turn into a jungle, for predators and crime to claim or reclaim the land on which the buildings stood. Turf was everything in environments like these.

Bolan stopped at the end of the alley, just short of the corner of the building. The block of flats backed against another building very similar to it, creating a canyon between the two through which the residents had strung clotheslines. The pavement between the buildings was littered with debris and stinking piles of garbage. There were dark streaks beneath the windows on the upper floors. The tenants were dumping their trash out the windows.

The smells of refuse and urine were overpowering. Bolan flattened himself against the wall inside the alley and crept as close as he dared to the corner. Then he took a small dental-type mirror from inside his jacket and poked the round lens past the wall.

It was as he had suspected. A metal landing resembling a fire escape was visible on the rear of the building, rickety iron steps leading up to it. Sitting on the steps, smoking a cigarette and balancing a sawed-off double-barreled shotgun in his lap, was a young man in a black leather jacket.

The watch cap on his head could easily have been a black ski mask rolled up, but that didn't matter. Whether an ES terrorist or a gang member, it was a good bet he wasn't merely a neighborhood punk out for a quick drag. Not with the shotgun evident for everybody to see.

There was no point in waiting. Bolan walked out from cover, his right hand on his M16, his left hand up. He spoke in English. "Hey. Is this where I buy drugs?"

The sentry spit out his cigarette, leaped to his feet and pointed his shotgun. Bolan ducked back behind cover. The shotgun boomed, coating the soldier in concrete dust as the shot ripped fragments from the corner of the building.

"Because I heard," Bolan said calmly, cupping his free hand beside his mouth, "that this was where you buy drugs—"

The second shotgun blast struck six inches below the first. Bolan immediately whipped around the corner and charged the shooter, who was struggling to break open his now empty weapon.

Bolan smacked him in the face with the butt of the M16. The shotgunner grunted and went down, blood spurting from his nose.

The sentry had time to look up accusingly at Bolan before the soldier stomped him in the face with one combat boot. The impact of boot to head and thereafter head to pavement was enough to put him out cold but not to kill him. Under other circumstances Bolan would have taken the time to search him and secure his wrists with a pair of zip-tie cuffs, but the shotgun blasts would have already warned anyone inside the upstairs flat. Bolan could not afford to put himself in so vulnerable a position. Instead, he hurried up the stairs.

No sooner had he pressed himself against the wall by the door to the upper flat than automatic gunfire punched through the rotting wood. Well, that settled that. Anyone willing to draw down on the door with a full-auto weapon was neither law enforcement nor law-abiding citizen.

Stony Man had pegged this location as an ES safe-house, but if Bolan were instead taking down a cell of heavily armed criminals unrelated to the terrorists, he would lose no sleep over it. He risked rapping on the door with the back of his hand and was rewarded by another spray of fire. A fist-sized hole grew in the flimsy door.

Bolan took a canister grenade from his war bag, pulled the pin and popped the bomb in through the hole.

The gas grenade blew, filling the flat with noxious fumes—fast acting, fast evaporating. The gunman inside fired his weapon empty, leaving a random pattern of exit holes in what little was left of the door. Bolan took the opportunity to take a deep breath, lower his shoulder and splinter the remains of the barrier. He plunged through the entryway and into the flat's living area.

Inside—amid the swirling cloud of gas—he nearly fell on top of the gunman, who wore camouflage pants and boots. The man, maybe thirty, was shirtless and struggling with a chopped-down Krinkov-style AK. Tears were streaming down his cheeks, generated by the gas.

Bolan's own eyes were watering, but the gas was already dissipating through the open doorway. The stuff was like watered-down CS, a lightweight formula Cowboy Kissinger had recommended for dealing with crowd control…and for distractions like this one.

The two of them were not alone. Doors led from the living area to what seemed to be a bathroom and—visible through a hanging bead curtain—a squalid bedroom. The kitchenette area was open to the living room, delineated by a waist-high half wall of cracked drywall and flaking paint. In the kitchen area, another gunman was raising a Kalashnikov rifle, as he cursed in French.

The Executioner snapped up his M16 to his shoulder and triggered a single shot that punched through the gunman's right cheek. The exit wound sprayed crimson.

Bolan swiveled as the first gunner, the one with the

Krinkov, had managed to slam a fresh magazine into his weapon. There was no need to fire another shot; the shooter was well within kicking range. Bolan rammed the sole of his combat boot into the man's face. The blow snapped the man's head back. His skull cracked loudly on the wooden floor.

The soldier caught movement in his peripheral vision and threw himself to the floor, pushing the M16 before him. The target he was searching for was not long in coming.

The shooter in the bedroom was a man covered in tattoos, wearing only a pair of boxer shorts. While Bolan would never sympathize with terrorists and murderers, he did feel a pang of mild empathy. Nobody liked being caught unaware in the middle of a nap.

The would-be napper had an old .45-caliber pistol in his hand, a 1911-pattern that was coated with rust so bad Bolan could see it from the floor. The gunman shot wild and wide, his rounds whistling past his target a good three feet above the soldier's position. Bolan, for his part, simply stroked the trigger of the M16 in 3-round-burst mode, squeezing a total of nine shots that he guided in a horizontal arc. The rounds, parallel to the floor, chopped the gunman's ankles out from under him.

He was screaming when he hit the floor. Bolan put one more round through the top of his adversary's head, silencing him forever.

Bolan heard the steps behind him just in time to twist his body into a supine position. He was bringing up the muzzle of the M16 when he checked his fire.

"Do not move," said the man with the snub-nosed .38.

Bolan was half a step ahead of the newcomer. His visitor was wearing a rumpled shirt and slacks under an equally rumpled trench coat. An old felt fedora was perched on his head, and his tie was at half-mast. He could not have been more stereotypically a law enforcement officer if he were trying to invoke the imagery, and Bolan was willing to bet this man deliberately cultivated the look. The identification badge around his neck bore the letters DCRI.

Direction Central du Renseignement Intérieur was French for the Central Directorate of Interior Intelligence. Bolan knew the agency. Founded in 2008 by the merger of two other intelligence agencies, the DCRI was a surveillance, counterterror and counterespionage outfit.

"Cooper," Bolan said, using the cover identity on the identification Brognola had provided him. "Justice Department."

"Inspector Alfred Bayard," said the man with the .38. "To say your reputation has preceded you, Agent Cooper, would be an understatement."

"I'm sorry?"

"A moment, please," Bayard stated. He stepped aside as several special tactics soldiers in black gear, balaclavas and helmets, wielding FAMAS assault rifles, entered the room. They had been behind the inspector the entire time. Bolan's estimation of Bayard—who had chosen to take point with a revolver before a squad of men with automatic weapons—rose quite a few notches.

The tactical unit spread out through the flat. One entered the bedroom and began calling out instructions into a radio clipped to his vest. Another checked the man Bolan had knocked unconscious and began to secure his wrists with a pair of plastic cuffs. These were not unlike the ones Bolan carried, but of a heavier gauge.

"I would appreciate it," said Bayard, whose French

accent was thick but not impenetrable, "if you would please stop pointing your gun at me, Agent Cooper."

"The feeling is mutual," Bolan replied. He eased himself very carefully to his feet, mindful not to make any sudden moves. Deliberately he rested the M16 in a patrol carry position, the muzzle pointing at the floor in front of his left foot.

Bayard very slowly lowered his pistol and returned it to the holster in his waistband, where it was positioned for a cross draw. Taking a walkie-talkie from the pocket of his trench coat, he keyed it and gave the all clear in French.

"I take it these men are supposed to be members of Les Étrangers Suppriment," Bayard said. "No doubt you informed them of their rights under the French legal system before you began beating them senseless or shooting them dead. We took into custody at the base of the stairs a dazed young fellow who appears to be among the lucky survivors."

"Inspector Bayard," Bolan began, "I'm—"

"I am more than aware of why you are here," Bayard interrupted. "Your Mr. Brognola has been on the phone with the Central Directorate—and several other levels of the French government and its intelligence community—through the night. Specifically he was paving the way for what I gather is a—what is the English phrase?—a 'one-man wrecking ball.' And now I behold that one man."

Bolan raised an eyebrow. "Do we have a problem?"

Bayard snorted. "I am told, if I do have a problem," he said, "I am to hold my tongue about it, lest I disturb sleeping giants who rest well above my grade of pay. Does that sound familiar to you?"

"It does at that," Bolan agreed. "I'm here to get to

the root of the ES problem. I have the appropriate authorization to do so and nominal permission from your government to operate independently on French soil."

"That is a grenade launcher," Bayard said, jerking his head at the M203 mounted to Bolan's assault rifle. "It does not get much more independent than hurling explosives through the air. Your Mr. Brognola warned us that your methods are what I would consider extreme. Your President has spoken to our president. I always wonder how tense such conversations must be."

"Just so we understand each other," Bolan said.

"Explain to me your purpose here," Bayard requested. "My men have reported no contraband apart from the weapons these men carry. No explosives. No incriminating documents. No computers containing nefarious terrorist plans."

"I'm shaking the tree," Bolan explained.

"You are...what?"

"The ES has a network of safehouses in the city," Bolan explained. "Any of them could lead to what the terrorists are doing. Some of them won't. When you don't know which branch you want, you shake the tree until something falls out."

"How delightfully imprecise," Bayard said. "No doubt your approach to problem solving is unique in this way. Tell me, Agent Cooper, if you sought a needle in a haystack, would you burn down the haystack? Or merely find and torture the needle's comrades until someone gave him up?"

"I don't torture people," Bolan said. There was steel in his voice now; he had seen too many good people tortured and mutilated. "I fight for *justice,* Inspector. My methods are direct. They aren't immoral."

"Give me a good reason not to arrest you."

"I don't need one," Bolan replied. "And you know it. If you didn't, you wouldn't be here already. How did you find me?"

"Even in this place—" Bayard spread his arms, obviously referring to the desolate neighborhood in which they stood "—a man with a grenade launcher is noticed and remembered. And as bad as things are here, automatic gunfire is also noticed."

"Nobody's response time is that good in a ghetto," Bolan replied.

"No." Bayard eyed Bolan as if reevaluating the soldier's intelligence. "No, they are not. My men and I have been on alert, running a patrol through what we thought were the most likely target areas, knowing you would make your presence known. Mr. Brognola seemed to think a great deal of cleanup would be required wherever you went. I can see he did not underestimate that need."

"He doesn't sugarcoat things. Neither do I."

"What do you mean?" Bayard asked.

"I mean that obviously you wanted to intercept me, because you don't like the thought of me wandering around alone in your city."

"Right again," Bayard said. "I've come to offer my... assistance. As liaison."

"Or babysitter. But that's all right, Inspector. As it happens, I could use a guide. I want to get the lay of the land around here. Get to know this neighborhood and the others like it. Knowledge such as that could make the difference between success and failure. Are you up for it?"

"It does not matter," Bayard said, "because I am required by my government to offer you whatever assistance I may. Understand one thing, Cooper. I resent your presence here. I resent your cowboy ways. I resent the violence that I know you will bring to my city."

"Sometimes violence is the only way," Bolan told him. "Predators understand little else."

"Until I have seen differently, Cooper, I will categorize you as one of those predators."

"Do what you have to do, Inspector."

"I shall, Agent Cooper. I shall."

CHAPTER THREE

Bolan sat in the passenger seat of Bayard's unmarked Peugeot, watching through the open window as he had done through his own vehicle, while the inspector drove. They had no specific goal. The soldier was marking time until he judged he could mount another safehouse raid. While logistically there was nothing stopping him, politically he needed to let the dust from the bank assault settle. He had received several secure text messages from the Farm already, warning him to go easy for a few hours.

The director of the DCRI in Paris, Jean Vigneau, had been flagged in Stony Man's systems. He was a person of interest in no less than three corruption investigations. Nothing had stuck, and no hard evidence had been found, but flags like that remained in the system precisely as a forewarning for future missions. The ground on which Bolan stood could indeed become considerably more hostile if Vigneau decided to target Bolan.

So much for hitting them full force and as fast as he could. Still Bolan understood the exigencies of the field. Brognola was, according to Price, once again on the phone with French authorities, smoothing feathers and reassuring them that the heavy-handed tactics of one Agent Matthew Cooper were justified under the circumstances. Once Bolan got the all clear, he would pull out all the stops again.

Complicating matters was the fact that Agent Cooper's previous exploits in France were a matter of record to the intelligence agencies here. Bolan was starting to wonder about the longevity of his cover identity, given that Cooper was developing a storied history to rival Bolan's own. It had been that cumulative effect that had prompted him to forego previous aliases, such as the Mike Belasko moniker.

Bayard had been huffing and growling his way through the past several blocks, scowling at the people they saw on the streets while pausing to peer into the darker alleys. He kept up a pretty good running commentary on the players in the neighborhood, but it was obvious he thought little of Bolan and wanted just as little to do with him.

The soldier's impression was that Bayard was a man of duty, who did as he was told as a point of principle, but who had his own opinions about right and wrong that he was not afraid to express.

"There, that one," Bayard said, pointing. He was hunched over the wheel of the Peugeot because the car was simply too small for him.

The inspector was a big, rawboned man with thinning gray hair, wire-framed glasses and angular features. His jaw was covered in short white beard stubble. He smelled of cigarette smoke, although he had not indulged while in the car with Bolan.

He was pointing to a dark-skinned man in an oversize leather coat, whose gold chains were so numerous they had to have been weighing him down. The man had shoulder-length dreadlocks and wore louvered white sunglasses.

"That one?" Bolan asked.

"He is Razor Fayini," Bayard said.

"That's original."

"But deserved," Bayard replied. "Fayini runs prostitutes for a gang leader named Roelle. The gang is called "Suffering" in English. It is a brutal Zulu gang, fighting for dominance with one of our locally grown criminal syndicates, La Mort Rouge."

"The Red Death," Bolan said, raising an eyebrow. "Really?"

"They are criminals." Bayard waved a hand dismissively. "They are not known for their modesty or their good taste. Their territory ranges for several blocks north and west."

"And Razor?"

"A lieutenant to Roelle. He carries a folding razor blade, what the British call a 'cut-throat.' He enjoys using it. It is his primary means of maintaining discipline. If you entertain a whore who has scars on her face, you find yourself with one of Roelle's women, courtesy of Fayini's tender ministrations."

"I'll keep that in mind," Bolan stated.

Bayard brought the Peugeot to a stop across from the alley's mouth. He reached across Bolan and took a pair of field glasses from the glove compartment, which was empty of everything else except—Bolan blinked—an actual pair of gloves. The inspector brought the binoculars to his eyes and adjusted the focus knob.

"Something is going on," Bayard said finally. "I do not like it. He moves with purpose and speed."

"And?" Bolan asked.

"And if you knew Razor, you would know this is unusual. Never have I seen him on the street before noon and never in a hurry. He and his blade will catch you when he finds the time, they say on the street. I have never seen him so agitated."

"Something to do with his gang?"

"It can be little else. He answers to Roelle and to no one else."

"What do you have on Roelle?" Bolan asked.

"Almost nothing," Bayard admitted. "Not a country of origin, not a real name. Always he uses others, like Fayini, to shield him. Of course we know he is behind the group's operations. But we cannot prove it, and he has access to skillful lawyers. Drug profits have their advantages. His gang is powerful, violent and well equipped. I have lost two men in attempts to insert covert operatives within Suffering. The second of these was tortured to death."

Bolan considered that. "If something odd is going on, let's get after it."

Bayard lowered the binoculars and looked at him. "But Roelle is not connected to your terrorists," he said. "This I can guarantee. I know his group very well. Terrorism is not among their interests. Money is their motivator."

"But this is unusual," Bolan replied. "You said so. If it's not related, it's not related. But if we stick a wrench in whatever Razor Fayini has going on, it just might help some people. And that's worth doing."

Bayard blinked as if looking at Bolan for the first time. "You would do this?"

"Make your play," Bolan said. "I'll back you."

"Very well." Bayard nodded. He removed his revolver from the holster in his waistband, checked it and replaced it. "Follow me. Bring your many weapons. You may as well bring the assault rifle. We might need it."

"What about my penchant for heavy-handed tactics?"

Bayard jerked his chin at the assault weapon as Bolan hefted it. "Rarely do I leave my vehicle in the darker

alleys of this place. You will find backup is slow to respond here. We may require heavy hands. I am neither
stupid nor suicidal."

"Fair enough," Bolan said.

The pair exited the vehicle, which Bayard locked,
before making their way across the street and taking
up positions on either side of the alley's entrance. Bolan
cast a glance back at the vehicle. His own car—which
the local kids had, in fact, kept unmolested for him—
was now parked at the DCRI satellite branch from
which Bayard operated. No doubt the inspector had
quietly ordered his lab boys to go over the vehicle for
prints and any other clues they could find. Bolan could
not fault the man for that. Bolan would have done the
same if their roles were reversed.

"You are thinking I should pay some local urchins
to watch my car?" Bayard asked.

Bolan shot him a look. "You saw that?"

"I see everything, Agent Cooper," Bayard said. "At
least if it happens around here. And I have agents watching the car from the other block." He shot a glance
down the alley. "Razor is entering a doorway on the
left, at the end."

"Then let's go knock," Bolan suggested.

Bayard nodded. The two men entered the alley, the
inspector walking slightly behind Bolan.

"I would prefer this not turn into a bloodbath if we
can help it," Bayard said.

"Can we expect your agents watching the car to back
us up if we need it?"

Bayard paused. "If they were not imaginary."

Bolan had suspected as much from Bayard's tone
earlier. Well, it wasn't his car to worry about. But it
did mean, if they encountered resistance, in whatever

Fayini and his gang were up to, that resistance would need to be dealt with decisively.

"I may not be able to prevent a mess," Bolan said. He jacked open the M203 grenade launcher and thumbed in an M576 buckshot round.

Bayard nodded, eyeing the launcher warily. As they had at the alley, he took up a position opposite Bolan next to the door Fayini had used. The alley was close and fetid, smelling of urine and rot.

Bolan looked to Bayard. The Frenchman nodded once more. "Go," he said.

Mack Bolan reached out and rapped on the door with the back of his hand. The hollow-core wood rattled under his knuckles. The door would come down easily under his combat boot.

There was an answering shout in French. Bayard yelled something back. As Bolan opened his mouth to speak, automatic gunfire began spraying them both with splinters. The rounds chewed through the door as if it were paper. The gunman quickly went dry.

Bolan was about to reach into his war bag and remove a stun grenade when Bayard swiveled. Lowering his shoulder, the Frenchman drew his .38. He was crashing through the damaged door before Bolan could tell him otherwise.

Nothing to do now but back the inspector's play.

Bolan brought his assault rifle to his shoulder and stepped through the opening. The door had come apart in pieces, leaving jagged debris behind. As he took in the room beyond, Bolan had an impression of threadbare, broken-down furniture crammed in a room strewn with garbage and empty liquor bottles.

The inspector was ahead and to Bolan's left. Bolan swung the barrel of his assault rifle to the right and immediately found targets. Several dark-skinned men, wearing gang colors and tattered jeans, were scrambling for an assortment of automatic weapons on the coffee table in front of them. Bolan saw a MAC-10 and an old Polish submachine gun amid the loose rounds of ammo and other weapons.

The Executioner triggered his grenade launcher.

Nearly two dozen 24-grain metal pellets ripped the gunmen to pieces as the grenade launcher belched death. Bolan immediately triggered follow-up bursts from the assault rifle, dropping to one knee to lower his profile. Several of the gunmen fell.

Bayard's .38 barked. A man screamed horribly. Bolan followed the sound and dumped another bullet into the wounded man's head, snapping his skull backward. Bayard winced and went to the floor.

The inspector's instincts were good. There were two more shooters, rushing into the room from the attached kitchen. Their weapons were identical to the one that had unleashed the opening salvo, at least to Bolan's experienced ear. They were French MAT-49 subguns, developed in the late 1940s and produced for the next thirty years until they were phased out in favor of the FAMAS assault rifle.

"Bayard!" Bolan shouted as he dumped the M16's magazine and swapped it with a fresh one from his war bag.

"I am not hit," Bayard said from the floor. "Are you clear?"

"Clear. How long do we have?"

"Before police response? All the time in the world."

"No," Bolan stated. "Before the gunfire brings more like these."

"Considerably less. But they will not be so eager for a few minutes."

"Then we better check while we can," Bolan told him. "What did we walk into here?"

The inspector pushed himself to his feet. The front of his trench coat was stained with something dark and wet that was not blood; he frowned and started to rub at it, then thought better of it. Looking around the wreckage of the ground-floor flat, he opened his mouth to speak, then he stopped.

"None of these men is Fayini," he said. "They wear his gang's colors, but he is not here."

The pair scanned what was left of the apartment. Bullet holes pocked every wall. There was at least three weeks' buildup of garbage, including fast-food wrappers; trash bags of lumpy, rotten leftovers; a few empty boxes of 9 mm Parabellum ammunition and even piles of pizza boxes.

Bolan shook his head at that; it was universal among flops and safehouses of this type. There was also a lot of broken glass, much of it colored. Bolan bent and inspected one of them. He found himself holding a colored glass tube the length of his forearm. It reeked of hashish. There was evidence of other narcotics around the flat, as well.

The two men surveyed the rooms, checking the corpses to make sure there were no gunmen still alive. The place was small; there were few places a man could hide. Bolan did check the bathroom and the filthy tub, sweeping the equally filthy plastic shower curtain aside with the barrel of his rifle. There was nothing in the tub except an inky black ring that looked as if it were made of tar.

The tile, the commode and the tub itself might once

have been porcelain, but they were now ash gray, covered in mildew and oily grime. The smell in the bathroom was so bad it nearly made Bolan's eyes water.

Returning to the living area, the soldier made a more thorough search of the corpses. He photographed each one with his sat phone, which was programmed to upload the photos immediately to the Farm for cross-referencing.

His search of the dead men's clothing wasn't very helpful. He found a cheap folding knife, which he discarded, and some extra magazines for the MAT-49s. There was also a magazine for a weapon not in evidence, but that looked like it belonged to a Browning Hi Power. He thumbed the rounds out of the gun and dropped it on the floor. Then he set to emptying the submachine-gun magazines before field-stripping the MAT-49s themselves.

"What are you doing?" Bayard asked.

"There's a lot of hardware here," Bolan replied. "Enough that I'm not comfortable leaving it lying around for the neighborhood kids to play with." He removed the firing pin from first one, then a second weapon, tossing the pins into one of the leaking bags of garbage on the floor. Then he scattered the parts of the guns around the room.

"You do not care much for preserving evidence, do you, Agent Cooper?" Bayard did not sound overly troubled.

"We both know you're not going to bring a forensic team into this no-go zone and pore over a bunch of dead gangbangers for clues."

"True enough." Standing in the hallway, Bayard spread his arms to indicate the flat. "Where could he have gone? We have searched everywhere. Fayini entered and disappeared. What was his mission?"

"What sort of cell phone surveillance are you running locally?" Bolan asked.

"The usual," Bayard replied. "We have reasonably good coverage and keyword recognition throughout the city. The gangs use prepaid phones and satellite. The prepaids are no problem. Satellite, much problem, but these are expensive and require a line of sight to the sky. Unlike your own very special phone, it would seem."

Bolan did not respond to that, other than to note that Bayard had to have been watching him closely as the soldier took his photos. "So if Roelle wanted to communicate something to his people quick, he'd probably send a runner. And if it was big, his runner would be somebody high up the chain. Like his trusty lieutenant."

"Yes," Bayard said. "It would be Fayini."

"So he hurried here with a message and then turned to vapor."

"A passable theory."

"And that message is something Roelle didn't want intercepted." As he spoke, Bolan was feeling his way along the rear wall of the flat. The bullet holes had ripped large craters in the drywall. He paused, turning his cheek to the wall.

"There's a draft here," Bolan said. "Another room on the side of this one."

"Then Fayini left through a hidden exit—"

"Found it," the soldier announced. He pressed in along the seam he had felt in the rear wall. A section of the plaster facade, its edges disguised by a network of cracks, moved smoothly inward. Bolan let his assault rifle lead the way as he pushed through, expecting at any moment to begin taking enemy fire again.

An upholstered chair, the only furniture in the small

room, moved six inches across the filthy shag carpet on the floor.

Bolan snapped a savage kick into the chair, knocking it over. The tunnel beneath looked like an old sewer access. The wide eyes that looked up at the soldier from just above the lip of the tunnel belonged to Razor Fayini. He disappeared, either jumping or sliding down. Bolan threw himself into the tunnel, trusting that Fayini would break his fall.

The bone-cracking heap in which they landed brought shouts of pain from Fayini, who had absorbed Bolan's two-hundred-plus pounds of weight. Bolan drove the butt of his assault rifle into his quarry's head, but the man ducked and managed to snake a hand into his pocket.

Steel glittered in light reflected from above. Fayini pushed himself against the ladder, his left arm cradling his chest and what were probably a couple broken ribs. The straight razor in Fayini's hand weaved back and forth before the gang lieutenant in practiced, fluid motions.

He might be injured, but he was far from harmless. Bolan noted the shadow above as Bayard loomed at the tunnel entrance. No doubt the inspector's .38 was trained on Fayini from up there, but killing the man would tell them little.

Fayini's eyes drifted to something on the tunnel floor.

Bolan stepped back two paces before letting his own eyes fall. There was a short stack of photographs on the grimy concrete.

Kids. The pictures were all of children.

Razor lunged.

Bolan batted the folding blade away from himself

with the barrel of his rifle. He followed through with a strike from the weapon's butt against Fayini's face, driving the man into the side of the sewer tunnel. The folding razor hit the ground, and Bolan kicked it away. He planted the toe of his combat boot in Fayini's face for good measure.

With the criminal stunned, Bolan scooped up the photographs. He thumbed through them.

"What is that?" Bayard called down.

"Every one of these is a scared-looking kid with today's newspaper held in front of him," Bolan called up. "There's writing on the back. Looks like each one has a surname on it. Some have first and last names."

Bayard reached down. "Let me see." He took the photos from Bolan.

Fayini began to reach for his waistband. Bolan kicked him savagely in the ribs, doubling him over, before pushing him onto his stomach and patting him down. He found a small Beretta .380 pistol. It was an old model, its blued finish worn off almost completely.

Bolan unloaded the gun and tossed it away, then strapped Fayini's wrists together with plastic zip cuffs from his war bag.

"I recognize this name," Bayard said. His voice was very soft, as if he had just realized something horrible. "'Aguillard'… Cooper, this is the name of a highly placed enforcer in the Red Death."

"Coincidence?" Bolan asked. He began to climb up the ladder, hooking an arm under Fayini's to pull the captured man with him. The gang member writhed in agony as he was dragged up through the sewer opening.

"One perhaps. But I know more of these names. Moubray. Pagel. There are others. I do not recognize them all, but the ones I do are known to be members of the Red Death."

"Then these kids…" Bolan said. "These are ransom photos."

"Mon Dieu," Bayard said. "Roelle has kidnapped the children of his rival gang. We are close to the Red Death territory here, farther away from Roelle's headquarters. It would explain sending Fayini with dispatch to this location. The men here were perhaps to act as messengers, as well, or perhaps to provide—what is the term you use?—muscle for Fayini, protection as he distributed his photos.

"Were I Roelle and using such diabolical methods, I would make sure these photographs circulated far and wide in this neighborhood. I would want not only the Red Death but also the residents and the customers for my drugs to know I had done this. 'Mess with Roelle, and he will steal your children and hold them, to do with as he will, unless you comply.'"

"What will the Red Death do?" Bolan asked. "Will they respond?"

"They may well," Bayard said. "They may attack Roelle's headquarters, the one place he would keep the children. It is where he is strongest. A block of flats north of here, completely owned by Roelle and controlled by his people. It is yet another area of the city the police dare not tread too heavily."

"So it's going to be a slaughter," Bolan said. "With a bunch of innocent kids trapped in the middle."

"The two gangs have grappled with each other for a long time. It is not surprising that Roelle would take decisive measures. But this…"

"Do we know for certain he would hold the kids on his home turf?" Bolan asked.

"Anywhere else would be too vulnerable," Bayard said. "He must know their location will be ferreted out. There are spies and informers everywhere. No location could be kept secret for long. Once known, only strength will preserve it."

"Will he kill those children?"

"He will," Bayard said. "Without hesitation. And to show that he is merciless. The parents of the children will understand this, too. They will know that their only hope is to fight back, to take the children from Roelle if they can."

"We're taking an awful lot on faith here," Bolan pointed out.

"I know this man," Bayard said. "As well as any law enforcement officer in Paris can know him. I understand the gangs and how they think. You are on my 'turf,' as you put it, Agent Cooper."

"Then we'll dump Fayini at the DCRI on the way to Roelle's headquarters," Bolan said.

"This is not wise. We will be caught in the middle of a war."

"Story of my life."

CHAPTER FOUR

"The entrance is there," Bayard said. He took the compact binoculars away from his face and handed them from the driver's seat to the passenger seat. Bolan took them and adjusted the little focus knob, surveying the end of the block.

"When the riots happened," Bayard began, "the burning cars? The worst was not far from here. You are deep in the heart of one of what your media would call 'ethnic enclaves.' There will be no help for either of us here. And we do not know for certain that Roelle is holding the children in this location."

Bolan swiveled in his seat to face the inspector. "You just got through telling me—"

"I know," Bayard said. "I am trying to discourage you. Cooper, I cannot enter that building. There are certain political realities involved here. I will not stop you if you go. And I am in your debt for supporting me in my suspicions. Fayini has been caught in the act of assaulting law enforcement officers and will now see at least some time in prison. I admire what you are doing."

Bolan held up the photos. "I'm going in."

"And as I said, I will not stop you. But I risk running afoul of delicate political agreements already in place if I step into Roelle's lair and insert myself in this gang war. These are matters left to the denizens of this place." He spread his hands. "I have been thinking as we drove here. You will stop nothing, Cooper. Even if you rescue the children, the gangs are vast. And if all of them fell dead at once, others would take their place."

Bolan shook his head. "I'm going in."

"But, honestly, as fierce as you are, as well armed as you are, do you believe you can triumph against an army?"

"I can," the Executioner said, "and I will." He stepped out of the Peugeot. Over his shoulder, he said, "And Bayard—the car. You didn't have agents watching it."

The Frenchman paused. "No," he said.

"They leave your car alone because you take payments from someone. You're a known quantity. You look the other way, and they don't hassle you when you make an appearance down here. One of those 'delicate political agreements' you were talking about."

"It is true."

"Were you ordered to assist me?" Bolan asked. "Or did you sniff me out in order to stop me?"

"Everything I told you about that was true," Bayard said, bristling. "As was everything I said and believe about your methods. I am a dedicated man, Agent Cooper. I believe in the law. I believe in maintaining peace. But a man must face reality. A man must understand that there are things that cannot be changed, not by one man alone."

"That's fear talking. You should be better than that."

"Perhaps. But fear is a powerful emotion, Agent Cooper. It keeps a man alive."

"There are limits to fear," Bolan told him. "And you're wrong, Inspector. One man can change the world if he tries. If he fights past the fear. If he goes forward, toward the danger."

"Goodbye, Agent Cooper," Bayard said. "I cannot

say it has been a pleasure knowing you so briefly. But you are a brave man."

Bolan nodded and walked away.

The inspector was a complex man. That complexity complicated matters somewhat. He would have to consider that on the other side of this particular mission was mercy.

Right now those kids needed Bolan. They might be the children of vicious gang members, but they were innocents. They did not deserve to be puzzle pieces in some gang war. To say nothing of what might happen to them if the Red Death showed up and tried to dig them out. Caught in the cross fire, they would be killed just to spite the enemy gang.

Bolan was disappointed, but not surprised, that Bayard was staying out of the fray. It was just as well. Bolan could not be entirely certain where the man's loyalties rested if the official admitted to being on the take. There was a toughness to the inspector that Bolan could sense, something that men of action could simply intuit in each other. That made Bayard's surrender to the status quo that much more disappointing. Clearly the man could do better if he chose.

Well, the man would live his life as he believed he should, and nothing Bolan did would make Bayard's choices for him. At least, thanks to Bayard, the Executioner knew what was going on and could do something about it. His mission to intercept terrorism in Paris and to ferret out whatever was going on with the elections was no more important than the lives of innocent children.

The neighborhood block was typical of World War Two–era public housing: multiple stories high, of crumbling brick, with a roof that looked like slate but could be anything else. Bolan had entered the address of the building into his smartphone and now checked the message that he had gotten from the Farm. No plans on file in network, it read. Satellite photos cross-referenced to news article, attached.

A brief news report from the previous year was appended. The overcrowded six-floor tenement, described as a "courtyard building, with no street access," had been the scene of a fire. The layout had proved to be a problem to fire crews and rescue efforts, although Bolan got the sense from the copy that these had been slow to arrive and halfhearted in execution.

Residents of the tenement were described as "North Africans, many of them migrant laborers." Whether the composition of the building's residents had shifted as Roelle consolidated his hold there, or whether he had long been there and the report was spun to be politically correct, Bolan didn't know or care. It fit with what he knew already.

He would likely catch hell from Brognola for the ruckus he was about to raise, but that was just something the big Fed would have to accept. Brognola knew, and Bolan made sure to emphasize from time to time, that he was an autonomous operative, not an employee of the Sensitive Operations Group or the Farm. Not anymore. Those ideas had died with…well, with someone he would remember for the rest of his life.

The only visible entrance or exit to the block-sized tenement was a metal door at the east end. There were no sentries evident on the street. Bolan scanned the windows on the end of the building. They were clouded with years of grime. In broad daylight he couldn't see any shadows moving within, but there would be gunners there.

They would be wondering who on earth had the audacity to approach, openly and without fear, and think he would not be seen. It was entirely possible that, since solidifying their control here, no one had dared confront Roelle in his lair. And why would they? It would be suicide to try. A man like Roelle ruled his fiefdom through fear and violence. He counted on that fear, needed it, traded in it.

Bolan brought up the M16 with its M203 slung beneath the barrel and jacked a round into the launcher.

Slow response time. The watchers at the windows should have seen that, should have hurried to react to it. Bolan was prepared to dodge, to duck and weave; he was expecting heavy resistance and had come loaded for bear.

The perimeter of the building would hold nothing of value. Predators, when building their redoubts, did so on an instinctive level. The hostages and anything else to which Roelle assigned high value would be buried deep in the tenement, somewhere heavily guarded, behind multiple barriers. That meant there was nothing to stop Mack Bolan from punching a hole in the outside wall.

Time to open the dance.

Bolan's 40 mm grenade hit the door and blew it inward with a good chunk of the building. The blast reverberated across the street facing the tenement. Sheets of glass, blown to fragments, rained down onto the pavement at Bolan's feet.

The return gunfire started.

The first few shots were tentative, as if the gunmen were trying it on for size. Bolan was already close enough to the building that they couldn't hit him without hanging from the windows and shooting straight down. Bolan cleared the rubble of the door with a burst from the M16 against his shoulder.

He emerged from a cloud of dust, surveying the layout before him. With no floor plans available through the Farm—which was not uncommon, as many municipal networks did not include digital building plans—he would have to improvise as he went. That meant clearing each room to which he could gain access, working his way from floor to floor. But on the periphery of the tenement it was not necessary to search every cell and chamber of the maze, for again, the valuable hostages would be secured deeper within the building.

The hallway stretched before him. Doorways punctuated the corridor on either side. The walls were probably plaster, given the construction's apparent age. The load-bearing walls would be concrete, he suspected. Overall the interior of the building would afford more protection from bullets than modern drywall construction, but that was not saying much.

Doors opened on the left and the right ahead. The soldier wondered if perhaps Roelle's gang were coordinating with phones or two-way radios; the attack was well timed. From both sides the shooters aimed their MAT-49 submachine guns in Bolan's direction, unleashing long, undisciplined bursts that went well high. Plaster dust was ripped from the ceiling above.

Bolan dropped to one knee, aimed carefully and punched a 3-round burst through the neck of the left-hand gunner. Swiveling smoothly Bolan punched another 5.56 mm round through the forehead of man on the other side. The right-hand man unloaded his weapon into the floor, tearing up stained carpet and the hardwood floor beneath, as his finger clenched on the trigger.

Bolan kept going.

The dead men had dark skin and sported a variety of tattoos. Their clothes were a mixture of expensive and threadbare. Criminal chic. One of the dead men sported lines of ink on his neck, trailing across the corpse's throat, spelling "Suffering" in French. Bolan was definitely in the right place.

At the end of the corridor he headed toward the stairwell, then stopped, turned and hit the floor. From the chambers at the opposite end, a trio of gunmen piled into the hallway. It didn't matter whether these men, too, had been detailed to watch the street or were simply on hand when the gunfire erupted. Bolan raked the barrel of his assault rifle from left to right, stroking the trigger repeatedly, blowing the shooters' ankles out from under them. When they hit the floor, he perforated them from front to back, aiming for their skulls, putting them down for good.

Up once more, the soldier snapped a kick into the fire door at the stairwell. The door, like the walls on either side of him, was covered in layers of graffiti. The effect was almost psychedelic. As he walked, his boots crushed fast-food wrappers, broken glass and aluminum beer cans.

The Executioner almost missed the trip wire.

The silvery thread was stretched taut across the third step leading up. On one side the wire was attached to a bent nail rammed into the wall. On the other side, a soup can just large enough to accommodate a vintage World War Two pineapple grenade was duct-taped to the wall. The wire was wrapped around the body of the grenade, beneath the spoon; pulling it free of the soup can would release the spoon and cause the grenade to detonate on the stairs.

The booby trap was incredibly dangerous. There was

no way a grenade that old could be considered reliable. It might not explode at all when the spoon released, or it might explode simply while sitting there. The presence of the trap told Bolan much about what to expect of the gang leader and his people.

The soldier heard steps in the corridor behind the fire door. Bending, he snagged the trip wire, pulled the grenade free and watched the spoon clatter to the steps. He yanked open the door with the grenade still on its wire. The other end of the wire snapped under the force of his pull.

He was not sure where the gang members in the hallway had been hiding, but it didn't matter. He saw their eyes widen as he whipped the grenade through the open door. Then he slammed the fire door shut and hurried up the stairs.

The explosion behind him made his ears pop and threw the fire door into the stairwell. The door was stained black and red. It steamed as it gouged a black line in the floor.

Bolan checked the second and third floors as he ascended the stairwells. These were blackened and scorched from within, their corridor doorways sealed with plywood nailed haphazardly across the burned openings. Evidently the fire that had occurred here had taken out a portion of the building, and repairs had not been attempted. He moved on.

His adversaries were waiting for him on the fourth floor. As Bolan entered the corridor, they rushed him, coming at him in a wall of running, screaming, shooting hostiles. There was no logic or reason to it; they were as likely to shoot one another—as they ran the corridor with guns blazing—as they were to hit their target. Bolan saw the charge and hit the floor on his back, pointing the M16 between his legs. He emptied his weapon's magazine, neutralizing at least four of the oncoming gunmen as their rounds scorched the air above his face.

The fifth man fell on him.

The blow to Bolan's ribs nearly drove the breath from his lungs. The gang member was an enormous man, with black skin and a shaved skull. He wore black leather pants and a vest with no shirt. His weight pressed against the soldier, pinning the M16 to Bolan's chest, making it impossible for him to draw the Beretta 93R from its shoulder holster.

He didn't need to.

His right hand found the Desert Eagle in its Kydex inside-the-waistband holster, where it rode on his strong side behind his hip. He drew the weapon and, with the heavy triangular snout of the hand cannon pressed against his body and angled into the enemy, Bolan pulled the trigger.

The .44 Magnum round was muffled beneath the gang member's body, but the effect was immediate. The huge man jerked as the round tore a tunnel through his abdomen and out his back, digging through vital organs, ending his life with brutal finality. Bolan shoved off the dead man, rolling the corpse aside, feeling the moist warmth where the man's blood had begun to soak through the front of Bolan's shirt.

It was a familiar feeling.

There were more shooters, hiding in the doorways farther down the hall, and they opened up on the big American as he tried to rise to a sitting position. Bolan simply carried his motion through, diving into a forward roll, popping up at the end of the roll to come up on one knee with the Desert Eagle leveled. The enormous weapon thundered, rocketing heavy hollowpoint slugs through the space between him and the gunmen.

He did not target the door openings. He targeted the walls near the openings, where he calculated the gunmen would duck behind cover. The slugs bored through the plaster, leaving craters in their wake, splashing the doorways with flecks of blood and bone.

Screams echoed through the corridor.

The Executioner walked the blood-soaked hellscape that he had created, his combat boots leaving crimson prints in the creaking wooden floors. Something moved in the doorway to his right. He swiveled and triggered a round that cored through the throat of the gang member as the gunner tried to level an ancient bolt-action rifle at him. The weapon hit the floor.

Bolan reached the end of the hallway, emerging in the opposite stairwell. Below him the access had been blocked by a pile of old metal bed frames. Above, numerous warnings in French had been spray-painted on the walls in bright red against splotches of white. Obviously he was closing in on Roelle's sanctum, or at the very least nearing something the gang held more securely than the lower levels.

The door leading into the next floor was rigged with a bomb.

Bolan saw it easily; it was meant to be visible, to dissuade intruders. Several sticks of what looked like ancient, sweating dynamite were simply taped to the fire door. Wires led from the dynamite to an electronic detonator of some kind. Unless Bolan missed his guess, the detonator was a modern mercury switch. That made a certain sense. Opening the door would disturb the switch and detonate the explosives.

Bolan examined the bomb closely. He was keenly

aware of the crosshairs on the back of his neck. An enemy could easily take advantage of his focus on the bomb to attack him from behind, if he were not careful. He listened intently as he examined the bomb. Any sound from the stairs below him would prompt him to brace the new threat.

He reloaded the Desert Eagle almost without thinking about it. His muscles were well trained by years of experience. The weapon was an extension of his body; firing it was as natural to him as breathing and required almost as little conscious consideration.

Bolan reached out and plucked the detonator wires from the dynamite.

It was as simple as that. He shoved the fire door open, letting the Desert Eagle lead the way through the gap—and nearly fell to his death.

The floor was gone. The fire that had burned the lower floors had apparently been worse on this end of the building. Where the corridor should have been was a blackened chasm, beneath which the lower floors were visible. Across the gap, where the floor had not been destroyed, a makeshift barrier of wooden pallets and scrap lumber had been erected. There were sentries here, more gang members, and when they saw Bolan, they began firing with a mixture of submachine guns, pistols and rifles.

Bolan fell back to the stairwell long enough to holster the Desert Eagle and slam a 40 mm grenade into his launcher. Then he charged the doorway again, stopping short of the gap in the floor, launching the grenade from the M203 into the center of the opposition. The high-explosive round detonated, pelting the vicinity with wooden shrapnel. Screaming, burning men fell from the barrier to the floors below, tumbling through the holes burned in floors and ceilings.

Bolan expended a 30-round magazine from his M16 through the broken barrier, hoping to keep down any enemies who might be lying in wait. When there were no answering shots, he reached into his war bag and produced his folding grappling hook.

The hook was simple. It was two pieces of titanium nitride–coated steel held together with a swivel pin at the center of both limbs. He pulled the swivel pin, turned the limbs to ninety degrees and fed out the high-tension line attached to the bottom of the hook.

There was not a great deal of line, but there was enough for his purposes. He tossed the hook through the gap and then yanked it back, waiting for it to catch on the scrap of the badly damaged barrier. When he could tug on the hook with all his weight and not dislodge it, he judged it safe. Finding an exposed beam above his head, he knotted the opposite end of the line.

The soldier hoisted himself over the gap hand over hand, using the line to suspend himself. When he reached the opposite end, he reloaded the M16, let it fall to the end of its sling and drew his silenced Beretta machine pistol. He believed he was close to his goal now. He had spent enough time in enemy lairs to get a sense for such things.

The corridor ended in a pair of ornate wooden doors that had obviously been brought in from somewhere else. The hinges were cobbled together, crooked and jury-rigged. The portrait of a man had been painted on both doors. He was dark-skinned, with gold teeth and incongruously blue eyes. Long dreadlocks flowed from his scalp to his shoulders. The face on the twin paintings bore a beatific grin.

It could only be Roelle. The portraits brought to mind the giant paintings of dictators in third-world nations. Bolan paused long enough to make sure the doors were not rigged. Heavy chains and padlocks through the iron handles of the doors secured them to each other. Bolan stepped back, switched the Beretta to his left hand and drew the Desert Eagle with his right. He triggered the weapon several times, shattering the padlocks and sundering the chains.

Bolan lashed out with his boot, kicking in the doors, smashing the flimsy internal lock that was all that remained to hold them together. The hall into which he emerged was, he surmised, overlooking the courtyard at the center of the tenement. It had probably been created by smashing out several of the interior walls and then paneling the walls to create the impression of continuity.

Massive banners that were simply painted sheets had been hung on the walls. They bore French slogans and, frequently, the word *Souffrir*. At the center of the hall was a massive enclosure made of hastily nailed wood and chicken wire. Within this enclosure were maybe twenty children, huddled together under the watchful eye of several gang members acting as guards.

At the rear of the hall was a gilded antique chair. It looked like a throne, which, Bolan realized, it most assuredly was, and was occupied by the man Bolan recognized from the paintings on the doors.

It had to be Roelle.

"Kill him!" the gang leader barked in French.

CHAPTER FIVE

Bolan charged the throne, dodging gunfire from the Kalashnikov and FAMAS rifles held by Roelle's guards, until Bolan was close enough to try for a flying tackle. The shooters couldn't target him if their leader was in the path of the gunfire. Roelle raised one hand and snapped his fingers.

The gunmen standing at the perimeter of the room immediately trained their weapons on the enclosure full of children.

Bolan stopped in his tracks.

The gang leader's face split into a wide grin. He had several gold teeth. His dreadlocks were thick and long, larger than in the paintings on the double doors. He wore what appeared to be a silk caftan. His chest was layered with gold chains; heavy gold rings adorned each of his fingers. His hands were thick and gnarled. They were the hands of a boxer.

"They fire," Bolan said, "and you die."

Roelle's smile grew wider. "English," he said. "And American! Are you CIA, little man? Always meddling everywhere, your Central Intelligence Agency. What is your business here, American?"

"Those kids are keeping you alive," Bolan said. "Free them, and I'll walk out of here."

"Do you believe there is any chance you will leave here alive, American?" Roelle's smile turned feral. "I will bring you down like a dog. I will torture you for days. You will beg me to kill you. I command an army, American. And you walk in here as one man?"

"Your army didn't stop me from getting this far," Bolan pointed out. "And I'd say you're a few men shorter than you started this morning."

"Enough," Roelle roared. "No man defies me, American. All Paris fears *Souffrir*. They fear me because they know I will bring them suffering and pain. Pain is power. Pain is truth."

"You're a coward," Bolan said. "A coward who hides behind children as human shields."

Roelle frowned. "I will give you the same honor I have given all of my enemies," he said. "The honor I will grant the leaders of—how would you say?—the Red Dead."

"Death," Bolan said.

"Yes," Roelle replied. "Death." He snapped his fingers again. "Shamir! Tehrab! Put your blades to him!"

Bolan was watching carefully; he saw Roelle's eyes cut to each of the henchmen as he called their names. Shamir was a brute, well over six feet tall, wearing camouflage fatigue pants, combat boots and a mesh shirt. Like Roelle, he styled his hair in dreadlocks. His face was covered with a heavy beard that also obscured his neck.

Tehrab, by contrast, was a head shorter. Where Shamir was thickly muscled, Tehrab was sinewy. His hair was close cropped, his face heavily scarred. One of his eyes was a dead, milky white. He wore black jeans, faded and ripped. His black tank top clung to him tightly.

Both men held well-used machetes.

"Put your guns on the floor," Roelle said. "I will let you live if you can defeat these two."

No you won't, Bolan thought. But there was nothing to be gained by arguing now. He unclipped the M16 from its single-point sling and placed it on the floor at his feet. The Beretta and Desert Eagle joined it a moment later.

"I like mine better," Roelle said. He held up his own weapon, a .50-caliber Desert Eagle plated in gold. He waved the barrel of the pistol almost casually. "Begin. Save your life if you can."

Bolan drew his combat knife.

The two gang members circled him. Bolan bent his knees, dropping into a half crouch, his blade in front of his body. He was at a distinct disadvantage wielding his knife. The machetes were eighteen inches at least, and the men who held them would be experts in their use.

As Bolan moved slowly in an arc that paralleled his opponents, Bolan ran the numbers in his head. The children were his priority, and if necessary, he would give his life to free them. He could see no way, however, to make that exchange. Yes, he could give his life but not in a way that would free the hostages.

Besides Roelle and his .50-caliber pistol, there were four other gunmen stationed around the room, all of them obviously stamped out in whatever metaphorical factory supplied *Souffrir* with Zulu gun-thugs. Two of those shooters were within Bolan's line of sight, but the other two were blocked by the chicken-wire enclosure and the terrified kids within it. Bolan would not be able to draw a proper bead on either of them from where he now stood.

The bigger man, Shamir, attempted a deep, circular strike that cleaved the air where Bolan's collarbone had been a moment before. He slipped aside from that, stepping away, only to catch the edge of Tehrab's blade along his left forearm. The machete bit, but not deeply, and as it did, Bolan made the man pay for it. He brought his fighting knife's false edge up under the gang member's arm, slicing deeply, cutting in and around the arm. Tehrab screamed horribly. Blood splashed the floor.

Shamir was not impressed. Possibly this was not the first time Roelle had played this game with his men and his enemies. It was likely, in fact, that all concerned had seen knife fights of this type played out with bloody and predictable results. The huge man tried to carve a hunk from Bolan's flank, striking forward and laterally, his weapon almost at waist level. Bolan arched his back, avoiding the tip of the blade, and spread his arms wide as he stepped out and left.

There were two ways to fight a man with a blade. One, he could use his off hand to shield his body and, in the process, absorb damage with the arm that might kill him eventually from blood loss. Two, he could make an effort to keep his vital organs, his body's center line, out of the strike zone. It was not feasible to battle through Roelle's defenses and continue with Bolan's mission if he were spraying his own blood everywhere.

Of course, the foolishness, the fundamental stupidity, of a knife fight was that it was not possible to win every duel. Sooner or later the law of averages was bound to catch up with you, as Tehrab, likely scarred from previous knife battles, had just learned. The smaller man was effectively out of the fight, cradling his deboned arm and turning shark-belly pale as his blood soaked through his fingers.

All those thoughts flashed through Bolan's mind in an instant as he formulated his plan. He required precise timing for this to work; he also needed to know that every one of his shots would count. That meant the Beretta, with its custom sound suppressor attached, was not the best option. While accurate and reliable, the weapon's lighter 9 mm cartridge did not have the knock-down power he required.

Bolan's eyes went to the Desert Eagle on the floor.

He knew the weapon was primed to fire. He had placed it on the floor with the safety off and the hammer cocked, knowing he might need to scoop it up and fire it quickly. Now was the time to do that. He just needed to line up two very important variables.

"Stop dancing around and kill him!" Roelle shouted impatiently. "Or I will do it for you!" The gang leader gestured with his ostentatious pistol.

Bolan had used the .50 AE Desert Eagle himself on more than one occasion. He was dimly aware that the big, distinctive weapon, in all its calibers, was a favorite of television and movie producers. A gold-plated gun like Roelle's was a status symbol.

One rarely saw the fall of a third-world dictator that did not involve triumphant rebels waving around the elaborately engraved sidearms those tyrants invariably possessed. Roelle, who undoubtedly saw himself as Paris's crime lord and master, would carry his for the same reason.

While Bolan had no doubt that the monstrous gang leader had used his pistol to kill others, it was unlikely such a man would put in the time to master fast, accurate shooting with so heavy a round, at 300 grains. The weapon would be a handful to use on a quickly moving target, which the Executioner was about to become.

Bolan's own .44 Magnum Desert Eagle, and the man who wielded it, was a considerably different prospect.

The pistol had been action-tuned and mated to its custom-loaded rounds by the Farm's weaponsmith to provide optimum muzzle energy and accuracy. Shamir attempted to flank the soldier, which gave Bolan exactly the trajectory he needed.

The Executioner dived into a forward roll, still holding his combat knife. With a grunt of pain he absorbed the impact on his shoulder, coming up on one knee next to his temporarily discarded weapons, hurling his combat knife as hard as he could in Roelle's direction.

Snatching the Desert Eagle, Bolan popped to his feet, standing at full height, shot his arm forward as he turned his body into a classic target-shooting posture and pumped a single round from the .44 Magnum pistol through Shamir's left eyeball.

The 240-grain bullet exited Shamir's skull and struck the guard standing in line and beyond the machete-wielding corpse. Bolan turned and fired, not pausing to watch his next round take the second of the four guards in the face. He then raised his arm and angled the pistol down, riding out the painful recoil in his bent wrist, forcing himself to hold the weapon rigid despite the poor form.

His shots, angled high and down to clear the prisoner enclosure, struck the third and fourth guards. One took a round through the chest and fell as if poleaxed. The other was struck in the base of the neck on one side. He went down gurgling, drowning in his own fluids. The bullet had to have ruptured the subclavian artery as it cored through him.

Bolan couldn't stop, wouldn't quit, didn't dare cease his motion. Bolan rolled again and missed a left-handed slash from Tehrab. The man was ashen now and would probably die on his own if his wound was not treated.

He swung at Bolan again, unsteady on his feet, his eyes wide with dawning recognition that his body was failing him.

The children were screaming. A part of Bolan's mind noted that, adding to his urgency, prodding him to run for the perimeter of the hall so as not to put the hostages between Roelle and himself. The thunder of the gang leader's gold-plated pistol was not unexpected when it began.

Bolan had never intended to make a kill shot with a thrown knife while on the move at that distance. It was virtually impossible. But the knife had been accurate enough, and come hard enough, that it had forced Roelle to put his head down, fouling the gang leader's shots while Bolan took out the guards.

The soldier tumbled and landed on his back, bringing up the Desert Eagle in both hands, targeting the gilded throne. He would see to it that Roelle died in that chair—

But Roelle was not there. He was running across the space between his chair and the enclosure, shooting at Bolan as he ran. Before the soldier could draw a bead on his quarry, Roelle had reached a section of the chicken wire that only appeared to be attached to the rest. He peeled it back with one arm and, reaching in with a roar, emptying his gold weapon in Bolan's direction, he snatched the nearest cowering child.

As he did so, he tossed his pistol at his attacker. The weapon was empty, and the gang leader knew it. With both hands he ran with the child, back in the direction of his throne.

Bolan could do nothing but push to his feet and give chase. He rammed his Desert Eagle into his beltline as he ran past his other weapons, snatching up the Beretta and the M16 in separate hands, thrusting the Beretta back into its shoulder holster with muscle memory born of thousands of repetitions. Still running, feeling his heart hammer in his chest, he kicked open the hidden door behind Roelle's throne, which the gang leader had opened and closed in attempting his escape.

The door had been behind one of the wall hangings, but Roelle had ripped that free in passing. The tight hallway into which Bolan pursued him was some kind of maintenance manway, cluttered with exposed pipes that forced Bolan to duck and dodge lest he knock himself unconscious by colliding with one. The pipes also obscured his view of Roelle.

They were heading out of the building.

Bolan's sense of direction told him that much. They were on a direct course for the exterior of the tenement, several stories up, and there was nowhere to go....

The square of sunlight nearly blinded him. Roelle had opened a door to the outside and now stood on what Bolan surmised was a fire escape or similar landing. The square of light began to recede. Bolan raised the M16 and prepared himself for the difficult shot he would have to take.

The door closed.

Bolan poured on the speed. He hit the door with all his weight, smashing it open again. The sunlight outside, compared to the dim interior of the tenement and the darkened manway, dazzled him for a moment. On the fire escape below him, Roelle was already making access to the street level. His hostage, a hysterical girl of perhaps three years old, was tucked under one arm like a football.

Bolan raised the M16 once more.

Roelle was running. His forward motion would make

the shot that much more difficult. Bolan caught another figure approaching in his peripheral vision. Roelle saw it, too, and something about it forced him to stop short.

Bolan shot him.

The round punched a neat hole through the back of the gang leader's thigh. Roelle bleated, falling to one knee. Bolan slid down the fire escape's multiple levels, vaulting the landings and using the ladders like firemen's poles, until the soles of his combat boots were on the narrow street, and he was charging toward the would-be child-murderer.

"Drop that kid!" Bolan shouted. "Drop that kid or the next round will find the back of your head!"

Roelle turned, snarling. As if remembering something, he pivoted to whatever had caught his attention before.

Bayard stood there, his .38 pointed at the gang leader. His weapon belched flame, once, striking Roelle in his free arm. He shouted in pain and grabbed at the wound, dropping his hostage in the process. Bayard ran forward and scooped up the child, turning to put the rest of his body—and his revolver—between Roelle and the child.

"It is over," Bayard said. "You are defeated."

The gang leader dropped his head to his chest. On one knee he looked almost as if he were praying. The pool of blood beneath him was growing, but slowly. It would take time for his wounds to kill him. A hospital could save his life easily.

When Roelle raised his head again, it was to laugh.

Bayard almost flinched. He looked to Bolan, then up at the fire escape. Black smoke was beginning to pour out of the manway exit. Bolan saw it, too. The combat inside, the explosions, perhaps even the action of some unseen gang member who had chosen not to confront the soldier's invasion, had started a fire within the tenement.

"Watch him!" Bolan ordered. Before Bayard could protest, Bolan was back on the fire escape, pulling himself up the ladders, making his way inside once more. He nearly brained himself on a low-hanging pipe in the manway, but avoided it at the last minute, emerging once more in Roelle's main hall.

The smoke that was trailing through the manway and into the sky outside was coming from the corridor beyond the doors. He couldn't do anything about that now. The lock on the chicken-wire cage was easily smashed with the butt of his Desert Eagle.

Telling the children in French to hold each other's hands, he managed to form a chain of the hostages. At the head of that chain, he led the kids out of the hall, through the manway and then carefully down the fire escape. By the time he was on the street once more, he was fighting a cough. The smoke was thick above him.

Roelle's cackling echoed off the nearby buildings. Bolan listened for sirens, for movement, for any other sign that the battle in the tenement had drawn official attention. He detected nothing. Only Roelle's deep, sonorous laughter reached his ears.

"What have you to laugh about?" Bayard demanded. The girl he held was crying. He brought her to the others and began checking each one for injury, all the while keeping one eye on the gang leader.

"You have stopped nothing," Roelle said. "All know the name of Roelle and my organization. In a day's time twenty more will flock to my banner. In a week, fifty. You have saved the spawn of the Red Death, yes. Congratulations. They will grow to be adults and fight you themselves. You are in our territory. This is the way of suffering."

"We need to get the fire under control," Bolan said. "This block will burn out of control if we don't."

"Were I confident that only this fetid tenement would become ashes, I would let it do so," Bayard stated. He sighed. "I have made certain calls. Help is coming."

Bolan's head snapped up. Multiple vehicles were converging on their location. He put his back to Bayard and raised his M16.

"Cover Roelle," Bolan said. "I still don't hear any sirens."

"You won't," Bayard said. "Lower your weapon for a moment, Cooper. Or we do not leave this block alive."

Bolan shot the inspector a look. "You're out of your car," he observed.

"A rare thing here," Bayard told him. "As I warned."

The vehicles that arrived were all expensive imports. The men who emerged were Caucasians, their clothing casual, even slovenly, compared to the cars they drove. Each had a red bandanna somewhere on his person.

"The Red Death," Bolan said. "You alerted them."

"I made certain calls." Now, in the distance, a siren's wail could be heard. "The fire will be dealt with."

The Red Death gang members were pointing automatic weapons, most of them Beretta 12-series guns, at Bolan and Bayard. Several came forward and took the children in tow. With quiet words in French they guided the former hostages to the vehicles.

"Their parents will be waiting," Bayard said. "A few are perhaps among these rescuers."

"Rescuers," Bolan repeated.

"Yes," Bayard said. "Keep your weapons low. They

will grant us safe passage regardless. They owe me a debt now. But that debt comes at a terrible cost."

"What cost?" Bolan asked.

"I have taken sides," Bayard said. "Against *Souffrir* and for the Red Death. It puts me in a very difficult position. Red Death will expect me to side with them in the future, and if I do not, I will be judged a traitor to them. This is worse than avoiding involvement altogether. And of course I have made a mortal enemy in whatever remains of *Souffrir.* You have waged a very effective one-man war, Agent Cooper. I must say I am surprised."

"You don't sound happy." Bolan took his smartphone from his pocket. There were several messages from the Farm, received while he was engaged in battle. One of them informed him that there was breaking news of some kind coming in the media. This news was significant. He should stay alert, the message informed him, and stand by for the aftermath.

"Would you be?" Bayard asked. He indicated Roelle with a jerk of his chin. The gang leader was no longer laughing. He was watching the Red Death members as they returned to their cars and drove away without giving Roelle so much as a second glance. "My life will have quite a price attached to it now. I do not look forward to the dangers this will pose to me. I told you. The politics are…"

"Delicate," Bolan supplied. "I remember. And him?" Bolan pointed to Roelle.

"I will take him to the DCRI," Bayard said. "But he is correct. He will be out only too soon. And when he is, the streets will run red with blood. A war between *Souffrir* and the Red Death will claim many innocent lives. Some of them may be the very children you saved today. In the end, very little will be gained by this and much trouble."

"So you would've just let it be?" Bolan demanded. "Let the two gangs work out their problems together, no matter how many children they used as pawns along the way? No matter how many innocents were slaughtered like sheep? They were housed like penned goats in there, Bayard."

"I do not dispute that. I am simply explaining that your actions, while incredibly brave, are futile. The gangs will murder each other tomorrow as they did today. And Roelle, free of the system once more, will be more vicious than ever."

"That is right," Roelle said. "It may take a year or two." He grinned, showing his gold teeth. "But I will make you pigs, you snakes, a promise. Perhaps when I am free once more, I will go to the finest neighborhood in Paris, perhaps find a child. Maybe I will murder that child in vengeance for what you have done here today. Blood will be on your hands, for you have dared to defy the mighty Roelle, here where he is most powerful. I will murder a child because—"

The Executioner snapped the Desert Eagle from his holster, extended his arm and shot Roelle in the face, blowing the man's brains through the forest of his dreadlocks and onto the street behind him. The body stood for several moments before toppling to the pavement.

"Get back in your car, Inspector," Bolan said. Bayard's jaw had dropped. He looked on in horror and astonishment.

"But…" he said. "You…"

"Get back in your car," Bolan repeated. "It's time to go."

CHAPTER SIX

"He's talking to his superiors now," Bolan said. He spoke into his smartphone as he sat in an interrogation room in the DCRI office from which Bayard was based. "I suspect he's giving them his account of how a gangster and would-be child-killer named Roelle met his maker."

"I read your text report," Barbara Price stated. The Farm's mission controller sounded more concerned than usual. "Striker, I know it was necessary."

"The kids are with their parents," Bolan said. "It was necessary."

"I know. But you've inserted yourself in a gang war."

"Wouldn't be the first time," Bolan said. "Nor am I going to let that stop me from doing what's right. You know that."

"I do," Price agreed. "What's going to happen now?"

"Probably nothing," Bolan said. "Roelle is gone, and his organization is fractured. The Red Death owes me a debt, although I doubt I'll get to collect on that."

"Watch your six just the same," Price urged. "You got our communiqué about the news?"

"I did, but it didn't tell me anything. What's going on?"

"That's because we're not sure of the implications. French media is worked up like a hornets' nest," Price told him. "We're monitoring internet traffic and wireless telecommunications. Whatever it is, it's big, and they're getting ready to go nationwide to announce it."

"Can I assume Hal's managed to clear the way for me again down here?"

"It's more complicated than that."

"How so?" Bolan asked.

"The French have stopped talking to us," Price stated. "We've received several complaints from Director Vigneau of the DCRI. Even if he's clean, Striker... Hal thinks they're worried about the trouble you've stirred up by raiding one of the ethnic enclaves. It's an unsteady, unspoken truce they have with the power elements down there at the best of times. Now you've created a power vacuum while flouting that agreement. They're worried."

"You can't appease evil," Bolan said. "You can't cut deals with murderers, with child-killers."

"Hal says he understands. But he's reached the limit of his influence for the moment. He says if you keep on, the Man won't complain, and Hal will of course support you...but he's got no more leverage with the French."

"Long-term damage?"

"None," Price said. "You know how these things work. They'll make a big stink now, then forget all about it the next time international interests align. But Hal can't push them any further. He said to say as much. Said he thought you knew what that meant."

"Yeah," Bolan replied, "I do. A friend called such politics 'delicate.'" He paused. "You know, Barb, this upcoming news could have nothing to do with the mission here."

"Striker, how long have we been doing this?"

"A long time. Why, Barb?"

"What are the chances it has nothing to do with your mission?"

"Understood. I'll see if I can find a television. Striker out."

"Good hunting, Striker," Price said, closing the connection.

Bolan stretched his arms wide, rotating them, making a conscious effort to loosen the knots in his muscles that were always the result of adrenaline, combat and all the crashing and bouncing around that accompanied his battlefield existence. He took off his leather coat and draped it over his arm. Then he ducked out of the interrogation room—where Bayard had asked him to wait—and into the adjacent conference room.

There was a long, low wooden table there, with a media center at one end on the facing wall. Bolan unclipped his M16/M203 combo from its sling and put it in the corner, resting on its stock with the barrel pointed toward the ceiling. He switched on the television and jabbed his thumb at the input switch until he got what he thought was local television, then changed channels until he found what looked like a twenty-four-hour cable news station.

The running news ticker at the bottom of the screen was his clue. He found the switch that activated captions and cycled through these until he got English, as he knew he wouldn't catch much of the rapidly spoken French. The captions were delayed, but they would suffice.

Downtimes—in his work—were few and far between. Bolan knew to take advantage of them when he could. Keeping one eye on the screen across from him, he draped his three-quarter-length leather jacket over the next chair.

Then he unslung his canvas war bag, placed it on the table before him and took his Desert Eagle and Beretta 93R from their holsters. He also stopped long enough to take his combat knife from the sheath clipped to the off side of his shoulder holster, behind and below the spare magazine pouches for the Beretta. He put the knife on the table, as well.

From one of the side pouches of his war bag, he took a folding diamond rod, a rag and a ballistic nylon cleaning kit. Breaking open the kit, he removed from it a spray bottle of pressurized solvent and a pair of brushes.

The key to managing stress, Bolan had once read—probably while killing time recuperating from a gunshot—was to find something about which you felt nothing. The examples cited in the book had been mundane things like folding laundry. The idea was to do some activity that was emotionally neutral, something that allowed the mind to calm itself while the body was occupied with the purely mechanical.

For Bolan, maintaining the weapons that had saved his life time and time again was not exactly "neutral," as such, but it was as valid a way to find one's center as any other.

It was certainly efficient.

Bolan methodically cleaned and reloaded his guns. The spare magazines in his war bag had been loaded by Kissinger. There were boxes of loose rounds, as well. It was from these that Bolan reloaded the spent magazines he'd dumped in the bag to that point.

As he worked, Bolan was doing more than maintaining his guns. He was feeling every portion of his body, rotating his ankles beneath the table, flexing his calves and thighs, making sure he had taken no injuries that would interfere with the continued pursuit of his mission.

Setting aside his guns, Bolan unfolded the diamond rod. From his war bag he took an antibacterial swab and cleaned the blade. Then he dried it with the cleaning rag and ran the diamond rod along the knife's polished edge, returning it to razor sharp. He was just sliding the knife back into its sheath when the door of the conference room opened.

"Agent Cooper?" asked one of the two men standing there. Both wore dark suits bearing DCRI identification tags. Bolan scanned the tags. The one who had spoken was Musson. The one just behind him was Flagel. Musson's French accent was only barely perceptible. He had probably been bilingual since childhood.

"Yeah," Bolan said. He stood to face the two inspectors.

"Agent Cooper," Musson said, "I'm afraid I must ask you to place both your hands on the table. You are under arrest."

"I'm what now?" Bolan asked. "Inspector, I'm operating under the aegis of the United States Justice Department, in cooperation with the French government. This arrangement—"

"I'm afraid that the cooperation of my government has been rescinded. Based on the testimony of Inspector Alfred Bayard, we have determined you to be a threat to the general peace and welfare of this nation. We are arresting you on multiple charges, not the least of which is the murder of French citizens. You will be transported to a secure holding facility to await trial while we compile a full record of your activities on French soil."

Bolan sighed. "That isn't going to work for me," he

said. He looked down at his weapons, which were still on the conference table, and then back to the television, where the promised "big news" still had not broken.

"Make no move for your weaponry," Musson said. "We will use force if we must."

"Inspector," Bolan stated, "I would never kill a law-enforcement officer."

"Place your hands on the table, Agent Cooper," Musson ordered. "We will not ask you again."

"No," Bolan said. "You won't."

The two inspectors looked at each other. Bolan watched the almost imperceptible nod that they exchanged. Musson's hand went for his jacket. The Executioner had already spotted the telltale bulge, which gave away the shoulder holster.

Bolan's hand snapped like a rattler, pinning Musson's arm against his chest before the man could complete his draw. Behind, his partner, Flagel, sucked in a breath, probably to shout for help. Bolan took his free hand and shoved Musson's skull with a vicious palm heel, bouncing the back of Musson's head off Flagel's face. The blow knocked Flagel's head into the doorway in which the two lawmen stood.

The soldier followed up with a powerful close-range knee strike to Musson's groin. The inspector turned purple and dropped to his knees. Flagel, whose nose was streaming blood, managed to rise behind Musson and yank his own pistol from under his jacket. Bolan clapped the weapon out of Flagel's hands as if taking it from a child.

The result was that the gun was snapped from Flagel's grasp and sent spinning to the carpeted floor. Bolan kicked it away, then rapped his adversary in the bridge of his already bloody nose with his wristbone. Flagel collapsed within the doorway.

Musson managed to surge to his feet and collide with Bolan, pushing the soldier into the side of the conference table, knocking him against the table's surface. The Beretta and the Desert Eagle skittered across the polished wood.

Musson's hand found the combat knife.

"Don't," Bolan said, as Musson, who was a large man, struggled to pin the equally large Bolan to the tabletop. "I'm trying not to hurt you, Inspector."

The blade came up. Bolan snagged Musson's wrist and forced the knife into the table at the point. Then he clenched his fist and punched the inspector across the jaw with a good old-fashioned haymaker.

The shot struck the inspector right in the knock-out button. Bolan thought, just for a moment, that he could see the man's eyes rolling into the back of his head before he slid off the table.

Flagel was up again. The backup revolver he held had a four-inch barrel and looked to be a heavy caliber, probably a .44 Special. It was an odd choice for a French inspector, but Bolan had seen more idiosyncratic selections in personal firearms. Bolan's eyes narrowed as he watched the set of Flagel's arm, the tension in his hand.

The man was about to shoot him.

"Put that down, you fool," said another voice. Alfred Bayard stood in the doorway, holding his own .38 Special in front of him. The weapon was not pointed at anyone in particular, but neither could Bolan say it was not aimed in his general direction.

Flagel stared at Bayard. "But…Alfred, this man is a murderer."

"This man is an American agent in our country under the auspices of both our governments."

"Not anymore, he is not," Flagel stated. "The orders came through moments ago, while you were still debriefing. Agent Cooper is to be detained."

"You won't be detaining me," Bolan said.

"Do not touch those weapons!" Flagel ordered. Blood trickled down his face from his smashed nose.

Bolan snatched up his Beretta, turned in a tight circle. The gun blast that came was not unexpected. The shot dug a furrow in the conference table. Above them, a smoke detector began to beep. Bolan was jacking back the slide of the Beretta on a full 20-round magazine as he turned again. When Flagel tore his gaze from the table to Bolan, his eyes widened.

Bolan's gun was pointed right at him.

"You said you do not kill law-enforcement officers!" Flagel insisted.

Musson groaned on the floor.

"He said *what?*" Bayard asked.

"I won't kill a cop," Bolan said. "But if you don't lower that revolver, I will fire a round that takes a piece off you. An ear, maybe. Or the pinkie finger of your gun hand. Whatever it is, I guarantee it will be something you'll miss."

"Please," Bayard begged. He turned to Flagel. "This man risked his life to save those who could not possibly have meaning to him…except as innocent lives. I have watched him for just long enough to know that, if he wanted the pair of you dead, you would be dead.

"In fact, knowing the little that I do of this man, I think he exercised what was for him considerable restraint. Please lower your weapons. There will be no more talk of arresting Agent Cooper. He will leave here and go on his way."

"But, Alfred—" Flagel began.

"Enough!" Bayard ordered. "Enough, or it will be on all of us. You fools, look at the television! It was coming through just as I left my debriefing."

Flagel turned his face to the set that Bolan had switched on. His jaw dropped, and, a moment later, he lowered his gun.

The news was staggering. The reporters seemed scarcely to believe it themselves. After a period of what Bolan took to be the usual vapid time-filling commentary—as people with nothing new to add to a story struggled to fill minute after minute and retain curious viewers through shock value—the report began to cycle through from the beginning once more. Video footage then rolled.

The scene itself was nothing terribly distinctive. Shadowy figures sat in cars in some dark alley. The corona of a street light was playing hell with the camera. Whatever device had recorded the conversation was attached to some kind of zoom lens, so the footage was grainy, heavily pixelated and color-distorted.

The conversation involved a discussion of the ES and its terror attacks. Talk turned to potential targets, a mixture of public places and rallies belonging to Henri Gaston. This squared with what Bolan knew from his briefing. The ES has been targeting civilians but paying special attention to Gaston's events in order to put pressure on Gaston to quit.

Evidence of the terrorist involvement in the French elections was certainly a big story. As the graphs in the next set of videos obviously showed, support for Gaston was rising. But support for Leslie Deparmond was plummeting, which made less sense. What could take voters away from the ultranationalist candidate so quickly? The underdog effect explained rising numbers for Gaston, but there didn't seem to be any reason for Deparmond's subterranean poll numbers.

Then the video changed again. This time it depicted a close-up of one of the men in the cars. The footage had been digitally enhanced, the reporter said, and as a result the interference fluctuated wildly while the images turned several shades of green and brown.

There was no mistaking the face of the man sitting in the car, however. The man who was spearheading the meeting, the man actively discussing the selection of targets with men identified as high-ranking members of the ES, was instantly recognizable. Bolan knew it from the campaign posters that had been supplied with his briefing.

The man was Leslie Deparmond.

"I do not believe it," Flagel said.

"What…what is going on?" Musson asked as he rose from the floor. He looked at Bolan and flinched as if he expected to be hit again. Bolan shook his head.

"Well," Bayard said. "This explains a great deal."

"But it makes no sense," Flagel stated. "The terrorist attacks have helped Gaston. They make him look like a victim, make the voters determined to defy terrorism by supporting a candidate the terrorists do not wish them to support."

"Fear," Bolan said. "They count on fear to influence the election."

"But the people are brave and will fight for freedom," Flagel said.

"Are we not arresting this man?" Musson asked.

"Be quiet, Musson," Bayard ordered.

"After a terror group carried out coordinated train bombings in Spain," Bolan said, "the voters ushered out the current administration and voted in a new government. It's widely believed that's what the attacks were carried out to do. Fear works, Inspectors."

"So you think this is true?" Flagel asked. "You believe Leslie Deparmond is a terrorist sympathizer?"

"I'm not offering speculation," Bolan said. "I deal in facts. Facts as real as a bullet or a blade." He jerked his combat knife from the table, shot a look at Musson and Flagel and sheathed the knife. Then he holstered both his pistols and slung his war bag back over his shoulder, across his chest.

Bayard sighed. He had stowed his own weapon. "Cooper, I wish something understood."

Bolan turned to him. The inspector went to the soldier's leather jacket and picked it up, turning it left, then right, as if examining both sides against the light.

"I am surprised," he said, "that there are not at least a few bullet holes. The way you live your life, Agent Cooper, I should think that would be a constant hazard."

"I didn't get shot," Bolan said.

"No," Bayard agreed, inspecting the coat. He turned it over and over in his hands, clearly mulling something over. "No, you did not. But a man who fights as you do must see bullets pass close enough to perforate his clothing at times."

"I'm not saying you're wrong," Bolan said. He held out his hand. Bayard passed him his coat.

On the television, the reporters had turned their attention to speculation that Deparmond would now face charges for his actions. They had begun calling him the "mastermind" of the attacks. Gaston was poised to secure an easy victory, and the surging support for his party meant that his moderate regime would take the reins of the French government.

That was what the Man wanted, Bolan knew, or at least what the folks in Wonderland thought they wanted, which would work out pretty well for everyone concerned. That was provided the ES didn't interfere, and Bolan thought it likely they would. Seeing their designs thwarted would not sit well with the terror group. They would try to reassert their control of the situation.

The course ahead of Bolan seemed simple enough. He would resume his attacks on targets of priority per the ES safehouse list provided by the Farm. Sooner or later, he would either eliminate the ability of the ES to prosecute its agenda, or Bolan would find some clue leading him to the leadership of the group, where he would attempt to do the same thing in neutralizing the enemy.

So why did Bolan feel uneasy about it? Something just felt too pat, too easy. It was tickling his sixth sense for combat. He had learned to pay attention to those instincts.

"Cooper," Bayard said again.

Bolan shrugged into his jacket. "I'm listening, Inspector."

"I will see to it you are allowed to leave the building unmolested. Understand that I cannot guarantee anything further beyond that. If you do not leave the country immediately, I cannot say what will happen to you in an official capacity."

"I get that," Bolan said.

"But I wish to say one thing more. Please understand that I did not report your actions to my superiors because I wanted you apprehended. I did so because I disagree with your methods and because our procedure dictates that I keep this organization informed of such matters. I will not maintain secrets from the DCRI. But as futile as I believe your effort with Roelle to be in terms of…politics, Agent Cooper…in terms of humanity, it was the right thing. I wish for you to know that."

"Thanks, Inspector. Do me a favor and call downstairs."

"Agent Cooper?" Bayard looked at him, confused.

"So I can get my car back without a shoot-out," Bolan explained.

"Oh. Yes. I will see to it."

"Take care of yourself, Inspector. Perhaps we'll speak again before I leave Paris."

"Go with God, Agent Cooper. I think you will need Him."

CHAPTER SEVEN

Paris Suburbs

The car was a Mercedes, several years old, dented and careworn. The two men sitting in it were wearing civilian clothes, which by itself told Bolan nothing. But he had watched them for an hour as they sat, unmoving, watching the house and the street beyond Bolan's vantage in the Paris suburb. They were chain-smoking cigarettes and dropping the butts out the open window of the vehicle. The pile on either side told Bolan that the car had been parked for hours, if not days. That meant the men sitting in it were probably taking shifts, and that made them sentries.

He could not be certain of that, of course. The Mercedes sat some distance from the large home in this densely populated residential area. It was the spot Bolan himself would choose, if he were positioning lookouts before the safehouse. From the car to the house, the configuration of the street and the neighboring yards formed a natural bottleneck. It would be difficult, if not impossible, to approach the house without being seen.

Bolan parked his rental vehicle on the street two car lengths away from the sentry sedan. The men in the vehicle did not expect so brazen a maneuver. They were focused on looking anywhere but at him when he walked up to the car, and so they did not notice the M16 barely concealed under his coat.

They also did not notice him place the weapon on the ground next to the four-door vehicle before he simply whipped out his combat knife in his left hand, his Beretta 93R in his right, and smashed out the rear window behind the driver's side.

Safety glass pebbled the upholstery. Bolan wrenched open the door and sat in the backseat, placing the suppressed barrel of the Beretta against the neck of the driver. The blade of the knife he placed against cheek of the man on the passenger side. Both men froze, their hands inches away from what Bolan assumed were guns under their windbreakers.

"I'm operating under the assumption that both of you are members of the group known as Suffering," Bolan said in French. "Do either of you care to deny it?"

The two men exchanged glances. Bolan looked down. On the floor beneath his combat boots, behind the driver's and passenger's seats, were a pair of folding-stock Kalashnikov-type rifles. The passenger began to move, slowly.

"Don't go for that gun," Bolan said. "No matter how fast you think you are, you can't make it. I'm guessing these automatic rifles aren't what the Paris fashion set are carrying around these days. You couldn't leave some black ski masks lying around to clinch it for anyone who happens to look in?"

"We will kill you," the driver said. "You and every other stinking foreigner. You don't belong here."

"Well, that settles that question," Bolan said. "You're going to very carefully step out of the vehicle, and then I'm going to secure you in the trunk."

The passenger went for his handgun.

Bolan shoved the knife into the side of the man's neck, then thrust it forward. He did not have to look at the driver to know that he, too, was going for his gun. As the knife came through the passenger's neck, the soldier triggered the silenced Beretta. The windshield of the car was suddenly blotted out in a crimson wash.

Bolan paused to strip out the bolts from the AK-pattern rifles and unload the pistols. He tossed the bolts and magazines into a nearby gutter.

There could be no doubt now that he was in the right place.

He took up the M16 and clipped it once more to his sling. Wiping his knife on the shirt of the dead driver, he sheathed it, then holstered the Beretta. The assault rifle would be his primary weapon for the entry to the safehouse.

It was not likely the yard would be mined, given that explosions would draw immediate attention should a stray dog or unaware jogger happen by. There might be passive sensors in place, however. Infrared beams or simply surveillance cameras would be enough. There was not that much territory to cover.

There was a grim task to complete before he hit the safehouse, but one would facilitate the other.

Bolan found the keys in the ignition. He popped the trunk and, one at a time, dumped the two dead men in it. There was a camouflage BDU jacket on the backseat of the car, which he used to wipe the windshield reasonably clear. It did not have to be spotless; he just needed to be able to see where he was going.

He started the car, put it in gear and slammed his foot on the gas pedal.

The Mercedes leaped forward. Bolan jammed on the brake, shifted into Reverse and sent the car speeding down the street, away from the safehouse. When he judged the distance sufficient, he tromped the brake pedal again, then shifted into low gear, put his left foot on the brake and put the gas pedal to the floor.

The engine roared in protest. Bolan sent the car shooting down the street and across the lawn of the safehouse, cutting deep gouges in the grass, building speed as he hurtled toward the front of the building.

He reached across his chest and put on his seat belt as he drove.

Shoving the M16 out the window, he braced it against the driver's side mirror, aiming it with his left hand. As the wall of the safehouse loomed, he saw the first orange-yellow fire-blossoms from the windows. They were muzzle-flashes, from the guns of the ES terrorists. The blood-smeared windshield cracked and spiderwebbed as bullets struck it. Bolan bent as far as he could below the dash, pressing the trigger of his M16, sending controlled bursts into the windows.

The Mercedes struck the safehouse.

The front of the car crumpled with the impact, driving the hood up and folding it in on itself, causing the engine to scream at high revolution as the drive train did its best to eat itself. Before the heavy sedan came to rest, it crushed the safehouse kitchen and pulled a man in camouflage fatigues—who had been seated at a table in that kitchen—under its wheels. A micro Uzi, lost from the ES gunman's hand, struck the windshield. Bolan heard bones cracking before the man's scream was cut off.

The Executioner released the seat belt and stepped out of the car.

The shooters came fast. They were wearing camouflage fatigues, the uniform of the ES, and they carried

AK-47 assault rifles as well as other small arms and pistols. Bolan threw himself over the hood of the car, putting the engine block between himself and the rest of the kitchen, then fed a 40 mm grenade into the launcher slung under his assault rifle.

He raised the weapon from behind the Mercedes just long enough to let fly with the HE round, which punched into the wall opposite the kitchen, before ducking back behind the engine block. The explosion sent the hurrying gunners airborne, spreading them around the dining room, scorching and blackening the kitchen as it blew the cupboards to splinters.

Bolan waited long enough for the explosion's aftermath to settle. Then he left the shelter of the much-abused Mercedes, moving in a combat crouch through the wreckage of the kitchen and into the slaughterhouse that was the dining room.

Two men began to shout at him in French.

They were hiding behind furniture in the living room, waving guns at him. Bolan ducked behind the corner of the entrance to that room and waited. Bullets tore the floor near his feet and chewed through the wall above his head. He crouched lower.

It was called the "fog of war." Bolan had heard the term many times, and it could mean different things… but among them was the confusion that sometimes led men to do foolish things when threats arose. In the stress, the adrenaline dump, the rush to do something, anything, they sometimes behaved in ways that, objectively, made no sense.

One such irrational act was to use upholstered chairs as cover.

There was cover, and there was concealment. The furniture in the living room, made of wood and springs and foam, would provide neither. Bolan let his M16 fall to the end of its sling, drew his pistols and snapped off their safeties.

"Throw out your guns," Bolan called in French, knowing that the order would not be heeded by the ES terrorists. "Throw them down and surrender."

The response was a blast of gunfire.

Bolan threw himself to the floor in the doorway, rolling to avoid any shots that might come low, as a barrage of bullets ripped apart the facing wall of the dining room. From the floor, he pumped two rounds each from the Beretta and the Desert Eagle, aiming for the center of the two upholstered chairs behind which his enemies sheltered. When the nearly dead men fell to either side of those chairs, he fired once more into their skulls, making them completely dead men.

The clatter of footsteps on stairs drew Bolan's attention. A wooden door opposite his position was thrown open and a gunner appeared, apparently coming upstairs from the basement. The Executioner extended his Beretta 93R and fired a single round. The 9 mm slug drilled into the terrorist's right eye.

The body fell backward, toppling the next man on the stairs. Bolan rose to a combat crouch, fished a grenade from his war bag, armed it and tossed the bomb into the stairwell.

The explosion was muffled; the grenade had bounced all the way to the bottom of the stairs before detonating, Bolan judged. He holstered his pistols and lifted his M16 again, stopping short of the stairway to expose just enough of his left eye for a quick look down. The steps were scorched and ripped to pieces near the bottom. The sublevel, which appeared to be a dug bunker and not a true basement, was dark. Bolan removed the modular combat light from his war bag and affixed it to the forward rail of his weapon. There he could trigger it with his support hand.

It was necessary to jump the last few steps to the basement's dirt floor. Bolan bent his knees to absorb the impact. His combat boots left heavy prints in the dirt.

The sublevel was a workshop. Heavy wooden benches—rough-hewn from cargo pallets—held cartons, plastic bins and tools. The components on the benches were, to Bolan's practiced eye, exactly what was required to make improvised explosive devices. He saw black powder, pipes and caps, fuses and a stack of cell phones, probably burners, to be used as detonators.

Wireless bomb detonation had made great strides in the past few years, thanks to the widespread use of improvised explosive devices in battle zones like Iraq and Afghanistan. There was a time when the would-be terrorist had fewer options for causing his bombs to go off. He could use a timing device of some kind, which meant the bomb might go off when there were no high-value targets nearby. It was also impossible to abort a timed device, at least under common circumstances. Physical fuses were even more difficult to mess around with and easily circumvented.

Wireless detonation was far more reliable, but the common problem in all bomb factories was prematurely blowing them up. Any number of cowardly home bomb technicians had blown themselves to hamburger while assembling explosive devices or testing detonators. That was the problem with radio detonation; it was too easy for an errant signal to blow the whole works sky-high.

The bombers had turned to wireless phones as detonators for several years now. These presented their own issues, of course. Anyone with a cell-phone jammer, or authorities with access to the wireless grid, could shut it down, effectively creating a zone in which the bombers could not ply their trade. Something as innocent as a wrong number could trigger the bombs prematurely, and electromagnetic interference of multiple types presented problems.

Bolan went to the table and examined the materials there. None of the bombs were in their finished state, but this was obviously one of the cells from which the ES was running its attack operations. The terrorist operations had been—according to the briefing files on his phone—a mixture of remote bombings and direct actions. Typically both were deployed.

The ES would use a bomb to inflict casualties and incite a media response, then follow up with armed men to inflict more damage before they withdrew. Bolan's assault on the bank had been the first effective counter, although the French authorities had attempted more than once to mount a meaningful counterterror operation. The death toll among their operatives had been among the reasons the French government had originally accepted the insertion of "Agent Cooper" in their midst.

The withdrawal of French sanction for his mission complicated things considerably. He did not blame the French government, or the DCRI, or any of the other elements with whom Brognola had been playing diplomatic tug of war. These things happened. But it meant that Bolan was on his own and dodging more than the original complement of foes.

This was nothing new to him.

When he had finished his inspection of the bomb-making shop, he went to the last doorway, which was crafted from a table, something heavy with an ancient Formica surface. There was a rope pull, but no handle.

He grabbed the rope and gave it a yank, reasoning that this was probably not a booby trap within the safe-house's inner sanctum. Nothing happened when he tugged on the door.

The hinges were exposed, an artifact of the crude construction of the barrier. Bolan backed up, palmed his Desert Eagle and drew a bead on the top hinge. He blew it apart on the first shot and used two more bullets on the hinges below it.

His ears rang with the volume of the gunshots at close range. Another tug on the rope brought the heavy table-door falling to the dirt with a muffled thud.

The bullets that burned past him seemed almost perfunctory. Bolan stepped to the side, snapped up his rifle and triggered several bursts into the chamber beyond. Dancing lights flickered more brightly as electronic equipment flared and buzzed. Bolan triggered another burst and yet another, before the yelling in French from the next room prompted him to stop.

"Throw your gun out," Bolan called in French. "I'm going to put a light on you. If that light reveals any other weaponry, or you make any sudden moves, the assault rifle attached to that light is going to end your life." He opened the M203 and inserted a buckshot round. "Specifically the weapon has a 40 mm grenade launcher. The grenade inside will blow you apart."

"Don't shoot. Here is my weapon." Bolan heard the thud of a gun as a weapon hit the floor.

The soldier entered the room with the M16 ready. In the circle of illumination cast by his combat light, a man in camouflage fatigues cowered behind a desk. On that desk were multiple monitors, some dark, some still operable. These were surveillance screens. The images that Bolan could see depicted the house above and the yard beyond. The image of the kitchen area showed the Mercedes among the debris.

"You're ES." It was not a question.

"We are freeing France from evil," the terrorist spit. "We are burning out an infection that—"

"Spare me the party line," Bolan said. "You're going to tell me everything you know."

"You are the police?" the terrorist demanded.

"No," Bolan said. "But I'm on their side. You're going to tell me everything you know about the ES and its plans in Paris. And you're going to look at a list of addresses here in the city and surrounding neighborhoods. You're going to tell me where I can find more of your friends."

The terrorist looked at the enormous muzzle of the M203. "You cannot make me talk."

"This isn't going to go like you think it will," Bolan warned.

The terrorist's arm snaked up. In his hand was what Bolan thought, at first glance, was a knife. But as the man tried to aim the blade like a gun, Bolan realized he was looking at an ballistic knife, a spring-loaded weapon that could hurl its razor-sharp blade hard enough to pierce body armor.

He pulled the trigger on the M16, maintaining a sustained burst.

"I warned you," Bolan said a heartbeat later. But there was no one alive to hear him.

The Executioner turned and left the surveillance room.

Vaulting the hole at the bottom of the stairs, he ascended to the main floor, checking the ground level and then finding the stairs leading to the next story. As he climbed, he listened for sirens. It was curious that there were none yet, especially in this quiet suburban environment. Was it possible that the local authorities had been plied with bribes, as the responders in the ethnic enclave had been? He supposed so. But if that was the case it pointed to a level of corruption even worse than his conversations with Bayard had revealed.

The combat light on his M16 led the way. Two silvery trip wires on the stairs caught the light, and Bolan stopped to examine each one. They were connected to electronic devices that were not bombs, at least as far as Bolan could tell. He guessed they were early-warning tools intended to alert those upstairs that they were about to have visitors.

Bolan stepped over the wires, mindful of pressure plates in the floor. He had walked into more than one elaborately booby-trapped enemy lair in his time on the battlefield. If he had learned anything from this, it was that human malevolence and human ingenuity knew no limits. If he could think of it, someone else could think of it, and find a way to make it reality.

At the top of the stairs he was confronted by two iron security doors, one to the left and one to the right. Shrugging, he took a pair of grenades from his war bag, popped the pins and dropped the bombs to the floor by the doors. Two quick leaps down the steps put him back on the first floor.

The pressure wave from the explosions made his ears pop again. Overlapping thunderclaps reverberated through the abused structure. Bolan, M16 in hand, crept back up the stairs, avoiding new damage to the steps caused by his grenade assault. The doors were off their hinges and lying like ramps before the openings.

Behind the doorway on the left, a single ES gunman stumbled around, holding his ear with one hand and shooting blindly from a revolver with the other. Bolan felt a round from his gun cleave the space in front of his nose. He snapped a single 5.56 mm round into the shooter's forehead. A short scream escaped the man's lips before his corpse hit the floor.

Bolan almost didn't hear the man who tackled him.

The repeated explosions and gunfire had done little permanent damage to Bolan's hearing over the years, but he was as susceptible to the temporary effects of gunfire as anyone else. The big ES man who collided with Bolan from behind was three hundred pounds easily—a bearded, shirtless mountain who wore camouflage pants tucked into heavy boots.

Bolan hit the floor next to the corpse. The M16 was wrenched from his hands. He heard the quick-release clip on his sling give way, as it was meant to do. Using his hands for balance, he fired a powerful kick from the floor, catching the big man in the midsection. With a groan, the bearded goon dropped Bolan's rifle. Undeterred, the ES man drew a KA-BAR knife from his belt and brought it plunging down at Bolan's face.

The soldier rolled away. The knife dug deeply into the floorboards next to him. His own knife was in his hand as he sat up, close to the enemy, and plunged his knife into the man's kidney and ripped upward. Bolan's opponent screamed in agony.

Then it was over.

The Executioner pushed his enemy off him, retrieved his rifle and stood. Entering the adjacent room, he discovered it dark. The windows were covered with blackout curtains. It was a bedroom, dominated by a queen-size bed. There was yet another door here, leading to what Bolan assumed was an additional bedroom.

Given the dimensions of the house, it could not be particularly large.

He paused, pressing himself against the wall. The soldier had no particular desire to absorb yet more bullets and splinters. "Whoever is in there," he said, "come out. Do it now, or I'll put a bullet in you and be on my way."

"I will not come out," a voice said. "But please enter. I assure you I will make no hostile moves."

"Do you surrender?" Bolan asked.

"I do not. But…neither will it matter. I am not a threat to you. Please come in."

Bolan reached down and very carefully grasped the knob.

He threw the door open.

CHAPTER EIGHT

The bedroom was indeed small. The smell of cigar smoke was so thick that it made Bolan's eyes water. The room was dark except for a single electric lamp on a corner of a writing desk. Seated at the desk was a large, heavyset man. He had turned away from the lamp and was cloaked in shadow, but as Bolan took a step farther into the room, the burning cherry of the man's cigar blazed with new life. In the illumination of the cigar, the stubble-covered face it revealed was thick and ruddy. Bolan lowered the barrel of his weapon fractionally as the large man blew a smoke ring with obvious pleasure.

"Gerard Levesque," Bolan said. "The head of the ES."

Levesque smiled. He was heavier than in the photos provided in the electronic dossier from the Farm, but it was unquestionably him. On the writing desk before him was a Browning Hi Power pistol. The slide was locked back and the magazine had been removed. The weapon was no immediate threat and had obviously been prepared deliberately to appear that way.

"I am Gerard Levesque," he said. He spread his hands, careful not to reach for the pistol. Then he took another leisurely puff of his cigar. "These are Cuban. Some of the finest available. Would you like one? I have more."

"No, I don't," Bolan said. "You're coming with me, Levesque. You've got a lot to answer for."

"So it is true," Levesque stated. "You are an American. I received reports from some of my men in the field. Observers who saw you hit the bank and also one of our network's safehouses. Men tasked with reporting to me the goings-on. Our suspicion, based on your methods, was that you might be a CIA troubleshooter."

"It doesn't matter who I am."

Levesque laughed. He had a deep, throaty laugh, like a man without a care in the world. He was dressed in a tailored double-breasted suit, his silk tie at half-mast. The gold chain of what was probably an expensive pocket watch trailed from his lapel to the pocket of his jacket.

He took another long drag from his cigar and blew a smoke ring that floated above his head. "These," he said, gesturing with the cigar so that ashes fell on the floor at his feet. "These were going to kill me. I was told this by a doctor some years ago. I believed him. I stopped smoking them. Out of fear, American. I, a man who has lived without fear. I became afraid. I let my fear of death make me forget what it was to live."

"Time to go," Bolan said. "I'm not interested in hearing philosophy from a murderer."

"I don't think you understand. But neither do I begrudge you this, American. Please do not shoot me until I have finished explaining myself. And then…then I will shoot myself for you. It is fitting that I do it. It is a weakness to allow others to do these things for you. But I was afraid again for a moment. I allowed myself to be protected here. To be shielded from what I have done. But you cut through them as if they were nothing. You did what the French authorities have not been able to do. Or what they have been unwilling to do. I have never been certain."

Gunfire sounded outside. Bolan hit the floor. Several rounds penetrated the walls of the windowless room. The shots were coming from the street. Bolan looked up and was astonished to see Levesque calmly sitting at his desk, smoking his cigar, as if a firefight had not just flared to life scant yards from him.

"Stay here," Bolan ordered. "If you stick your head out of this doorway, I will blow it off."

"I am not going anywhere," said the French terror leader. "I have nowhere to go."

Bolan crawled on his belly out the door of the bedroom, holding the assault rifle in front of him. Navigating the stairs took some work, but once on the ground floor, he made it past the wrecked car and to the gap in the side of the house. There he was able to pick out the shooters from their vantage on the street. It was a second car—another Mercedes, in fact—with shooters located behind the engine block and, ridiculously, behind the midsection of the vehicle. One of the gunmen was wielding an FN FAL rifle with a bipod and had braced the rifle on the roof of the Mercedes.

The ES were supposed to be well trained, but within every group of trained men, there were bound to be a few "fliers," a few men who, under the adrenal stress of a real altercation, did foolish things.

In battle, they would die for that stupidity.

Bolan used a portion of the wrecked wall to brace his weapon. The gunmen had not seen him; they were shooting at random in the same location on the upper floor. Bolan did some quick math in his head. Their trajectory had them pumping bullets into more or less the spot he had been standing, in the small, window-less room where Levesque was waiting.

And what was that all about, exactly? Rarely did his enemies simply grab a chair and wait for him. There was no trap that Bolan could detect, unless these gunners now attacking the house, obviously shooting for whomever had breached the structure with a car, were someone's idea of a clever deadfall. Bolan doubted that.

Aiming through the red dot sight of his assault rifle, he briefly considered punching a 40 mm grenade through the car, but there were too many other residences nearby. He could not be certain of the damage that would be done by shrapnel from the vehicle. Instead, he calmly sighted over the roof of the newcomers' car and waited for the gunman there to stick his head up.

When he saw the man's eyes, Bolan fired.

The bullet dug a hole through the center of the gunman's forehead. The corpse's skull bounced off the roof of the car before the deadweight of the rest of the body pulled it back behind cover. It was several more moments before the second shooter noticed that his comrade had fallen.

"Wait for it," Bolan said quietly to no one.

Bullets began to rattle against the ravaged wall of the house, raising splinters near his head and shoulders. These weren't important. The gunman had rightly divined the angle of Bolan's shot but had no real clue exactly where the soldier was located. The panic fire that resulted was the action of a desperate man.

All Bolan had to do was wait. His opening came soon enough. The shooter paused to duck behind the car and reload. A less-experienced man might use this opportunity to break cover and go after the car, lining up a shot on the gunner, but Bolan was concerned about

Levesque waiting upstairs. He was not about to give the French terrorist leader a target, letting him fire a clean shot between Bolan's shoulder blades.

The soldier aimed lower, for the pavement ahead of the car's bumper. Then he began firing single shots from the M16, walking the rounds in, bouncing them off the pavement. The ricochets began peppering the front bumper and grille of the car.

A headlight exploded. The gunman screamed in defiance and raised his weapon, a Kalashnikov assault rifle. As the terrorist shot wildly at the front of the house, Bolan finished his arc, walking the spray of bullets right into the man's thighs. The gunner toppled, howling in pain. His head was just visible beyond the front bumper.

Bolan put a bullet through it.

The realization that he was being played stopped him from leaving the wreckage of the house to check the body. Instead, he retraced his steps, hurrying back upstairs, expecting to find that Levesque had let himself out by some alternative route. He would be forced to pursue the terrorist leader and reacquire him—

Except Levesque had not escaped. He was sitting precisely where Bolan had left him, finishing his expensive Cuban cigar.

"I take it," Levesque stated, "that you've just killed more of my men."

"I have. Wasn't that your plan?"

Levesque shook his head. "Again you do not understand. I did not call them. They responded to the attack, nothing more. The local residences are under our nominal control. My men have visited every household previously and given them a telephone number to call."

"You forced them to play informer?" Bolan asked.

"No," Levesque replied. "We put them under our

protection. The trade was simple. Call us, not the police, should anything occur in this neighborhood. A few bribes, a few threats. The combination works well. You make them fear you, then you salve their consciences with money. Natural greed does the rest. They can hardly complain too loudly once they are, as you Americans say it, 'on the take.'"

"And that's why there are no cops here?"

"We bribed the local authorities," Levesque said. "As an added measure. There is much corruption here. But you knew that."

"I want answers, Levesque. It's time to go."

"As I said," the terrorist leader stated, removing another cigar from inside his coat, "I will die here. I am tired, American. It is my time. But I will make a full explanation to you before I do. Will that suffice?"

"You don't want to know the different ways I can lean on you to make you do what I say."

"I have no doubt of that," Levesque said. "But please allow me to share with you the story that is…me."

Bolan had no response for that. Finally he gestured with the barrel of his rifle. "Go on."

"What do the authorities know about me?"

"You're fully aware of what your file must say," Bolan told him. "Formerly with the Basques, among many other terror groups. You'll kill anyone for money, support any cause if the price is right. Your men have a reputation for being ruthless. I kept that in mind when dealing with your little hostage drama at the bank."

"I had hoped to preserve the hostages' lives just long enough to have them killed for news cameras," Levesque said. "A vulgar display, but the trade of terrorism is built on them."

"Trade?" Bolan asked. "That's what you consider it?"

"You protest, but I do not hear it in your voice. You know as well as I do that violence produces money. Focused violence. All men pay for what they desire. Some purchase women. Some purchase drugs. Some purchase and use weapons. Some pay the men to use those weapons. Political power generates the desire for anonymity, for plausible deniability. That is the service provided by a man like myself."

"You're a mercenary and a murderer," Bolan said. He glanced at the military chronograph wristwatch he wore. If Levesque was stalling for time, his specific purpose was unclear.

"Please, have a cigar," Levesque repeated. When Bolan shook his head, the terrorist leader set about lighting the second cigar for himself. He used a wooden match from a box of matches on the writing desk. "It is unthinkable to consume a second one so soon after the first," he said. "But I do not have much time."

"Spill it, Levesque," Bolan said. "Or I'll kill you myself and be on my way."

"Very well. Leslie Deparmond is my employer."

"Deparmond."

"Yes. I have been working with him for some time. It was Deparmond who sought me out, told me of his plans to purge France of foreign interests. Years ago he was but an ambitious man with nothing but a plan and a great deal of money. As his political career accelerated, so did our activities.

"With the financing provided by Deparmond, I built Les Étrangers Suppriment. I recruited and trained the men. I armed them. I tested them. I made sure that when the time came they would be an effective fighting force. And as I expanded, I delegated these duties to my second-in-command. Our hierarchy has grown. Our organization is truly a power."

"Your men are better than average," Bolan admitted. "But that doesn't make them good."

"No," Levesque said. "Clearly not. You have been to them as the scythe is to the wheat. Are all Central Intelligence agents so formidable?"

"I'm not with the CIA."

"I will not insult you by calling you a liar."

"Enough," Bolan said. "Why are you telling me all this? Why give up now? A last-ditch attempt to save your life?" Even as he said it, Bolan knew it didn't wash. If Levesque were simply turning informant to stop Bolan from killing him, he would have tried to escape while the soldier was occupied with the backup forces outside.

"For some time," Levesque stated, "I have been debating my course of action. I have lived much in my time on earth. It has been a shorter life than I pictured for myself. But an eventful one."

Bolan took a step closer. He drew his Desert Eagle and pointed it at Levesque. "Five," Bolan said. "Four."

"Please, bear with me, American. What is your name? I would like to know."

"You can call me Cooper."

"Agent Cooper, did you know I was born not far from here? Well, 'far' is a relative thing. But I was born a short distance outside Paris. My father was a common laborer. I never knew my mother. She left when I was a baby. My father never spoke of it. I would ask, and when I was old enough to demand, he began beating me when I persisted.

"But late one night, after the factory had closed and he had been sent home with the miserable sum that was his final pay allotment, he got drunk. He had spent all afternoon in a tavern, working up the courage to come home and tell me that we would be forced to leave our home. And when he did, he cursed my mother's name. He called her a whore who abandoned us while I was but a squalling infant, and suddenly I understood.

"I was a burden to him, you see. A nothing. Dead-weight. He resented my being left behind almost more than he resented being left. Many was the night he came home to fix me with a stare that I now realize was his hatred of the inconvenience I represented. But there was something else there.

"Beneath the hatred was an overwrought sense of duty, which he used like a weapon. Duty shackled him to me, and he wished me to know it. And so when I asked about my traitorous mother, he beat me for it, before and after…with the exception of that single bitter night. It was worse that night."

"Three," Bolan said.

"Staring into the barrel of your gun," Levesque went on, "I find that even one more day suddenly seems precious to me. And that is also a weakness. Just as I wished to hide myself away behind locked doors, with my men to protect me, hoping that whatever assassin the Americans had sent would not find his way to me or get through them…I realized that the only way to defeat weakness is to confront it."

Bolan stopped counting. "Forward, toward the danger."

"Yes," Levesque said. "That's it. That's it exactly. I hate the weakness in myself, Agent Cooper. I hate that it has reduced me to this. But I am telling you now. Deparmond engineered everything that has happened to this point in order to ensure political victory."

"Why tell me this now?" Bolan asked. "What possible benefit could there be to you to admit it?"

"Perhaps I think you're going to torture me for information," Levesque replied. "Perhaps I have a weak constitution, and I hope to spare myself the pain I know a man of your worldly abilities can cause me."

"I don't torture people."

"No, of course you don't. You're not the type. I could tell it the moment I saw you."

"Then why? Why give up the plot?"

"I'm sick," Levesque told him. "I learned of it just last week. You see before you a large man, yes? I was larger. When I began losing weight for no reason, I thought it was merely the demands of my work."

"Murder for hire isn't work," Bolan said.

"But, damn you, you follow what I am saying to you," Levesque spit, throwing the cigar down. "My lymph nodes are swollen. I feel pain in my back. I'm sick to my stomach all the time. I am *dying,* Agent Cooper. It is pancreatic cancer. There is no more certain death sentence. Adenocarcinoma, it is called. The pain will grow greater, and I will be dead."

"How long do you have?"

"It will come soon. And frankly I have no desire to end my days as the tool of some ambitious fool. I have done nothing with my life. Nothing but pursue money with the only skills available to me, those being aptitudes for violence and for the organizations of those who specialize in it.

"Even now you look at me, and I can see in your eyes that you would kill me in a heartbeat if you thought the act justified. I have met your type before. You believe you live by a moral code. You believe that I am corrupt and you are incorruptible. Perhaps that is even true. But

Deparmond looks at me the same way. He stares down at me like you or I would stare at a noxious insect, at the leavings of an animal."

"So you want respect?" Bolan asked.

"Do not be a fool. I will not have respect. There is nothing I can do to achieve that. But I wish no longer to be a gear in the machine of Deparmond's ambition. He will pay a price for his disrespect of me. I will soon be dead but so will be his political career."

"And you think telling me this will put nails in Deparmond's coffin?" Bolan asked. "You overestimate the power I have."

Levesque almost glared at the soldier. "No," he said. "I do not think I do. I think one such as you would put a bullet in Deparmond's skull upon learning of this betrayal...if not for the fact that men like you do not run the world. You are closer to me than you are to Deparmond or Gaston."

"I'm nothing like you," Bolan said.

"And yet it is Deparmond or Gaston, and men like them, who rule," Levesque replied, grinning. He bent, groaning and holding his back, and picked up his fallen cigar.

Bolan waited as the Frenchman lit the cigar again.

"I would like to see Deparmond pay for his crimes. As I most assuredly shall pay for mine. If you will entertain a simple request from a doomed man."

"I'm listening."

Levesque picked up the magazine for his Hi Power. With his thumb he began snapping rounds out of the magazine. The brass-cased rounds hit the floor and rolled. Levesque kept popping the cartridges free until there was just one round in the magazine.

"I am going to load this into my pistol. I would ask

only that you give me the privacy to take my own life. And in return for this gift, the gift of a dignity I do not deserve, I will give you the name and address of a man who can authenticate the video evidence I have of Deparmond. I recorded our meetings with him, you see. The video is ironclad proof of his complicity in the terror attacks. I think you want this very much."

"I do," Bolan said.

"I thought as much. For a man like you must bend his knee to unworthy masters. Politicians. Bureaucrats. Men in power. A man like you, he will be on a leash, yes? And the video evidence would give you the proof you require to make your leash just a bit longer, to go after Deparmond in the name of justice.

"Making Deparmond's crimes public will rob him of support. It will destroy the election. Bringing about the very result your government probably wishes, yes? The moderate, Gaston, in power? An administration in Paris that continues to heed your government's wishes?"

"Who is it?" Bolan demanded. "This video expert."

"His name is Tessier. Edouard Tessier."

"How do you know this Tessier can validate the video?"

"He stores them for us," Levesque said, "because he helped us record them. He can verify that they have not been tampered with, that the man appearing in them is Deparmond. Tessier is well-known in his industry, specialized though it is."

"And why will he cooperate with me?"

"You called me a mercenary," Levesque said. "A man who does things for money. Money is Tessier's only god, too, but he is not like me. He is a harmless man. A civilian in every respect. He will do as you ask simply because he has no reason not to do it. Do we have a bargain?"

Bolan paused. "All right," he said. "Give me the address."

Very carefully Levesque reached into his pants pocket and produced a business card. He handed this to Bolan. "Goodbye, Agent Cooper."

"Good riddance," Bolan said.

"I am going to load my gun now. I will wait until you leave before I chamber the round."

Bolan nodded. He backed out of the room nonetheless. When he was on the stairs, he heard Levesque rack the slide on his weapon.

The French terrorist was under any number of death sentences, not the least of which was Mack Bolan's. Allowing the man to take his own life rather than face Bolan's guns or the lethal cancer from which Levesque suffered was certainly a mercy. The Executioner was a merciful man, as much now as when he had earned the nickname, Sergeant Mercy.

Levesque had not been. Levesque would not have offered mercy to any of his victims. But a single bullet through his brain would remove him from the equation, would stop him from ever again harming another human being. He would die at his own hand; there would be no political blowback to American interests. And letting the French terror leader commit suicide meant he would cease to exist in mere moments.

All in all, Bolan thought, that was a worthy trade for whatever dignity the terror leader thought he was buying.

A single gunshot rang out.

Levesque said he would shoot himself. Bolan wouldn't leave until he saw the man's bloody corpse.

CHAPTER NINE

Somewhere in Paris

The sound of the gunshot was so loud that Anton Lemaire ripped the headphones from his ears.

"Merde!" he shouted.

He had done it. The crazy bastard had done it. Levesque, that coward, had shot himself and ended his pathetic life.

Lemaire sat back in his chair. As if without conscious thought, his hand found the switch for the radio microphone receiver and switched off the unit. The sound feed from the bugging device—hidden in Levesque's writing desk—was cut off in a burst of static. There was no one to hear it and nothing to be heard now.

While Lemaire felt vindicated for having planted the bug in the first place, there was still the bitter sting of proof in Lemaire's mouth. He hated the certainty that Levesque was broken, a turncoat. But the knowledge did clear the way for Lemaire to take his rightful position within ES.

The urban safehouse around him was abuzz with activity. Operatives of the ES in camouflage uniform were stripping, cleaning and loading weapons, as well as preparing explosive satchels for more raids in the city. Now more than ever it would be important to pour on the pressure.

This Cooper, the American CIA agent, would be quick to report to his masters that the head of ES had taken his life. Lemaire would not allow the ES to be dismissed as irrelevant. It was time for a show of force, and, more important, it was time to transmit a message that would make all of Paris take note of their resolve.

As for what Levesque had said in his dying confession…this was information that had not been shared with Lemaire, even given his position within the group. Levesque had been a man of many secrets. He had never revealed from where exactly his finances came, nor had he let on to his troops that he was motivated by anything but belief in their cause, belief that France should be purged of foreign influence.

Clearly these were lies. Levesque was a traitor to the cause. But the revelations changed nothing. The sooner Lemaire's troops forgot their former leader, the better.

As the second-in-command of ES, Lemaire had taken it on himself to call to arms those men among the organization who counted him as their leader. Over the years, Levesque's considerable influence had waned with a portion of the men. That group was large enough that the ranks of those recruited by, trained by and therefore loyal primarily to Lemaire were a considerable force.

There were others of the ES loyal to Levesque, particularly those recruited and trained by Levesque. Lemaire, in calling ES to arms at this, one of its last remaining safe havens in Paris, had offered these Levesque loyalists a place at the table. They had refused, and as far as Lemaire was concerned, the organization was well rid of them.

Weakness bred weakness. Lemaire had harbored doubts about Levesque for some time. Suicide simply confirmed every suspicion in the second-in-command's mind. Only a weak man did his enemies' work for them. Only a weak man betrayed his comrades before taking a bullet and avoiding the consequences of his betrayal. The ES was stronger without such a man at its head.

News of Levesque's death would have to be carefully managed. Only Lemaire knew of it; only Lemaire had been present, a disembodied listener for this final, unworthy act. He would have to capitalize on that if he could. Perhaps he could pass among his men the idea that Levesque had been assassinated by the CIA.

The American government wanted weaklings to run France, after all. It made a certain sense. The American CIA was forever meddling in things that it had no business with. Only Lemaire need ever know the truth of Levesque's ignominious end. Lemaire could build up Levesque's memory, make him a martyr, and thus use him to motivate his loyal ES troops.

The size of the network that was ES was more vast than most suspected. The public knew only that the danger was real. Law enforcement probably had its own theories, and in truth Lemaire had no idea what the American CIA or INTERPOL or other governmental agencies thought about the ES. He was not connected to international politics. He understood the realities of the streets of France. He had been born and bred to them.

Anton la Bête, they called him. Anton the Brute. Anton the Beast. Anton the Animal.

It was a street name. Street names were earned. Anton Lemaire grew up on the streets of Paris an orphan, one of many such urchin children. He never knew his parents; his earliest memories were of living alone in the shelter of doorways. Sometimes he wondered if his mother had been a prostitute.

Or perhaps his parents were rich but killed in a tragic automobile accident, their son the only survivor, with no family to claim him. As he grew older, he stopped making up such stories. There was no point to them.

There were always homeless, always beggars, always children among the dispossessed. Such was the way of cities. Paris—despite its reputation across the globe—was no different in that respect. It had its crime. It had its decay. It had neighborhoods where no man dared walk, if he was of the wrong color or of the wrong gang or simply not counted on a list of names.

It was in the streets of Paris that Lemaire learned to hate all foreigners.

As a very young boy, he was small. Quick, yes, as were most small boys. But speed was not enough when you were outnumbered. The block that the young Anton and his friends called their own, the territory to which they laid claim, was invaded by dark-colored foreigners.

It was long enough ago now that Lemaire had allowed himself to forget their exact nationality. The nation, the boundaries, the borders of their…otherness… were not important. The fact of their alien natures was. The fact that they did not belong burned him, galled him, made him hate.

They began taking the block, slowly at first, then more brazenly and in numbers. While in those days the deliberate police avoidance was nothing like it would become in Paris's ethnic enclaves, already law enforcement was learning to avoid the area. Lemaire remembered the first time he saw one of the dark-skinned gangs pelt a police car with rocks, driving the police back, showing that men in uniform, men of *authority,* were not always men of *power.*

Much as he admired such a demonstration, he was

quickly reminded of its source. The interloper gangs beat first one of his friends, then another. Marcel, a boy roughly Lemaire's age who often watched Anton's back in exchange for the same protection, was clubbed so badly in an alley that he died three days later.

The act demanded retaliation. But it would be years before such retribution could be wrought.

Despite the privations and the occasional malnourishment of living on the streets, Lemaire experienced a growth spurt. As he entered adolescence, he became a strapping bull of a young man. His hunger was insatiable. He devoted most of his days to stealing food from markets and stands in an ever-widening radius from his home block.

When he was too well-known to the shopkeepers and vendors, he began focusing on other street children, preferably those with skin darker than his own. Soon he learned that this was much more efficient. He could steal food and sometimes money or other precious items without making enemies of the local merchants.

The police, on their increasingly rare forays into the neighborhood, did not care about depredations among the outcast class. If no productive citizens were involved, no crime had been committed. Not as far as the authorities, impotent as they were, believed.

Then came the day Lemaire stole a knife from a black gang member.

He remembered vividly the feeling of crushing the young man's skull beneath a piece of paving stone. Going through the enemy's pockets, he found the long double-edged knife. He knew immediately what a prize this weapon was.

He took the sheath, a handmade one of cardboard and adhesive tape, and put the weapon in his own waistband. He would use it to stab to death two more enemy gang members, and in so doing, he would discover yet again the gift of efficiency. Just as stealing from his fellow street urchins was more efficient than stealing from shops, stabbing a man to death was quicker and so much easier than using his bare hands.

Lemaire became bigger and more powerful as he grew to manhood. But he never forgot the lessons of efficiency. And he never lost his love of knives. The longer and the sharper they were, the more he adored them.

There came the raining afternoon in which Lemaire —holed up in an abandoned storage house with a leaking roof—had begun throwing his knife at a broken barrel. He was simply bored. But the moment the knife struck, tip first, in the barrel, he was hooked. He practiced whenever he could. He obtained many more knives.

And then he learned savate.

As huge as he was, as strong as he was, he found the dynamic kicking of savate only made him deadlier. He began taking part in street matches. These were brutal, illegal events, exactly the sort of outlet he required. As he became a man, he left behind the need to scratch daily for sustenance; he began to feather his own nest, building a gang and organizing small criminal enterprises. The most natural was a protection scheme among the neighborhood shops.

He was almost disappointed when one frail, old man proved to be a baker he remembered from his childhood. He was tempted to hurt the man badly despite the business Lemaire was trying to build. He could remember this same man calling him worthless as a child. To survive as a child, Lemaire had stolen from the old man's bakery.

But, no, if Lemaire had learned anything from his street battles, from his time in savate, from using his fists and his blade and his will to claw his way up in the world, he had learned discipline. He would spare the baker's life and take his money instead.

But he charged him double.

Standing behind his secondhand steel desk, Lemaire walked across the otherwise empty second bedroom of the large Paris safehouse. He could still hear his men in the larger bedroom across the hall loading and maintaining weapons. Similar sounds could be heard downstairs. The building was an armed camp, which was as he wanted it to be.

On his belt Lemaire wore two large leather sheaths, one on either hip. Each sheath held three large throwing knives. They were bolo-shaped, with circular holes in the handles to yield perfect balance. They were razor sharp.

On the wall Lemaire had nailed an old cutting board. He took a deep breath, relaxed his arms and moved to stand in front of the board, as far away as he could without backing himself into the wall.

Then he turned.

With his back to the board, he let his hand fall to the sheath on his right. His fingers found the stainless-steel haft of one of the blades.

Lemaire spun and threw.

He had practiced the motion thousands of times. It was not hard to spin and to throw a knife. It was not even especially hard to do so while hitting the fist-sized circle he had drawn on the cutting board in black permanent marker. The true challenge was in doing so without telegraphing, without the telltale flicker of shoulder muscles, without the barely perceptible change in stance that would alert an enemy to his intentions.

Even before his time with the ES, even before he learned to carry and fire an automatic weapon, to use military tactics, he knew that it was his blades that would one day save him. He envisioned a moment when his weapon was empty, when the Tokarev pistol he carried in his waistband failed him, when all that stood between him and his death was his skill with a blade.

He could fight with a knife, of course. All of the ES men were trained to wield a blade in personal combat. Lemaire's own experience with street fighting had prepared him for fighting with a knife long before his time in the ES, too, but he had undergone the same training as all the men. He regularly engaged in practice of the same type. It helped him keep his edge sharp.

He smiled at the words even as he thought them.

After throwing two more blades he turned again, now facing the target. He took his time, planting the other three knives around the first three, making sure the blades went exactly where he wished them.

The key was not just the release. Releasing the knife had to be consistent, yes. The grip could not be too loose or too firm. The arm had to describe an almost lazy arc, throwing from the shoulder, not the elbow. The fluid throw was the fast throw. Rush it, force it, and the knife did not fly true.

The ritual—as it always did—calmed him. Now he had to turn his thoughts to the business of the ES…and of this American agent, Cooper, who would doubtless report to his superiors that the back of the ES had been broken. Such a message could not be allowed to reach the public. Paris lived in fear of the ES. The momentum built during the election could not be allowed to evaporate.

This presented a serious problem. Word would come out that Deparmond was a "criminal" in the eyes of the authorities. Lemaire scoffed at that. It was now "criminal" to fight the incursions of foreign trash who threatened to swamp his nation in a tide of dependence and scum. It was "criminal" to want to preserve his culture. It was "criminal" to see the decay created by those who did not belong on French soil, and long to do something to save the land of his birth.

Such was progress, Lemaire supposed.

To counter a message, he would send a message of his own. To battle the possibility that Gaston would suddenly find himself unopposed by viable opposition, Lemaire would make the public afraid to vote for him at all. With no one turning out to the polls, voices could be raised demanding a new election. A new candidate to defend France could be found.

But first the message had to be sent.

"Thomas!" he called out. "Michel!"

"Yes?" came the reply from the bedroom across the hallway. Thomas, one of his lieutenants, was holding a Kalashnikov assault rifle. Its cover had been removed, and its bolt pulled. Thomas held a cleaning rag in his other hand.

"Get the video camera," Lemaire ordered. "And find Michel. We will want him to run the recording to the press when we are finished." Michel was Lemaire's courier. He had never particularly liked the man; Michel had a ratlike demeanor and always perspired too much. But he had been a reliable courier, recruited by Levesque years ago. His loyalty was unquestionable. Such proven servants had value and were not discarded casually.

Still…Lemaire was in charge now. Levesque had always trusted Michel, but Michel had been loyal to Lemaire instead. And if Lemaire himself had misgivings, it might be wise to detail a group of men to keep an eye on Michel as he pursued his duties.

"The banner?" Thomas asked.

"Yes, the banner," Lemaire said, nodding. "Set it up here, in my office. Over the target."

Thomas hurried to do as he was told. He disappeared again and returned with a tripod, hastily affixing this to the small video camera. Once all was in readiness, Lemaire positioned himself in front of the banner. "A Kalashnikov," he said suddenly. "Bring me one."

Thomas nodded, returning once more with one of the assault rifles. He placed it in Lemaire's hand. Lemaire balanced it in the crook of his arm, angling it so that its profile and magazine were visible in profile for the camera. These actions were not taken without thought. One had to always project the right menace when sending ultimatums to sheep.

Fear. It was all about fear. Fear would keep the public in line. Fear coupled with the violence ES was about to bring about in the name of a pure, liberated France, unshackled by the chains of foreign lands and foreign people.

"One more thing," Lemaire said. "When Michel is dispatched with the recording, detail a group to keep an eye on him. If anything goes wrong, if he behaves suspiciously, he and anyone with him should be terminated."

"Yes, sir." Thomas pushed a button on the recorder. "Ready," he said.

"I am Anton the Beast of the organization known as

Suffering," Lemaire said. "I am speaking to you from within Paris. That is correct. At this very moment I am within the perimeter of the city. The authorities, weaklings that they are, have no power to stop me."

Lemaire turned and indicated the banner of the ES. It was a simple thing. The letters ES were spray-painted in white against a bloodred field. The banner was a rough-and-ready thing, crude and handmade. It projected exactly the message Lemaire wanted. Suffering was a group of rough men willing to do violence to get what they wanted. They were willing to dirty and bloody their hands to those ends. That was the message. It would be sent as such.

"Your protectors have failed you. Dirt, scum, the dregs of humanity, pour across the borders of a pacified France. Your police cannot even be safe in some parts of this city. They know it. You know it. We know it. Yet you do nothing. You vote for those who will continue the status quo. You vote for weakness. You give sanction to your own destruction! You are such fools you will never see the blade that lurks beneath the surface of your cowardice!"

With that, Lemaire reached under the banner and, as if by magic, produced one of the bolo throwing knives. Without hesitation he drew the keen edge down the palm of his left hand. A crimson line welled, dripping with the terrorist's blood.

"We are the knife!" Lemaire shouted. "We are the blade that cuts deep and flies true!" Then he turned and hurled the weapon at the banner. It stuck between the letters E and S, quivering slightly, pinning the banner to the wall and nearly pulling it free from the tacks holding it up.

Lemaire clapped his hands. Flecks of his blood

splashed his face. He rubbed his palms together in slow circles.

"We will not accept the election of Gaston," he said. "Any man, any woman who puts Gaston in power is taking his life in his hands. We will kill you. We will kill your children. We will leave bloody hands on your walls to show that it was we who took everything from you, as you would take everything from France!"

Dramatically Lemaire placed his hands on the banner, letting the Kalashnikov fall from the crook of his arm onto the floor with a clatter. He pressed his palms against the fabric and took them away to reveal two matching bloody prints. Then he charged the camera, causing Thomas to jump back. Lemaire grabbed the camera from the terrified man's hands and brought the lens to his face.

"Do not go to the polls. Do not vote for Gaston. Do not make the mistake of supporting the enemies of France. Suffering will stop you. We will make you pay. Right now our men are planting bombs all over the city. Some will be at polling places. Some will be in hospitals. Some will be in schools. Perhaps some will be in your shops and your libraries and your museums and your parks. They could be anywhere. If Gaston wins the election, these explosives will rock Paris. They will shake the city to its knees."

There were no explosives set. But there would be. Before the video was sent by courier to the press, Lemaire would have it played on the big screen television downstairs for all of his troops. It would rally them. Give them purpose. Then he would send his bomb makers to the basement of the safehouse, where they would begin assembling the charges. Then he could have the weapons distributed throughout the city. The explosions could be timed to coincide with any number of street attacks, on targets of high or low value.

Paris would never know what had hit it. The power of the ES, the power of an organization built by men of true faith in the ideal of French purity, would eclipse any betrayal committed by Levesque.

"This is your only warning," Lemaire said into the lens of the camera. "Do as you are told. Remember the lessons of violence taught you during past periods of political unrest. There is nowhere we cannot reach you. You could be at home. You could be sitting in an office. You could be riding a train or a bus. When the explosions and the bullets come, you will not know it until you are already dead. Do not let your last thoughts be of betrayal to France.

"I am Anton Lemaire. I am the new true leader of Suffering. I have always been the power behind the throne. I am the man who chooses who will live and who will die. Any government Gaston manages to form will be smashed from within before it can take a breath. We will strangle you in your beds. Gaston's government is stillborn. Remember that. And remember my face. If you make the wrong choice, if you put your vote with Gaston, my face will be the last thing you see."

He switched off the camera and tossed it to Thomas. The device was covered in blood.

"Get me a towel," Lemaire said. "And have the men assemble downstairs. We will play them the recording."

"Yes," Thomas said, nodding.

Michel stood in the doorway, his eyes wide. He took a handkerchief from his pocket and gave it to Lemaire. The terror group leader mopped the blood from his palm, made a face and threw the bloody handkerchief in the corner of the room.

"I am sending you to the press," Lemaire told Michel. "See that you are not followed back here. It wouldn't do to have anyone discover the location of our last sanctuary. Not when there is so much work to do." With that Lemaire left the room, calling over his shoulder, "Hurry. We have much ahead of us."

Michel nodded, though no one remained to see him do it.

He paused just long enough to snatch up the bloody handkerchief.

CHAPTER TEN

Downtown Paris

"There he is," Bayard said, pointing through the open driver's window of the Peugeot.

"I see him," Bolan replied.

The Frenchman was understandably surprised when Bolan phoned DCRI headquarters to collect his unofficial liaison. Bayard had also seemed reluctant to set out with "Agent Cooper" once more, given Bolan's now very gray status with the French government, but that changed quickly when the inspector learned from Bolan that Agent Cooper's superiors and the DCRI's intelligence network had produced the same piece of data: the ES was on the move—and issuing an ultimatum to the people of Paris.

This information had come to Bolan shortly after his departure from Levesque's hideout, by way of the Farm. The Farm's information was, in turn, a data intercept from the DCRI intelligence network... something Bayard's superiors were, according to the Frenchman, none too pleased about. The French inspector had done nothing but complain about that fact during the drive to the mixed residential and commercial district downtown.

Bolan did not rise to the bait, however. There was nothing he could say that would make the French authorities feel better about the fact that some unnamed agency had free rein over their bandwidth. He supposed he could blame it all on the CIA, the agency for which everyone seemed to think he was working... but Brognola probably wouldn't appreciate the international inquiries and angry transatlantic phone calls *that* would generate.

The upshot of the intelligence from the Farm was that the DCRI had an informant in the ranks of the ES. Apparently that informant had been less than reliable; Bayard had indicated as much during the drive but would not elaborate. Bolan saw no point in idle speculation about it.

They would learn as much as they would learn, and he would act on that. Years in combat had taught him to be flexible. The old adage "No plan survives first contact with the enemy" was remembered by so many for a reason.

Bayard had insisted on driving his own car. Bolan's was stashed a few blocks from the DCRI. The soldier hoped this was not a mistake, but Bayard knew the area much better than Bolan did. It was why using Bayard had been a good idea in the first place.

The informant was a slight man wearing camouflage pants and a black T-shirt. The pattern of the pants matched the ES men's preferred dress. Not very subtle, showing up in partial uniform. Bolan frowned.

"I think this informant is not very bright," Bayard said, echoing the soldier's thoughts. Bolan shot him a bemused look. Bayard shrugged. "As I said. Unreliable."

The Peugeot was parked on one side of the street, opposite what Bolan thought looked like a quaint old-fashioned record store and a much more modern electronics retail shop. The electronics place was all glittering white with bright overhead lighting.

It was an American firm, now spread worldwide. Bolan had seen them before, and always they were blinding. The soldier could not imagine what was so important about tablet computers and MP3 players that they should be bright enough to burn out a man's retinas.

The informant, on the other hand, was standing at a pay telephone kiosk, probably trying to be inconspicuous and succeeding in being the opposite. The telephone looked ancient. It reminded Bolan that one did not see many public telephones at all, anymore—not when every man, woman and child carried a phone in his or her pocket. Bolan's own field operations had been greatly enhanced by the state-of-the-art technology the Farm issued him.

"What is he doing?" Bolan asked. They were waiting to make sure they did not blow the man's cover if he had been followed. There were several cars on the street, but there was enough traffic and enough pedestrians passing by, that it would be hard to spot any tail that was not grossly obvious.

"And what does 'unreliable' mean, exactly?" Bolan asked the inspector.

"His name is Jules Michel," Bayard said. "He is a creature of opportunity. No known political leanings beyond what is touted by whichever group he joins. No particular loyalties. A few debts, some to organized, unlicensed lenders here in Paris."

"Loan sharks," Bolan said.

"Indeed. He is, for all intents and purposes, a common street criminal. Quite unremarkable. Pickpocket, sometimes burglar. The occasional assault for purposes of robbery, although not too much of that. The sort of trash one regularly recruits with money and promises of leniency. We turned him years ago."

"And?"

"When the ES was in its infancy, long before they began actively staging terror attacks, he was helpful somewhat. He gave us a little here, a little there. Enough to bring in an arrest now and again. But never did he give us a real feel for the true scope of the group's operations. A few weeks before things heated up around the elections, he dropped out of sight. This is the first we have heard of him on the streets since then. A traffic camera caught him and facial recognition software flagged him, although to his credit he did also call in."

"So why did he agree to spill now?"

"Technically he didn't." Bayard said. "Not specifically. He may just be hoping for extraction. We did promise him that eventually, although we were vague about the time line."

"Go on."

"Standard operating procedure, to prevent him being overheard or his communications traced, has been for him to find the nearest public telephone and place a call to an exchange that reports his location. He is then picked up by one of our agents, either in a civilian automobile or by a livery service. And that's really it. I'm afraid you know as much as I do at this point."

"Stop pouting," Bolan finally said.

"What?" Bayard looked incredulous.

"You heard me," Bolan said. "Intelligence is often porous. It happens at every level. Stop pouting about it."

Bayard actually laughed. It was the sound of a man who didn't find much funny and didn't allow himself more than a bark or two when he did.

"You have a point." He paused. "Although I wish I knew if I was going to walk into an arrest of my own when I return to the office. I'm not supposed to be here with you, Cooper."

"Tell them you were worried I'd run amok without your supervision," Bolan suggested.

"You *did* run amok without my supervision," Bayard said. "And I am worried you will do it *with* my supervision. Amok should be your middle name, Cooper. To be honest I only agreed to come because I have been thinking about your results. About the good you have managed to do. I still cannot agree with your methods. But the outcome was a positive one."

"I won't argue that," Bolan said.

"You wouldn't." Bayard sighed. "How long do you suppose we should make him wait?"

Bolan looked up the street, then down it. Something didn't feel right. "I'm not sure," he said. "But I think we'd better just shake the tree and see what falls out of it."

"You and your trees," Bayard grumbled.

The inspector started the Peugeot and put it in gear. He waited for a break in the traffic, pulled out, swung across the street and pulled up alongside Michel. The informant looked more nervous than surprised. He had obviously been waiting to be picked up.

"Get in," Bayard said.

Michel slipped into the back of the car. Bolan swiveled in his seat to hook one arm over the headrest. He fixed Michel with his most businesslike glare.

"Bayard," the inspector over his shoulder said. "DCRI."

"Cooper," Bolan added. "United States Justice Department. I want whatever you've got on the ES. Where are they based now?"

Michel rattled off an address, looking to Bayard with wide eyes. Bolan, meanwhile, checked the files on his smartphone. The address corresponded with what the Farm believed was one of the last of the facilities in the ES network. It was also one of the largest ones, a converted estate sitting astride residential and commercial neighborhoods in the middle of Paris.

"You have much explaining to do, Michel," Bayard stated.

"But I said on the telephone," Michel whined. "When I called for help. I already delivered the ultimatum video to the press!"

"Video?" Bayard repeated.

"What video?" Bolan demanded.

"I know I have not done my job well," Michel said. "They've had people watching me for weeks. I had the trust of Levesque, yes. But his second-in-command, this Lemaire…the Beast, they call him. He does not like me. Always he was watching. I had to wait for them to send me on a courier mission, and even then, I had to complete the mission to avoid raising their suspicions to the point that they dealt with me. I have been living in fear for weeks."

"So what's the story?" Bolan asked. "I want the short version."

"Anton Lemaire now commands the ES," Michel reported. "First he called to him all who were loyal to him. Those were his words. There was no sign of Levesque, and I dared not seem disloyal to Lemaire. So I rallied at the Paris safehouse, location Delta, our largest. There Lemaire told us Levesque was killed by foreign interlopers led by the American CIA."

"The ultimatum video?" Bayard prompted.

"I was tasked with delivering Lemaire's message to

the city, to all of France," Michel said. "He will bomb the city to ashes, attacking everything from polling places to hospitals, if Gaston takes power. He told us, privately, that the ES would now prepare for all-out war to carry out that message. We must fight Gaston's government and its formation with everything we have, he told us. To prevent France from believing that the ES died with Levesque."

"How much time do we have?" Bolan asked.

"He did not explain the timetable. Not to me. But preparations are being made even now. I believe he will attack swiftly."

Bayard and Bolan exchanged glances. Both men knew what that meant, although Bayard's calculations were likely a bit less direct than Bolan's. The French inspector was probably wondering if he could round up enough men and law enforcement backups to raid the ES facility. Bolan, however, was calculating the odds. As formidable as the Executioner was, he was one man. He could only be in a single place at once. Taking a facility as large as the estate Lemaire now used as his stronghold would require backup.

Pursuing the proof of Leslie Deparmond's guilt could wait. With the remnants of ES mobilizing, Bolan would have to come at them with everything he had to prevent more bloodshed among the public. One thing bothered him, though.

How had Lemaire and those loyal to him known that Levesque was dead? How had they known to blame Bolan, a supposed CIA operative? Was it a coincidence? Or had Lemaire had some way of monitoring Levesque's activities? How close had the two men been?

Did Lemaire know of Levesque's plans to take his own life, and was he now taking the organization in the direction he saw fit?

None of that mattered. The soldier had long ago learned to shelve these concerns, to catalog them in his mind, to be revisited and analyzed later, as data and time allowed.

For now it was time to fight. And for that, he needed...

"Help," Bolan said, as Bayard drove them to the DCRI headquarters.

"What?" Bayard looked at him, confused.

"We need to hit that location," Bolan stated. "It's going to take a considerable tactical team to cordon it off and secure it. Sweep for stragglers. Keep the terrorists boxed in while someone kicks in their door."

"And that someone doing the kicking would be you?"

Bolan nodded. "Can you run interference for me with the DCRI? Get us the uniforms we need?"

"That is asking a lot. I should not be here now assisting you."

"But you're here," Bolan countered.

"I think you should let us handle this," Bayard said. "It will take longer for official mechanisms to operate, yes, but—"

"I see someone," Michel cried from the backseat. "I think the men in that car—"

Michel's head exploded.

Bolan felt warm, wet blood on the back of his neck. He swiveled and lowered himself in his seat on instinct. Bayard, behind the wheel, stomped the gas pedal and sent the Peugeot careening forward and into a sliding, rubber-burning, gear-grinding U-turn. Pebbles of safety glass from the shattered rear windshield scattered across the backseat, glittering diamonds dotting the informant's corpse.

Bolan had stowed his assault rifle in the trunk of the car; it might as well have been back in the United States. Bayard swore and tried to get below the level of the dash as the chase car shot past them. It was an old-model Mercedes, spotted with rust and patches of unpainted primer. There were four men inside, wearing camouflage fatigues and black ski masks.

The snout of a Kalashnikov assault rifle protruded out the driver's side rear window.

They were close enough to see the muzzle flare from the assault rifle as the enemy gunner, sitting behind the driver, opened up with a long burst. Bullets walked up the flank of the Peugeot. A round narrowly missed Bolan's face, punching daylight through the roof strut behind him.

"Go," Bolan shouted.

Bayard grunted. The bullet-riddled Peugeot picked up speed. It was no race car, but the Mercedes was an old diesel model, heavy and slow. Bayard was able to stay ahead of the enemy as they weaved through traffic. More bullets found the rear of the Peugeot and struck buildings on either side of the street.

"It must be the ES," Bayard said. "He said they were watching him. They must have followed him."

"This is no good. We don't want to endanger civilians."

"I am open to suggestions!" Bayard shouted. His knuckles were white.

"There," Bolan said, pointing. "That alley. Hard left!"

The buildings on either side were tall, stone-facade structures. There were no windows facing the alley. It was the best location they were likely to find to screen passersby from gunfire. Bayard almost put the Peugeot on two wheels making the turn, but he managed it, goosing the parking break to bring the rear wheels around. It was nicely done. The inspector's skills as a wheelman were considerable.

"Brace yourself," Bayard said. "I am going to put the trunk in their faces."

Bolan nodded and pulled on his seat belt. Bayard did the same. The inspector slammed his foot down on the brake as the Mercedes entered the alley.

Even through the shattered rear windshield, the two men could see the Mercedes as it hurtled toward the Peugeot. Bayard slammed the gearshift into Reverse and tromped the accelerator again. Groaning, the Peugeot roared backward. Bolan tucked his chin in his chest.

Metal screamed as the Mercedes rammed the Peugeot, ripping the bumper from the inspector's car and crumpling the trunk. Bolan hit the seat belt release and went EVA. He could sense Bayard mirroring his motion on the driver's side.

The Desert Eagle filled Bolan's hand.

The heavy .44 Magnum hand cannon was just the weapon for punching through the Mercedes. As Bolan circled to the passenger side of the enemy vehicle, he let the triangular snout of the Desert Eagle do his talking for him, barking in hellhound fury as he fired a pair of hollowpoint rounds into the gunman in the front passenger seat. The man's skull came apart under the onslaught, spraying his blood and brains across the stunned man in the driver's seat.

Bolan did not have time to study the men in the vehicle; the shooters in the backseat were still very much mobile. He did notice, in the briefest of flashes, that the driver was slumped over the wheel, moving slowly. Doubtless he had taken the steering wheel in the chest when the cars struck. The Mercedes was old enough or in sufficiently bad disrepair that its airbag had not deployed.

Bayard pumped a pair of rounds from his snub-nosed .38 into the driver.

"Hands!" Bolan bellowed in French. "Let me see your hands!"

The gunmen were having none of it. They tried to pile out of the car on their respective sides.

For whatever reason, possibly from the adrenaline dump and the shock of the sudden collision, the man on Bolan's side did not try to bring his weapon to bear at first. Instead he swung the Kalashnikov like a club. The soldier ducked and the wooden stock sailed over his head.

Bolan rammed the man in the gut with the sole of his combat boot, employing a pistonlike front kick that had most of his body's power behind it. The gunman slammed against the car and then collapsed to the pavement in a sitting position. The barrel of the Kalashnikov scraped along the pavement as he tried to bring it around and up to point it at the soldier.

The Executioner punched the gunman in the throat with a .44 bullet. The expression on the abruptly dead man's face was one of horror.

Bayard stepped in and kicked his man in the nose as the gunner stumbled, but it was not enough. The ES man on the driver's side rear was bringing his Kalashnikov up to shoot the inspector when Bolan simply reached over the rooftop of the Mercedes with the Desert Eagle. He paused, not knowing if Bayard intended to take a prisoner. He had only fractions of seconds before he would be forced to—

"Shoot!" Bayard spit.

Bolan shot the gunman in the face. His Kalashnikov, too, hit the pavement.

Bayard let out a long breath. He looked down at himself, then at Bolan. Both men were spattered with blood that was not their own. The inspector's shoulders slumped, and he leaned against the enemy vehicle for support.

"The gunfire will bring police," Bayard said. "If you are still here, they will take you into custody, Agent Cooper."

"Are you all right?"

"I am fine," Bayard said. "We will need to make other arrangements for transportation. And we will… we will have to take poor Michel and see to it that his body is properly cared for."

"Yeah." Bolan nodded, feeling the muscles of his jaw twitch again. It was a brutal, sudden death. He had seen it countless times, had administered it countless times. Michel had been a petty criminal, yes. He had been mixed up with terrorists, certainly. But he had given them vital information when they needed it. Michel had served up to them the next step in the Paris campaign for justice in the elections. Michel had been doing the work of good men by serving better men than him.

"He did not deserve to die like that," Bayard said. "No man does. I will not leave him in the back of a car like so much refuse."

"Understandable. Once we've seen to him, there's a lot that needs to be put in motion." Bolan looked to the trunk and realized his assault rifle was back there. When he checked it, he discovered that the weapon had survived the collision intact. He put it on the floor behind the front seats of the Peugeot.

"Let's go," he said. "Take me to my rental car. It's not far from headquarters. You can arrange for the tactical teams, and I'll meet you on the street. We can go from there."

"A simple plan," the inspector replied, "but a workable one. I will do my best to keep you out of a cell until we can see this to the end. The ES must be stopped. They must be rooted out and destroyed."

"My feelings exactly."

"Do not mock me. I am not a juggernaut. I am not like you. I am a peaceful man trying to do a difficult job. That job sometimes requires violence. I am not born to it."

"No one is," Bolan said. "It shapes you. It makes you what you are, based on your choices. Your reactions to it. We all do the best we can. And I wasn't mocking you."

"Very well." Bayard sighed. "I will see to it that you have the tactical teams you require."

Bolan climbed back into the car. Bayard, behind the wheel, took a moment to massage the bridge of his nose, his head bowed.

"I do not know if I can live in your world, Cooper. I do not understand how you manage it."

"It doesn't get easier," Bolan said. "But you get better at it."

"Iron sharpens iron," Bayard whispered. He looked down and then started the Peugeot. Metal shrieked again as the two vehicles separated.

Bolan turned and looked at the dead man in the backseat. There *would* be justice for Michel, just as there would be justice for the people of Paris.

The Executioner would make it happen.

CHAPTER ELEVEN

As the briefing from the Farm had described, and per the plan and grid Bolan's smartphone displayed, the terrorist estate was a three-story stone building. It loomed over a commercial retail area and more traditional shops and side streets backed against rows of tenement-style structures.

The residential district was a mixture of historic Paris and new structures, representing the slow creep of more modern architecture that some Parisians believed was destroying the character of their city. If Mack Bolan spared any thought for this at all, it was to think that Paris's architecture and suburban sprawl issues paled in comparison to the threat of terror on French soil.

Bayard found Bolan standing at the edge of the tactical teams' cordon. The French operatives had erected a series of emergency barriers on the streets around the perimeter of the estate. Armored vehicles and men with automatic weapons dotted the perimeter. The French teams wore navy blue BDU-style uniforms and load-bearing gear as well as European Kevlar helmets. Their weapons were FAMAS assault rifles.

"There are already questions," Bayard said as he approached. "I have explained that you are a military adviser. That lie explains your weaponry—" Bayard nodded to the assault rifle Bolan once again wore on his single-point sling "—but as soon as you enter the estate, the illusion will be broken. I have not yet received authorization to send men in. My superiors at the DCRI are arguing over the advisability of a dynamic entry. I take it that is what you plan to do?"

Bolan simply looked at Bayard.

"Yes," said the Frenchman, his tone dry. "How silly of me to ask."

"Once I get things rolling," Bolan told him, checking the contents of the canvas war bag slung over his shoulder, "you should have all the probable cause you need to enter."

"That is a delightful euphemism for what I am sure will be wholesale destruction. Do not get killed or there will be more embarrassing paperwork for me to fill out after I am brought up on charges for assisting you."

"That's what I like about you, Inspector," Bolan said. "Your positive attitude."

The Executioner left the barricades, crossed the short strip of property spanning the distance between the street and the estate, and skirted the corner of the building. There were two entrances he could try; one was an ornate, columned affair. The other was a service entrance. He made for the latter, more from long habit than tactical considerations. He was walking directly into an ES stronghold. He was bringing the fight to the enemy, which meant the initiative was his. He simply had to keep it.

The terrorists opened up on him before he got halfway there.

The windows flanking the side entrance were broken out by the muzzle blasts. The hollow, metallic chatter was the old familiar song of a Kalashnikov assault rifle, the most copied and prolific select-fire military weapon in the industrialized world. As Bolan lay prone, lining up the shot with his assault rifle, the enemy gunners tore up the ground before him. They were walking their shots in. He would be dead in seconds.

He did not need that long.

The 40 mm grenade he fired blew the door in and scattered the remaining glass in the windows. Bolan pushed to his feet and ran for the opening. He had to cover the distance before someone could draw a bead on him.

The plan was so simple it was almost no plan, but the ES were expecting French tactical operatives if they were expecting anything at all. They were not prepared to have open warfare dropped on their doorstep.

Open warfare was what Mack Bolan did best.

There were two guards just inside the doorway, stunned and bloody from the grenade. They were trying to find their weapons on the debris-strewn floor. Bolan paused long enough to fire a burst into each one of them. Shell casings rattled on the floor.

The soldier stood in a hallway that appeared to run the length of the estate's ground floor. There were other corridors leading from it and several alcoves. A spiral staircase at the midpoint of the hallway led to the second floor. He glimpsed a wooden door in one of the alcoves that he assumed led to a lower or basement level.

There was a beat in which nothing moved, like the pressure wave of a storm about to hit. Bolan's sixth sense for combat tickled the back of his brain, and he threw himself to the floor.

The doors of the corridor flew open, almost in unison. Men in the camouflage BDUs of the ES—armed with a collection of assault rifles, pistols, submachine guns and shotguns—opened fire. Only the door saved him. Bolan scrambled for it as the wall of flying lead struck all around him. Plaster and wood cut him like shrapnel, raising bloody welts on the skin of his scalp and neck, and tearing into his left bicep, but he made it through the opening and fell roughly down a short flight of stairs.

He barreled into a terrorist and knocked him to the floor.

The man who broke Bolan's fall roared in anger as the Executioner's big frame crushed him. Bolan rolled, attempting to bring up his rifle, but when he pulled the trigger of the weapon, it did not fire. He dropped the M16 on its sling and yanked the combat dagger from its sheath on his shoulder harness.

The blade slid into the man's abdomen easily. Bolan wrapped the fingers of his left hand around the terrorist's neck and pumped the knife in and out, finally twisting and pulling as he gutted the man. He felt the strength leave his opponent's hands as the terrorist loosed his grip on Bolan's web gear and collapsed to the floor in a quiet death.

Bolan stood in a small chamber lit by a single bulb set in the wall.

Above him, against the ground floor that was the ceiling of this lower chamber, he could hear the rattle of thunder that was dozens of automatic weapons going off at once. A single bullet penetrated the door, which he had pulled shut as he fell. A second bullet followed the first. Then a third struck very near Bolan's knee.

Through a nearby closed and very heavy wooden door, Bolan heard a man tell someone that the building was under attack.

Bolan fired a kick into the door, smashing it open, shattering the jamb and the lock mechanism with the force of the blow. He lowered his shoulder and pushed through the doorway, planting the blade of the knife in the face of the ES terrorist on the other side.

The Heckler & Koch VP 70 was scuffed and worn, but the weight was right when he scooped it up from the floor. He fired twice into the nearest terrorist, a man standing at a workbench in the room beyond the entry chamber. It was another bomb workshop, and Lemaire's forces were hard at work constructing explosives for use on the people of Paris. There was no telling how many volatile substances might be arrayed here, but there were half a dozen men standing within, all of them moving to take cover behind the benches and their dangerous stock.

Bolan ripped the knife from his shoulder harness and cut through the strap of his canvas war bag. Dropping the bag on the floor, he reached in, took a single grenade and yanked out the pin.

He dropped the grenade back in the bag.

The Executioner wrenched the door open, made his way through the chamber and climbed up the ladder leading to the door. The moment the door opened, his ears found the sounds of magazines being changed and bolts being pulled back. In a fraction of a second the gunners on the ground floor would—

The entire building rocked as the explosives in the basement detonated.

Bolan rolled away from the door just in time. It was blown to fragments by the gout of fire that rushed up from below. The soldier could feel heat on his back through his jacket. Splinters pierced his flesh. The chain reaction of explosions beneath the floor shook fragments from the wall and ceiling, raining down still more plaster debris and pieces of the ceiling above.

The shock waves from below had sufficiently distracted the gunmen on the ground floor, allowing Bolan to expend precious seconds examining the M16. The receiver was bent and the selector switch jammed. The rifle had absorbed either shrapnel or a bullet meant for him; it had saved his life. He unclipped his sling and left the weapon where it lay, his borrowed VP 70 ready in his hand. He stood. Vibrations from the basement were still causing the floorboards to shudder under his feet.

Bolan ran.

He pushed himself through the corridor as quickly as he could, and at each doorway, at each alcove, he pumped bullets into the men sheltering there. The running, gunning blitz took the stunned gunmen completely by surprise. When the Heckler & Koch ran dry he let it fall, drawing his Beretta 93R and switching the weapon to fire 3-round bursts.

Four of the enemy met him on the stairs. They raised their guns; Bolan shot the closest one through the face.

The Beretta was empty.

Even as he shoved the Beretta behind his belt, he was drawing the Desert Eagle. The first of its .44 Magnum rounds blew a crater through the forehead of the second gunner. The dead man's fingers clenched and the MAT-49 submachine gun discharged, carving a furrow in the steps in front of Bolan's boots.

The soldier continued charging the stairs. He collided with the third man before the terrorist could acquire his target. Bolan shoved the barrel of the Desert Eagle up under the man's chin and pulled the trigger, blowing his skull apart.

Suddenly he was staring down the barrel of a .45-caliber pistol.

The muzzle of the 1911-pattern gun was huge in his vision. Bolan did not think about what he was seeing;

he simply reacted, snaring the gun arm and snaking his own limb up and through, driving himself through the last of this knot of enemy operatives. The gunman screamed as his elbow snapped. Bolan brought the butt of the Desert Eagle down on his adversary's face, crushing the bridge of his nose. His eyes rolled up into the back of his head and he collapsed.

The second floor door was another heavy wooden barrier with metal crossbars. Bolan hit it with his shoulder and grunted with the impact. Taking a step back on the landing, he kicked it hard. It did not budge.

Bolan's ears were ringing from the gunfire and the explosions. The air was heavy with smoke. The building was likely on fire; the conflagration he had started in the basement would have to be moving up through the floor and walls. It was only a matter of time.

He aimed the Desert Eagle and emptied its magazine into the lock mechanism of the door. The rounds chewed away at the wood and battered the locking mechanism into a shapeless lump of metal.

Bolan threw himself at the door again. It moved but did not give completely. He hit it again and finally the hinges gave, tearing away from the wall. The door crashed to the hardwood of the second floor. Bolan was now in an antechamber that looked like an improvised office.

A single terrified man stared back at him through the eye holes of his black ski mask. He started to raise a revolver.

"Put it down," Bolan growled.

The revolver continued to rise.

Bolan lunged and smashed the terrorist in the face with the heavy Desert Eagle. The blow caused the man's head to snap to the side. He collapsed to the floor in a heap.

The Executioner located the remaining loaded magazines among his gear. He reloaded both his pistols and, with one weapon in each hand, smashed through the door separating him from the rest of the second floor.

Already the air of the second floor was beginning to grow hazy with smoke. The acrid mist stung his eyes and made them water.

With the Beretta in hand, he checked the first of the bedrooms. It was empty. The second bore what had to be an ES banner tacked to the wall.

Farther on he found a pair of double doors that had been erected to divide the second floor of the estate. He put his ear to the door and listened for a moment. Silence had overtaken the building. Gunfire had been replaced with the distant crackle of flames.

Outside the tactical teams—speaking in French through a bullhorn—were broadcasting orders to the estate. Since they were talking, that meant they weren't attempting to breach the perimeter. Likely, with Bayard's input, they were waiting to see if Bolan—or anyone—emerged alive from the war zone Agent Cooper had created.

Some part of Bolan's mind could see the humor in that. He had performed exactly to Inspector Bayard's expectations.

The double doors gave way more easily than previous barriers. No sooner had he breached these than he found himself facing more terrorists with guns. There were three of them, only one of them wearing his ski mask. They were pointing French MAT-49 submachine guns at two men, presumably hostages, who had been stripped to their shorts and were kneeling on the floor with their heads bowed.

The hostages had their hands clasped behind their backs. Bolan quickly surveyed the room. What he estimated was a last set of doors—based on the size of the estate—waited beyond these men. The gunners screamed at him in French to put down his weapons or the hostages would be killed.

It was just too convenient for the enemy to have hostages on hand for such an emergency as a hit on the estate. And the two "hostages" happened to have interesting tattoos.

Mack Bolan had—in his time prosecuting his endless war—faced neo-Nazis and racist skinheads of every possible stripe. They were one of his more common foes. Over the years he had developed a real distaste for such men, for they were simply brutal murderers motivated by irrational fear and racial hatred. The "hostages" were covered in racist ink.

There were no swastikas. On this side of the ocean, even the criminal element wasn't as free with the old Nazi symbol as American racist gangs tended to be, given the sometimes very strict laws regarding expressions of the war-era National Socialist regime. But there were other slogans and symbols: including the numerals "88," a reference to Heil Hitler; or the initials *HH,* as the letter *H* was the eighth letter of the English alphabet; and other iconography that Bolan had seen before.

The men on the floor probably had weapons held behind their backs. Bolan needed only to spring the trap.

"Easy," Bolan said in French. "Everyone put down their guns, and this doesn't become a bloodbath."

"It already *is* a bloodbath," the man in the ski mask replied. "You have slain everyone below us. You have murdered our comrades."

One of the other gunmen spit on the ground.

"You know," Bolan said, "this whole hostage thing—"

"Silence!" the masked gunman barked. "This is your last warning! We will kill the hostages."

"Not if I kill them first." The Executioner snapped his pistols on target.

Both of the kneeling men had time to look surprised. One even managed to yank the snub-nosed revolver from behind his back and squeeze off a shot. The bullet went nowhere near Bolan.

The soldier let one of his legs collapse beneath him. He folded to the floor in a sitting, cross-legged posture known in some martial-arts styles as a "sit," a way to quickly lower the center of gravity while maintaining one's balance. The Beretta chugged out 3-round bursts as the Desert Eagle roared its .44 Magnum thunder.

The hostage on the right took a .44 bullet to the face. The hollowpoint round coated the hostage beside him with an oozing wash of dark red blood, bone and brain. The hostage on the left was nearly decapitated by the burst that stitched his neck.

Automatic gunfire hammered Bolan's eardrums as the uniformed gunmen doused the room in lead. The soldier simply opened his arms, walking his guns left and right, shooting each one of the ES men, pumping round after round into them when they would not go down, enveloped in the chaos of the moment and the deafening, blood-quickening storm of life-or-death close-quarters combat. Bolan continued to lean away and down until his back was on the floor and his legs were uncomfortably stretched beneath him. He could feel the burning in his thighs and lower spine.

The last of the bodies collapsed onto the floor.

Bolan's back was now wet. Blood was pooling beneath the corpses and spreading across the floor. The soldier looked up at the ceiling and could see smoke gathering. The sound of crackling flames was louder. Outside the estate he could hear the sounds of what he assumed were emergency vehicles responding to the fire. They were distant yet.

Bolan reloaded his weapons again. He was running out of ammunition. It had been necessary to sacrifice the war bag's payload, and to do it as quickly as he had, in order to end the threat of the bomb factory in the basement. But that did not change the fact that he would soon be outgunned.

Quickly he surveyed his body as he rolled and rose to one knee. He felt several different aches and pains. He was also covered in splashes of blood from his enemies, not to mention the wounds from splinters and shrapnel.

Beneath him, the floor was growing hot. Something in the flooring started to creak.

They were definitely running out of time. He went to reach for the nearest of the MAT-49s. They were an old design but serviceable. The gunmen had sprayed out their magazines most likely, but they might have spares somewhere on their bodies.

The double doors opposite him were thrown open. Bolan continued his roll. Bullets tore into the floor and into the pile of corpses. The shooters wore camouflage BDUs and were trying to acquire their target with AK-pattern rifles. Bolan was a sitting duck.

He did the only thing he could do: he stayed prone and fired his weapons with calm deliberation, despite the fury of the bullets striking all around him, despite the corpses jerking under the onslaught, despite the noise and the nearness of death and the knowledge, the ever-present knowledge, that he was one man against many.

When the discharge smoke from filthy, poorly maintained weapons finally cleared, Bolan was the lone survivor, and his guns were empty. He searched the corpses nearest him, but there was no time to be more thorough. He found no ammunition close to hand, no substitute weapon he could use. The submachine guns of the dead men were likewise empty.

He stowed his guns and drew his knife. Its blade was still discolored from the blood of already fallen men.

Bolan got to his feet and walked through the double doors.

CHAPTER TWELVE

"The house is on fire," Anton Lemaire stated.

"So it is," Bolan replied.

The French terrorist stood at the end of a largely empty room, his back to the door. He stood before a large window with an elaborate carved wooden frame. Heavy blackout curtains hung before it. Bolan noted the drapes; they would prevent a sniper from taking a bead on Lemaire, although Bolan had no idea what orders the tactical teams might have about initiating deadly force.

There were a few freestanding torso dummies here, of the type used in mixed martial arts gyms. There was also a weight bench and a rack of free weights. The room smelled of sweat and disinfectant beneath the odor of smoke.

Lemaire had stripped to the waist. His upper body was powerfully muscular. His hands were at his sides, concealing his belt line on the left and the right. If he had a pistol in his waistband, Bolan could not see it from behind the man.

The range was poor. It was not far enough that Bolan could expect to dodge gunfire, but it was too far for him to close the distance to Lemaire with complete confidence that he could reach the man before taking a bullet.

"You are the CIA man," Lemaire said. He was completely immobile, a statue. Bolan watched him for the slightest twitch, the first hint of aggressive action. "The man whom Levesque, that traitor, so feared that he took his own life."

"How did you know?" Bolan asked. If he could keep the man talking, keep his mind engaged, he might be able to take him by surprise. He inched slightly forward.

"I bugged his office," Lemaire replied. "As brilliant as he thought he was, he never thought to check himself or his environment for something so simple."

Well, Bolan thought. That certainly cleared that up. The simplest explanations were usually the correct ones.

"You know the old saying?" Bolan asked.

"That only a fool fights in a burning house?" Lemaire said. "I believe I saw that on television. A space fantasy program of some kind."

"You don't strike me as a big television watcher."

"No? I never was as a boy. I was too busy fighting to survive. I have much more leisure time now. But I hate it. I hate to rest, to do nothing. It breeds weakness. Weakness of that type is what made Levesque the creature he became."

"Lay down any weapons you have," Bolan said. "We'll walk out of here before the place burns down. The ES is destroyed, Lemaire. Your men are dead."

"Killed them all, have you? You. One man."

"The basement is gone. The first floor is full of dead men. You're standing on top of a pile of corpses."

"A pyre, American," Lemaire said. "A funeral pyre that you created."

"Last chance," Bolan warned. "Come with me or you leave here in an ashtray."

Lemaire threw his head back and laughed. "What

dramatic gesture would you accept, American? I have no gun to throw down."

"Then we have no problem," Bolan said. "Unless you have other weapons." His hand clenched on the grip of his own knife. He bent his knees, preparing for what was to happen.

"I'm going to turn around now, American."

"Do it slowly."

"I notice you have no gun in your hand," Lemaire said, glancing over his shoulder. "I don't think there is anything you can do to stop me. Is there?"

"Don't."

The smoke was growing thicker. The roar of flame was audible against the bullhorn shouts in French from outside.

The Executioner saw the flicker of movement he was waiting for.

It was more subtle than most men could pull off, but Bolan saw it nonetheless. The muscles of Lemaire's neck twitched almost imperceptibly.

Bolan threw himself forward.

Lemaire's thrown knife shot through the open doorway behind Bolan and lodged somewhere in the room beyond. Lemaire, to his credit, did not waste time cursing his fate or questioning his throw. He simply kept yanking knives from his belt sheaths and hurling them, his aim precise, his throws expert.

Bolan closed the distance, twisting and turning, narrowly missing the knives, almost dancing his way toward Lemaire. His knife was in his hand when the two fighters collided. The blade went in overhand, edge out, and sank in deep just past Lemaire's clavicle.

The terrorist leader jerked out of Bolan's grip. The haft of the soldier's knife jutted from Lemaire's body as if his left shoulder had grown a handle. He turned to look at the weapon.

"You were…trying for the subclavian," he breathed heavily.

He kicked Bolan in the face.

The blow took the soldier by surprise. While Lemaire's kick was no more nontelegraphic than what had to have been a practiced knife throw, it was damned fast. The edge of Lemaire's boot caught Bolan across the right cheek and snapped his head backward, hard enough that he saw a flash of light with the connection.

Lemaire had his right hand up now. The left hung limply at his flank, but otherwise he seemed not even to notice the knife rammed into his shoulder. His kicks were fluid, and his reach was long. He spun and kicked, his feet describing long arcs through the air. Bolan managed to avoid the worst of them but caught a glancing blow to his left arm before taking another solid kick to the side of his body. The small wounds he had incurred in his breach of the estate were starting to make themselves felt. Every nerve ending in his body was screaming.

Bolan had to get inside the range of Lemaire's legs. The style was savate, or something similar—Bolan recognized it readily enough—and it was most dangerous at long range, where the kicks carried the most impact. Close quarter combatives were a game of infighting, of getting right on top of the enemy. That would neutralize Lemaire's considerable skill and deny him his most powerful weapons, his leg muscles. Close in, Lemaire would be forced to fight with only one hand, for his left side was useless.

Bolan waited, ducking out of range as Lemaire threw several more kicks. Bolan stepped in, stepped back and repeated the maneuver as Lemaire found a rhythm. The terrorist was smiling. He had picked up on what Bolan wanted him to see: the soldier was coming just a little closer each time, seemingly giving the Frenchman the opening he needed for a power blow. Lemaire loved high kicks; that much was obvious. Bolan raised his chin slightly. He would draw Lemaire in for the throat shot the killer would be searching for.

Lemaire made his move. Bolan shifted, taking the sweep of the kick against his body, pushing forward so that his adversary's foot struck air beyond where the soldier stood. The Executioner brought his elbow down on Lemaire's calf. The Frenchman screamed.

He toppled to the floor, and Bolan went down with him. The large terrorist struggled beneath the big American, but soon the soldier had him pinned, mounting Lemaire's chest and raining down hammer-fist blows onto his opponent's face. It was a maneuver in sporting combat known as the "ground and pound," and while Bolan was no sporting martial artist, he understood the utility of pinning a man with his weight and smashing that man with the meaty undersides of his fists.

Lemaire groped for something concealed in the pocket of his BDU pants.

Bolan heard the snap of the knife well before he saw the weapon. The folding knife had a vicious hook-shaped, hawk-bill blade with a serrated edge. Bolan managed to clamp a wrist over Lemaire's before the Frenchman could begin carving away the flesh of Bolan's thigh.

Lemaire pulled his arm sharply inward.

Bolan was pulled closer to the Frenchman, which was exactly what the wounded terrorist wanted. He wrapped the fingers of his other hand around Bolan's throat. It was a battle of strength, now, with gravity pinning Lemaire, and the terrorist leader's fist squeezing off Bolan's air supply…as both men battled for the knife. If Lemaire managed to pull it free, he could maim or kill Bolan in an instant.

It was one of the truisms of fighting on the ground with another man in real life. A simple folding knife changed the entire game.

Bolan used his right hand to fight off the fingers around his neck, squeezing Lemaire's wrist. The Frenchman was incredibly strong, fueled by adrenaline and the knowledge that he was going to die on the floor of the estate. Bolan could breathe, but only barely. It was a stalemate.

The floor beneath them was growing hotter. Bolan's nose twitched. Smoke was now hanging like a bank of storm clouds on the ceiling. Somewhere at the other end of the floor, what Bolan thought had to be a smoke alarm was beeping furiously.

"The sounds of chaos, American," Lemaire hissed. "We die…together."

"Give up, and we can both walk out of here," Bolan said. "You've lost, Lemaire."

"Not for me the easy death," Lemaire whispered. "Not for me the coward's release. I will gladly take you with me, American. You and your government schemes and your foolish belief in your own superiority. You and your love for inferior races. We die in the fire, American."

"You'll die alone," Bolan gritted out. "You'll burn alone. And for nothing. And everything you've devoted your life to, all the hate that motivates you, will be nothing but ashes by tomorrow morning."

Lemaire screamed and struggled to bring up his

knife hand. The fingers of his other hand grasped more tightly around Bolan's neck. The soldier could no longer breathe. His vision was starting to blur. The world turned an amber-pink hue. Oxygen deprivation was claiming him. If he passed out, if his strength wavered even a little, Lemaire would finish him off.

The evil grin on Lemaire's face widened. "Which will it be, American?" he whispered. "The blade in your belly? Or the sweet release of the gray death, as you lose your grip and fall asleep? Shall I sing you a lullaby?"

Spots began to dance in front of Bolan's eyes. The folding knife with its wickedly curved, serrated blade was inching closer to him as he fought to keep it away. Worse, Bolan's eyes were drying in the heat, as if they were boiling. He knew the feeling. He had been in enough parched desert combat zones to know the effects of extreme heat.

So many ways to die. So many choices…none of them acceptable.

"Lemaire," Bolan growled. Orange light danced beneath the floorboards. The surface on which they fought was aflame beneath them. The flames had only to eat through the boards themselves and the room would be a furnace.

"Which lullaby would you like to hear, American?" Lemaire grinned. Would you like to—"

Bolan stopped trying to relieve the pressure from Lemaire's hand on his neck and instead wrenched his combat knife from Lemaire's shoulder and rammed it through the man's left eye socket.

The floor was shifting beneath him again when he finally staggered to his feet. Still shaking off Lemaire's attempt to choke him to death, he did the only thing he could do to prevent himself from being burned alive.

He jumped out the window.

BLACKNESS. MACK BOLAN swam through blackness. But the blackness hurt, which meant he wasn't dead. At least he assumed he wasn't. "Cooper!" Inspector Bayard said. His face loomed over Bolan's. "Cooper, can you hear me?"

"I could use some water," Bolan said.

Bayard's worried expression eased a bit. "Here. Let me help you sit up. Take this."

Bolan accepted the metal canteen cup of water he was given. It was cold and tasted of steel. He drank it anyway, enjoying the cool sensation that spread through his body.

He was on a compact bedroll that had been extended in the shelter of one of the French tactical teams' armored vehicles. He could see a dense cloud of thick, black smoke rising into the sky. Even from his position he could feel the heat and hear the flames. There were also fire department trucks working their way through the barricade. The sound of their emergency horns assaulted Bolan's eardrums.

Bolan checked himself. His pistols were gone. He had not expected that, but it was no surprise to him that he found no combat knife. That was back with Lemaire, probably still in the French terrorist's eye socket.

"My weapons?"

"Confiscated by the authorities," Bayard said, shrugging. He jerked his chin at the cordon around them. "Here."

The inspector passed a newspaper-wrapped bundle to Bolan. The soldier unwrapped it and discovered it contained a Glock 19 and several loaded 15-round magazines. He looked up at Bayard and raised an eyebrow.

"To whom do I owe the favor?"

"To me," Bayard said. "It is a loan from a friend that I suspect will not be returned. So you owe me the cost of the weapon. Among other things."

Bolan's leather coat was ripped and scorched and smelled of smoke. He shrugged out of it and left it in a pile next to him. He also took off his now useless leather shoulder harness and put it with the coat.

"I have battle dress uniforms in your color," Bayard said. "I believe I have judged your size correctly. Your clothing is not dissimilar to those worn by the tactical teams. You should thank me, Cooper. I have convinced them not to arrest you, telling them I already have you in provisional custody. Let me see your jacket."

Bolan handed the garment to Bayard. "Can you get me a windbreaker or something?"

"Yes," Bayard said. "And something else I suspect you will want." He disappeared around the corner of the vehicle for a moment. When he returned, he was holding a heavy messenger bag made of black canvas. He handed it to Bolan. "It is empty, this man purse."

"It's a war bag, not a man purse."

"As you say." The Frenchman shrugged. "Your wounds were cleaned and bandaged while you slept."

"I hope the nurse was pretty," Bolan said.

"His name is Helmut. Years ago he defected from East Germany. He weighs nearly three hundred pounds and is blind in one eye. He can also lift a truck by the bumper."

"Not my type," Bolan said. He stepped out, stood on the ground, steadying himself against the armored car. Turning, he surveyed the estate, which was now an inferno. The heat from the fire played across his skin, and he coughed, more by reflex than from a real need.

"How do you feel?" Bayard asked. "You may have some smoke inhalation."

"I'm fine."

"Tell me something, Cooper. Did you see Leslie Deparmond inside?"

Bolan stared. "No. It was Lemaire and what's left of the ES troops. They're dead. Bomb factory in the basement."

"This blew up prematurely?" Bayard asked.

"It had help."

"Of course it did."

"Why do you ask?"

"Because that coroner's vehicle there," Bayard said, pointing to the emergency vehicles moving through an opening in the cordon, "is carrying the corpse of Deparmond. It would seem that Gaston will be running more or less unopposed. Deparmond's party will furnish a last-minute candidate, probably, but such a man is unknown to the people. He will have no chance of victory in the wake of the scandal."

"Spell it out for me," Bolan said.

"He died here. Or so it has been made to appear. His body shows no signs that he was inside when the fire occurred. We found him on the grounds near a rear entrance."

"That doesn't make any sense," Bolan said.

"It does if his body was brought here for us to find. He has been shot with a single bullet at close range. The gun was found with him. It has been made to look as if, out of shame, he took his own life."

"Lot of that going around," Bolan stated.

"Eh?"

"Levesque," Bolan said by way of explanation. "Something's not right."

"Yes," Bayard agreed. "How would you say it? Something is of the fish, *n'est-ce pas?*"

"Fishy," Bolan corrected him, not really hearing the inspector. He was already considering the implications of what Bayard had told him, not to mention the fallout of Deparmond being killed. On paper, it wrapped everything up neatly. Gaston would surely take the election now. The Man's interests, and therefore Bolan's mandate to safeguard the United States' interests in the region, were satisfied. There it was, all tied up in a nice, neat bow.

"I don't like this at all," he said. "If Deparmond's a plant…"

"Then it means the enemy forces are actively working to build a narrative," Bayard added. "This begs the question—to accomplish what? As, seemingly, their goals have already failed, and the back of their organization is now broken."

"Can you get us a car?"

"I can. For what purpose? I was hoping you would allow me to drive you to the airport."

"You and I both know this isn't over."

"No," Bayard said. "Obviously not. But what can you do, Cooper? Your government's needs have been satisfied, have they not? And the threat of the ES is now ended. You have single-handedly destroyed their operation in Paris. I am amazed you lived through the experience."

Bolan shook his head. "I'm not convinced."

The soldier's secure satellite smartphone began to vibrate in his pocket. He took it out and flipped it open.

"Cooper here," he said. He was signaling the Farm that his conversation was being overheard on his end.

"We've received certain situation updates through

channels," Barbara Price stated. "The French media is going to run with news of Deparmond's death. Things are about to get even more interesting over there. And you probably already know that the French are demanding we pull you out. Director Vigneau of the DCRI has practically had a coronary on the phone."

"Not a surprise," Bolan said. "How is our mutual friend holding up?" He was referring to Brognola.

"He understands," Price replied. "But he's got a lot on his plate now. It's stressful. I'm sure you can relate."

"I can. Message received and understood. I'll make arrangements for extraction...but not yet. I have some confirmations I need to conduct."

"I trust your judgment," Price told him, "but you know I have to ask you if that's absolutely necessary."

"It is. There're some things I need to take care of right away. I'm going to have to call you later."

"Make it soon...Agent Cooper," Price said. "Everyone here is very eager to speak with you. Our mutual friend has other friends who are interested." That would be the Man, and by extension the United States government as a whole. In theory, the Sensitive Operations Group answered only to the President. In execution, SOG and Brognola were always playing a very complicated political game.

"I understand the...factors involved," Bolan said. "I'll do what has to be done."

"I know you will."

"Cooper out." Bolan closed the phone.

"I will pretend I don't understand what that was about," Bayard said.

"Good. Let's get moving."

"*Oui*. Let's get moving. I have done nothing insanely dangerous for entire *minutes*."

CHAPTER THIRTEEN

Outside Paris, France

The Citroën C4 Aircross carried Bolan and Inspector Bayard across the countryside in reasonable comfort. It was silver in color, fairly nondescript as modern sport-utility vehicles went and roomy enough that Bolan's big frame didn't feel compressed. The soldier had verified the name and then the address of the digital media expert Gerard Levesque had given him. They were on their way there now.

The plan was to engage Edouard Tessier and see what he knew. If he had evidence that would validate the videos of Deparmond—videos now in the hands of both the press and the authorities, thanks to whatever arrangements Levesque had made before his death—so much the better. If Tessier could determine them to be fakes, that would complicate things, but it would at least confirm Bolan's suspicion that something was amiss.

Tessier's home was some distance outside Paris. The inspector and the soldier had by now left behind what passed for suburbs and the sprawling semiurban areas around Paris proper. The drive gave Bolan time to collect his thoughts, which was to say, it gave him time to sleep on and off as Bayard drove.

"It amazes me," Bayard said, "that you sleep so

readily. Tell me, Cooper, how many men have you killed today?"

"Every time you ask questions like that," Bolan replied, without opening his eyes, "you sound less and less irritated."

"I told you. The results you have achieved have earned you a certain amount of respect in my eyes. But that does not explain how a man who has just destroyed a small army with his own hands can sleep as if he has not a care in the world."

"Easy," Bolan said. "Fighting small armies makes you tired."

"I suppose it makes you hungry, as well."

"I could eat." Bolan honestly hadn't considered it, but, at the mention of food, he realized he was indeed very hungry.

Bayard reached across the soldier and removed a package from the glove compartment. He handed it to Bolan. "Save one for me," Bayard said. "I will have something to eat later, perhaps."

Inside the foil package were several roast beef sandwiches. Bolan took two gratefully. There was already a bottle of water in the cup holder on Bolan's side. After checking the bottle for needle marks, he opened it and drank. Bolan's ingrained habit wouldn't stop a truly determined act of poisoning or drugging, of course; there were ways to seal a water bottle again after opening it to tamper with its contents. But he was not actually concerned about Bayard.

"That is odd," Bayard said, after they had driven in silence for some time.

"What?" Bolan asked. He was finishing his second sandwich.

"Men on motorcycles," the inspector replied. "Waiting by the roadside. If I did not know better, I would have thought they were wearing—"

"Woodland camouflage and black ski masks?" Bolan asked, sitting forward to check the rearview mirror on his side. "Trademark garb of ES."

Bayard, also looking in the rearview mirror, sighed. "Yes. That was it exactly."

"Maybe that wasn't it."

"Perhaps. Do you think we are that lucky?"

"No," Bolan said.

"Nor do I."

The whine of the motorcycles gaining on them was suddenly very loud. Bolan glanced at the GPS unit on the dash of the Citroën.

"If this map isn't too simplified," Bolan said, pointing to the moving diagram on the touch screen. "This is a bottleneck. This route leads to the address we want, and there are no major alternatives. This is the likely place to stage an ambush if they knew what to look for."

"To what end?" Bayard asked. He began to accelerate.

"I'd say somebody doesn't want us to talk to this Edouard Tessier," Bolan said. "And if there are still elements of the ES out there, it means the business with Lemaire wasn't the end of it at all. Maybe there are still some roots to this mess we haven't dug out and burned yet."

"You are a creature of dynamic metaphors," Bayard said. "Perhaps they are simply a motorcycle club with an ironic taste in fashion. It may be nothing. It may be coincidence."

Bayard's side view mirror was shattered by a bullet.

Bolan braced himself as automatic gunfire began

peppering the rear of the Citroën, shattering the window of the SUV's hatchback.

"You are bad luck, Cooper," Bayard said. "I am convinced of it. What is the word in English? Accursed?"

"Just cursed, I think is what you're looking for."

"Cursed," Bayard repeated. "But I must admit something." He stepped on the pedal and the Citroën roared as it revved to redline. The SUV quickly put distance between the two men and the motorcycles, but the bikes were faster and began to eat up ground in response.

"We are not going to outrun them," Bayard said. The motorcycles began trying to flank them. Bolan knew as well as the inspector that this could lead nowhere good. The men on the bikes would begin firing into the rear tires of the SUV and bring it to a halt, then fire away at the men inside. Bayard took evasive action, causing the SUV to yaw from side to side on shocks that were not designed for such violent maneuvers.

"Oncoming traffic!" Bolan warned.

Bayard saw it and overcompensated. The SUV nearly went up on two wheels, but the inspector was able to bring it back under control again.

"This is not good," Bayard said.

"On your left, on your left!" Bolan gritted out.

"I see it," Bayard said, narrowly missing an older Peugeot. Just then, one of the motorcycles took advantage of the opening and surged past the Citroën SUV. "*Mon Dieu!* He is going to—"

The motorcycle headed straight for a passenger car that was coming in the opposite direction. Bayard floored the gas pedal and succeeded in bringing the SUV alongside the bike. He rolled down his window and began shouting at the driver.

When he looked back up he realized his mistake.

The road was too narrow, the distance too short. There was no way to stop the ES terrorist on the motorcycle from striking the passenger vehicle that was coming. It was a small car, some sort of mini-import. If the vehicles struck head-on, innocents would be killed.

Mack Bolan could not permit that.

The soldier reached over and shoved the steering wheel with one hand.

The Citroën struck the motorcycle, pushing it out of the direct path of the oncoming car. There was still a collision, but it was not as severe. Bayard glared at Bolan but brought the SUV to a halt next to the other two vehicles. Bolan was immediately out of the SUV with his Glock in hand.

The man on the motorcycle was now pinned beneath his vehicle. The roar of the other pursuing motorbikes was very loud as they surrounded the crash scene. Bolan did not waste any time. He went to the fallen bike and put a bullet in the head of the man beneath it. The terrorist had been reaching for a holstered pistol strapped to the fairing of the motorcycle.

Bolan swiveled, went to one knee and engaged the other motorcyclists.

The ES terrorists split up, moving left and right around the SUV, using it as a barricade. Bayard unlimbered his .38 and took cover behind his vehicle's engine block. Bullets struck the hood. The motorcyclists had MAT-49 submachine guns and were doing their best to empty the magazines.

"They must have gotten a good deal on those things," Bolan muttered.

"What?" Bayard shot back.

"Nothing. Check the car! I'll cover you!"

Bayard nodded. He went to the vehicle and took up a protective position by it.

"Cooper!" the inspector shouted after a moment. He took a shot at one of the terrorists and succeeded in scoring a hit. Another of the cyclists took the man's place on the far end of the hastily parked SUV.

"What have you got?" Bolan shouted back.

"I have a man, his wife and their fifteen-year-old daughter," Bayard said. "The husband is having chest pains. I believe he may be having a heart attack!"

"Call for medical evac," Bolan said. "Can you get a hospital chopper in here?"

"I can," Bayard said. "But I must guide them to me. What about you?"

"I'll take this party down the road," Bolan replied. He ran for the Citroën.

"Cooper!" Bayard shouted. "Cooper! Wait!"

"No time!"

The Executioner shot another terrorist before making the driver's side of the SUV. Bullets pocked the driver's door. Bolan ignored the slugs ripping holes in the seats around him, put the vehicle in gear and slammed his combat boot onto the accelerator.

He needed to make sure the ES terrorists would follow him, not stay to exchange fire with Bayard. He hauled the steering wheel over and cut a tight circle, burning rubber with the SUV's all-season tires, and targeted the motorcycles. The Citroën crashed into first one, then another, sending the men aboard them falling and diving for cover.

The wheels bounced and the SUV bucked as Bolan crushed one of the gunmen under the vehicle.

Bolan rolled down his window. Glock in hand, he sprayed out most of a magazine into the scattered ES gunmen. Two of them fell, never to stand again. He deliberately drove the SUV over one of the corpses to anger the other ES troops.

His calculated act of disrespect produced the desired outcome. The remaining ES gunners were in a rage by the time they caught up with him farther down the road.

The GPS pinged. Bolan glanced at it. Apparently he was getting very close to this destination, but he had to deal with the men chasing him, the men who had been lying in wait to ambush him.

They were clearly ES operatives. That meant some part of the ES was alive and well, which meant his mission was not as far along as he had believed it to be. That pointed to a hole, a miscalculation somewhere along the way.

No plan survived first contact with the enemy, he reminded himself. Talking to Tessier was now more important than ever. The digital expert was the only lead Bolan had, the only thread he could pick up to put him back on task. He was accustomed to these moments. They occurred in many battles, in many campaigns. The key was to be as flexible as possible, to adapt to new adversities in order to turn them into opportunities.

He spared a look behind him and almost lost control of the SUV when another stream of bullets walked up the middle of the Citroën from outside. The dashboard was struck repeatedly, drawing a squealing metallic noise from just beyond the firewall. The dash fan had been hit apparently. The scraping noise was an automotive banshee under the Citroën's hood.

The GPS had not been hit.

Bolan was grateful for that. He noted the location ahead. He was almost on top of his target. One of the ES motorcyclists pulled up alongside him, leveling a

Makarov pistol, and Bolan swung the wheel hard. The Citroën crashed into the motorcycle and sent the driver to the pavement in a screaming, ripping, bloody mess. Bolan guided the SUV back into the center of the road.

The target address was now directly ahead of him.

Crushing the brake pedal beneath his boot, he succeed in stopping the SUV so suddenly that one of the remaining ES bikers crashed into the back of the Citroën. Bolan swiveled and, still in the driver's seat, extended the Glock. He fired through the opening of the broken hatchback and took the faltering biker through the right eye socket. Then Bolan rolled out of the Citroën.

Steam hissed from the SUV's engine. It was pocked and starred with bullet holes. Most of its glass had been broken out. The left rear tire was going flat before Bolan's eyes; a nick from a bullet had eventually become a leak.

The last pair of ES bikers rolled to a stop some distance from the Citroën. That was smart. They probably knew that, protected by the engine block of the SUV, Bolan could shoot them down as they approached on the bikes. There was no advantage to using the vehicles and much danger, so the two hardmen ditched their machines and approached on foot in a half crouch. They were still far enough away that Bolan was largely concealed behind the Citroën. They were gambling, he suspected, that they could get abreast of the SUV with their submachine guns and spray the interior before Bolan could mount an effective resistance.

The Glock 19 was a compact version of the Glock 17, the weapon that had seen the introduction of the Austrian weapon to America. While not a "true" compact weapon in that there were many who considered the Model 19 a more comfortable full-sized pistol, it was no sniper's tool. To fire precision shots at long ranges with the Glock required a man with considerable skill as a marksman, as its maximum range was roughly fifty yards, depending on windage.

Mack Bolan was one of the world's best.

He took a deep breath, let out half and held the rest. With his arms extended over the hood of the Citroën, he lined up the triple-dot pattern tritium night sights of the Glock on the first of the approaching targets. The Glock's trigger pull was notoriously light, it's "safe action" built for rugged performance. The weapon had never been intended for what he was asking it to do.

The Glock barked once.

The shot cored through the chin of the closer of the two terrorists, blowing apart his lower jaw, dropping him where he stood. His partner opened up, blazing away on full automatic with another MAT-49, charging the SUV. Bullets sang a metallic symphony along the body of the abused Citroën.

Bolan dropped to one knee, where he crouched before the grille of the vehicle. The angle was poor. He would need to leave the cover of the vehicle if he was to line up the shot. On one knee, he crab-walked from beyond the shadow of the truck.

The terrorist's weapon stopped firing. It was empty. He stopped moving and, almost comically, looked down at the submachine gun as if it had betrayed him.

Bolan pulled the trigger of his Glock.

The weapon did not fire. Without thinking, he slapped the magazine, ran the side back and noted the unfired round that flew over his shoulder when he racked the pistol. He acquired his target again and, as his arms reached full extension in a two-hand grip, he pulled the trigger—

Again, nothing happened.

Catastrophic malfunctions were rare in modern service weapons, especially those as reliable as the Glock autopistols, but they did occur. Bolan did not know the provenance of this borrowed weapon. He had no idea how many rounds it had fired, whether it had been properly maintained, or if it had a history of misfires. It was possible the firing pin had broken; excessive dry firing in training could produce such a malfunction over time.

The ES man yelled a battle cry, dropped his weapon and drew a wicked knuckle-guard knife from a sheath on his belt. He charged again, heading straight for Bolan, determined to put the blade of the massive black-coated trench knife in the soldier's body.

Bolan still held his pistol and, as the ES man came into range, he used it as a club, bashing the charging terrorist's temple with the heavy metal slide. The enemy ripped off his ski mask, revealing swollen, Neanderthal-like features. The terrorist was a large, powerful man sporting a blond crew cut. He had a teardrop tattoo on one cheek.

"I cut you," he said in English.

The heavy knife slashed patterns in the air, which Bolan managed to evade. The two men began circling each other. As large as Bolan was, the ES man was larger. In terms of raw strength and reach, the terrorist had the advantage.

"You're finished," Bolan said quietly. "The ES is broken. Get gone, and I won't follow you."

The terrorist grinned. "I cut you," he repeated.

Bolan lunged. He shoved the pistol forward as if he

were about to shoot it, but instead of pulling the now useless trigger, he smashed the barrel of the gun into the ES man's eye socket. The blow was hard enough to drive the slide back.

The terrorist screamed and dropped to one knee by the side of the road.

Bolan took a moment to survey the road in front of the target house. There had been no other traffic, but that could not last, not this relatively close to Paris. Sooner or later a citizen would see what was happening and call in the cops, if Bayard's call for a medical evac did not already prompt a law enforcement response. Bolan didn't have long to conduct his interview with Tessier before things got uncomfortable. On both knees now, the terrorist wailed. His hands were cupped over his injured eye.

Bolan threw an outside crescent kick that caught the injured man under the chin. He collapsed on the pavement, out cold. That was good enough for now. Bolan rolled him over and took a trusty plastic zip-tie cuff from his pocket. He had lost his Kissinger-supplied war bag and supplies, but Bolan still had a few items.

Satisfied that enemy resistance had been fought to zero, Bolan discarded his Glock, walked to the corpse of the other man he had sniped with the pistol and took up the man's MAT-49. There was a spare magazine in the dead man's belt. He took it, loaded it into the vintage French weapon and chambered a round.

He took up a position next to the front door of Tessier's home. Rapping on the door, he prepared himself to be greeted by a hail of gunfire or the boom of a shotgun blast. That had happened often enough over the years that he had become accustomed to it. It was almost a surprise when no such violent response came.

He tried the door handle. It moved. The door swung open. Cautiously Bolan entered the home.

The entryway opened to a living area that was filled with clutter. Most of it was electronics related. Some of it was recording media, such as disks and even a stack of magnetic tapes. There were boxes for the equipment, discarded cameras and microphones, and lots of wrappers for various fast-food restaurants, including one that was popular in the United States. No matter where you went in the world, apparently, you could gorge yourself on the burgers of a U.S. chain.

His sixth sense for combat was screaming at him. Something was wrong, but he wasn't sure what it was. Finally he found the locked door off the kitchen area. When it wouldn't budge, he kicked it open with one well-placed snap from his combat boot.

Tessier was sitting in front of his computer.

The arrangement was an elaborate one. No less than eight separate flat-screen monitors, two or three deep, were arrayed around the semicircular desk. There were at least three keyboards—each with its own mouse on the desktop—sitting in tiered stands. The monitors were switched on, but displayed nothing. No Input blinked on one of them.

"Tessier," Bolan said. "Don't make any sudden moves."

The French digital expert made no response. Bolan reached out and, very carefully, turned the chair around. It squeaked as it swiveled.

Tessier stared in openmouthed horror. His eyes looked at nothing. His skin was fish-belly white, almost blue. A single gunshot wound, directly over his heart, had left his shirt stained crimson from chest to waist. He had died in the chair. From the look on his face, he might never have understood why or how death had come for him.

Bolan sensed someone behind him.

He did not hear the man moving behind him; there was no telltale motion in his peripheral vision; he had no idea what had alerted him to the presence. He spun, his finger clenching the trigger of the MAT-49 as he turned.

He tasted blood when a gun barrel hit him in the face.

He felt himself falling, felt the blackness closing in, felt—if only barely—the floor come up to meet him. A man, the edges of his face blurring in Bolan's vision, peered at the soldier from above.

Bolan tried and failed to speak the man's name.

It was Gerard Levesque.

CHAPTER FOURTEEN

When Mack Bolan opened his eyes, he was lying on his back on a weight bench in what he thought to be the rear room of Tessier's country home. Bolan's jacket had been removed and dumped on the floor next to him. His wrists had been duct-taped to the legs of the weight bench. His feet were held immobile by more tape that bound his lower legs to the bench itself. He tested them, trying not to be obvious about it. They held fast.

"Ah," a voice said. "He is awake."

Gerard Levesque's face once more appeared, looming over Bolan as the terrorist leader stood above him.

"Levesque," Bolan said. "You look pretty good for a dying man who shot himself in the head."

"Honestly," said Levesque, "I had no idea there existed in the world men as honorable as you, Agent Cooper. It was the perfect lever to use against you. The only lever, I am quite sure…although we will find out just where your tolerances truly lie before this day ends. Perhaps you should have looked for an exit wound instead of just gazing at my slumped form."

"So what are you doing here, Levesque?"

"What am I doing here alive?" the terrorist leader asked. He wore a leather M65-style field jacket. From inside it he removed a silver cigarette case and opened it. He took a black clove cigarette from this, put it in his mouth and lit it using a small silver butane torch built into the case. Inhaling deeply, he paused before blowing a cloud of smoke into the air above Bolan's head. "Or what am I doing here in the home of the late, unlamented Edouard Tessier?"

"Take your pick," Bolan said.

"Cooper, I do not think you realize how valuable you have been to me. A man of my power, a man who commands a force with the strength of my organization, must always be on guard. I must always consolidate and jealously defend that power. A man I trust to command my troops, to operate my affairs one day… he can become a traitor the next. You know the story of Judas, yes?"

"You're talking about your boy Lemaire."

"Yes," Levesque said. "Judas killed his leader because that leader disappointed him. That leader was not the man Judas needed him to be. Lemaire's problem was something similar. I assume it was you who killed him? Personally, by your own hand?"

"Yes," Bolan said. There was no reason to lie about it. The knowledge of who had removed Lemaire from the earth would not help Levesque in any way.

"I would expect nothing less. You are an elusive man, Agent Cooper, but I have contacts in the intelligence community. An impressive record follows you. Many stories—most of which cannot be confirmed—have you everywhere at once, traveling the globe and making a great deal of trouble for…well, for men such as me."

"You know what they say about believing everything you read," Bolan said. As Levesque grinned down at him, he searched the room with his peripheral vision. Levesque was flanked by two uniformed, ski-masked men of the ES. There were other operatives in the house, too; Bolan could hear them moving around.

"So why did your men kill Tessier? Afraid he would make trouble for you?"

"Yes." Levesque drew deeply from his cigarette. "But not in the way you think. Tessier was killed by Lemaire's men. They were sent here to eliminate him and recover his computer's hard drive for safekeeping. Tessier, you see, manufactured the evidence that implicates Deparmond as my backer. It is thanks to his brilliant work that Deparmond's political fate has been sealed. Tessier did his work at my request."

"So Lemaire killed him to keep him from revealing that fact," Bolan said.

"Of course. If you wish to keep a secret, you kill all who may reveal it. Had Lemaire not sent his own people to do it, I was going to kill him myself and for the same reasons. His usefulness was at an end. As it was, we intercepted them just after they murdered him."

"Then why put me onto Tessier?" Bolan said.

"Why do you think?" Levesque laughed. "I know how dangerous you are, Agent Cooper. When your usefulness to me was at an end, I needed a way to pen you in. A predictable way to bring you to ground. What better trap than one you walk into voluntarily? I needed only to stage my men and have them wait. And in the meantime, you very obligingly cleaned house for me."

"You suspected Lemaire's loyalty."

"Indeed. When a man ceases to believe in you, Cooper, you feel it. You do not wish to believe it at first. But the patient man, the man of power, he senses the little betrayals. The degree to which a man's devotion… shrinks, if you will. Dwindles, to one day become nothing. But understanding that Lemaire was losing faith in me, suspecting that he was building troops loyal to him before they were loyal to me…this was not enough.

I needed to ferret out those ES members who believed in Lemaire. And I needed to eliminate them. But that presented a problem in itself."

"Purging the ranks might not sit well with the members on the fence?"

"Exactly, Cooper," Levesque replied. "I needed to give Lemaire a reason to believe that it was time to make his move. For all his bravado he was unsure of himself. Had I remained strong it might have taken him months, perhaps years, to oppose me. So I pretended to be sick.

"My symptoms progressed gradually and obviously. I made sure Lemaire saw. And saw me unsuccessfully trying to hide them. It was finely calculated, for I needed to make sure he would stay his hand until I was ready for him. Originally I had planned to hire mercenaries and make the defeat of Lemaire's men look like a military operation. But then you entered the picture."

"So you figured I could kill Lemaire and his people for you."

"A task for which you proved more than capable," Levesque said. "And I was aware that Lemaire had me under surveillance. He had been monitoring me closely for some time. It was a simple matter to arrange the drama I wanted him, and you, to see. I fed you the information that would eventually lead you here to be intercepted.

"And I made sure that Lemaire thought I was dead so he would move forward. You, in turn, predictably moved against him, for Lemaire knows only one way, and that is brute force. It was no great surprise that he would wage an all-out assault once he thought he had control of the ES. Those men loyal to me had orders to fall back and wait, out of sight and safe from any reprisals."

"And then you sat tight while we took them out for you," Bolan concluded.

"I could not have asked for more." Levesque laughed again, dropped his cigarette on the floor and crushed it under his shoe. "Your battle with Lemaire's men even gave me the opportunity to smuggle Deparmond's body onto the grounds. My team was disguised as special operations officers. We needed only to bribe our way past the cordon...and of course I took great pleasure in killing Deparmond myself. To be honest I always found him obnoxious."

"Why eliminate the candidate who would have given you what your group says it wants?" Bolan asked. "You're working against your own interests. Now that it's all public, there's no undoing it."

"Am I?" Levesque smiled. "You really are an honorable man. It doesn't surprise me that you wouldn't see the obvious political answer. Agent Cooper, it is *Gaston* who is funding us. I have just handed Gaston victory in the elections."

Bolan considered that. While he did, Levesque turned to the men flanking him. At his nod, they removed their masks. One was a gray-haired man with a cataract; he was obviously blind on that side. The other was younger, shaved bald, with tattoos on his neck. He was obviously a street-fighting type, muscle in Levesque's quasi race war. Bolan, in his mind, dubbed the two guards Graybeard and Skinhead.

He did so as a means of designating his targets.

Beneath him, the bench strained under his weight. He could feel his arms and legs pulling the duct tape taut against the resistance of the bench. It was not a particularly sturdy piece of furniture. It creaked and groaned beneath his heavy frame.

Given that Tessier had not looked particularly fit in death, Bolan had to assume the digital expert had ordered the bench via mail, or on the internet, or whatever people did these days to buy things they didn't need and that they would not bother to use. Probably the bench had been holding up Tessier's dirty laundry before the soldier had been strapped to it. There were enough discarded garments lying around the room to prove out the theory.

"Do you know the old saying," Levesque went on, "that the greatest deception Satan ever perpetrated was persuading the people he did not exist? So it is with Gaston. He is widely believed to be a moderate. He has the support of your government for this reason. Deparmond, with his hatred of foreigners, his inconvenient nationalism… Ideologically, yes, he was the better fit for my organization. But do you know Deparmond would not work with us? He was the rarest sort of politician. He was an honest man. A true believer in his cause."

"I can see how that might get in the way," Bolan said.

"Indeed." Levesque looked away, as if distracted. "But in truth it has always been Gaston behind my organization. It was Gaston who saw the value we could provide. He understood the backlash our terrorist attacks would create. Understood how good we could make him look, how solid would be his hold on the French government once he secured power.

"If you had to characterize him, Cooper, I think you would consider him power-mad. What is the word… sociopath? He will play any role to get what he wants.

He will use any maneuver that will lead to his advantage. And so we struck up a working relationship."

"What do you get out of it?" Bolan asked. "Where's the profit in it?"

"Power," Levesque replied. "Power is the only currency of any real value. The ES helps Gaston take power. Politically he was not necessarily going to win. There was a significant chance he could lose to Deparmond…to Deparmond and his damnable honesty. My organization helped position Gaston to earn political and public favor.

"And then we arranged for Deparmond to be disgraced and to die, an apparent victim of his own ill-considered political affiliations. In the wake of all this turbulent news, Gaston will take the day, and he will reward me with power. The ES will become a force for street justice behind the scenes. We will run Paris and all the major cities of France. Those I choose will benefit. Those I condemn will suffer. That is power, Cooper. That is profit."

"Something tells me I haven't heard the best part," Bolan said. He felt the muscles of his arms burn as he strained against the duct tape. His bench creaked. Levesque eyed him with something like amusement.

"Why, yes. You haven't learned of your ultimate role in all this. It is an important one, American, and one that cannot be faked. I would have thanked God for the intervention of your government in sending you here, if I believed in God. You are Deparmond's murderer."

"No, I'm not," Bolan said.

"Really, Agent Cooper? Let us not argue over such trivialities as what is true and what is not. Reality will be what the news records. And the reality is that you fit nicely into Gaston's plan. I told you he would play any role that would serve him. Posing as a moderate to get the support of your government simply puts him that much more ahead of the game. But the embarrassment *you* will cause cements everything."

Bolan glared. "I don't think so."

"Don't you?" Levesque spread his hands. "This is the last room you will ever see, Cooper. Gaston waits in his mansion, surrounded by luxury, a wealthy man who will soon be one of the most powerful figures in France. He is guarded by a force of my own men. He is untouchable. He has won. I have won. You are defeated, and after my men interrogate you, you will die. Your body will become another piece of evidence for the public narrative Gaston and I will create."

"I'm listening."

"Isn't it obvious?" Levesque asked. "Your corpse will be discovered somewhere conspicuous. Your complicity in Deparmond's death will be proved by documents found on your body. I am sure something suitable can be drawn up in time. Perhaps we will arrange for one last ES attack on a public place in Paris, where you will be presumed killed in reprisal for your assassination of Deparmond.

"Just like that, the machinations of the United States will be revealed. An American CIA operative found on French soil, having actively and through murderous violence changed the course of the French elections. How will that look?"

"You won't bring down anyone important in the United States," Bolan said. "I'll be disavowed. I'm no more an American agent than you are in the eyes of my government."

"Of course you will be disavowed. I have seen your 'improbable directive' movies. But it will not matter. Publicly your government will deny involvement. Privately they will grasp for any possibility of making amends. They will want the continued support of France's leader. They will offer concessions."

"Concessions?"

"Financial aid, most likely," Levesque said. "A few other considerations. A vote here or there in the United Nations, a promise of military support or cooperation in some crucial piece of statecraft. The options are really unlimited."

"Did you ever believe in the garbage you spew?" Bolan asked. "The ideology you claim? Or was it all just a means to an end?"

Levesque looked at Graybeard and Skinhead for a moment, then leaned in over Bolan's face. More quietly, he said, "Don't you see, Cooper? It doesn't matter. I get what I want. I get power. My organization will grow to recoup its losses. The losses you inflicted for me. And one day, with Gaston as our man within the government, we will rise to what you would consider 'legitimate' status. We will be a legacy. And in time, a dynasty."

Levesque snapped his fingers. Graybeard and Skinhead disappeared into the laundry nook attached to the rear room. Bolan could hear the sounds of metal and plastic as something large and hollow was jostled. Then the squeak of pipes was followed by the sounds of water being poured into a large container, likely a plastic bucket.

"You're not going to be a dynasty," Bolan said.

"You understand what comes next, I imagine," Levesque told him.

"You're going to interrogate me."

"Let's not mince words. I'm going to have you tortured."

"To gain what?"

"In truth? Probably nothing," the French terror leader admitted. "But as a highly placed agent of the American government, doubtless given much autonomy to make independent decisions that include the taking of lives among foreign nationals, I imagine there is much you know that would be useful. Perhaps you will part with some of it."

"If you're going to waterboard me," Bolan said, "you're not going to get anywhere."

"No?" Levesque asked. The sound of running water had stopped. Graybeard and Skinhead appeared on either side of the terror master. Graybeard held the bucket. Skinhead grabbed a dirty T-shirt from the floor and twisted it. He dropped it in the bucket and then followed it with his hand, soaking it.

"But then, I promised to torture you. According to your government, what my men are about to do is not 'torture' at all. It is merely an 'enhanced' form of interrogating you. Such a phrase. Cold. Austere. Robbed of truth and of emotional content. This is a politician's word, yes?"

"Waterboarding isn't a new technique. They used it during the Inquisition. It doesn't kill. It doesn't even really drown. It's possible to do it without ever getting water into the victim's mouth or nose. It's a psychological technique. You subject the victim to psychological stress in the hope that the simulation of drowning will snap him."

"My, my," Levesque said. "This is the authoritative knowledge I would expect from a Central Intelligence

Agent. I wonder, Agent Cooper, if you will be so non-chalant about this when your gag reflex takes hold."

He gestured to Graybeard and Skinhead. "Do it."

Bolan drew in a breath, careful not to gasp or gulp; he did not want them to know he was prepared. The T-shirt smelled rank. The cloying wetness on his face, as the cloth was draped over him, was both cold and oily.

"Tell me your orders on French soil," Levesque demanded. "Tell me why your people sent you here."

When Bolan made no sound, Levesque gestured to his henchmen. One of them, whichever one held the bucket, began pouring water over Bolan's face. The sensation of drowning was immediate. He could feel himself wanting to choke and sputter.

He did neither.

It was well-known in certain intelligence circles that those agencies operating within strict rules for interrogation would not waterboard a subject for greater than a specific length of time. The stricter the guidelines, the more easily the interrogation subject could withstand the procedure. There were documented accounts of terrorists simply counting off their time underwater, waiting for it all to be over, never giving up a word because they had cracked the secret of the game.

That was the psychological war that was "enhanced interrogation." It was useless if you couldn't get inside the subject's head, couldn't make him feel fear, couldn't make him believe the misery would never end unless he caved in, gave up, knuckled under.

They'd figure it out soon enough, realize that their game had no effect on Bolan because he knew what to expect. He was reasonably sure he could hold his breath long enough that they would worry about suffocating him before he actually ran out of air. He did not kid himself that his life meant anything; they were planning to murder him anyway. But they would want to keep him alive until he divulged something.

He debated, briefly, offering them some believable misinformation, some carefully concocted piece of intel that could be followed up later by the Farm. It could conceivably give the Stony Man teams some operable intelligence downstream of Levesque. Plant just the right lie and see who acted on it; that showed who was connected to those in possession of the lie that was divulged. It was a very old tactic.

The problem was that a plausible lie could easily become reality if field conditions shifted. There was no way to be sure, out of direct contact with the Farm as he now was. And there was no real need to resort to such a delaying tactic. Getting them to cease their interrogation would probably lead to them shooting him in the head where he now lay imprisoned.

That's what they would do if they were smart, anyway.

He had spent enough time suffering at the hands of would-be interrogators and, worse, seeing loved ones eviscerated under the scalpels of the criminal underworld's most brutal artists, to know that they might just go for broke next. If Bolan gave them something they thought represented value, they might dispense with the "enhanced" portion of the night's floor show and just start carving away on him with butcher knives or tools heated to red hot under blowtorches.

It was the way thugs' minds worked.

Mack Bolan knew how sessions like that ended, with quivering chunks of once-human flesh lying on tables, in beds, on concrete garage floors. A man or woman cut up by a really talented turkey doctor, as once such men were called, would live only briefly, but in horrific pain. For such a living vegetable, the release of death was a kindness, not a punishment.

That would not be Bolan's fate.

The soldier tested the duct tape holding him to the bench once more. He would need a distraction, something to give him enough room to make his play. Levesque was demanding some new piece of intelligence, but Bolan had tuned out his voice. He heard only a kind of hollow quacking, the sound made by unseen parents on long-forgotten children's cartoons.

The cloth was taken roughly from his face. Graybeard held it, red faced, while Skinhead took the bucket back to the laundry area to be refilled. Graybeard told Levesque in French that they were getting nowhere.

"I agree," Levesque said. "And he hardly seems impressed. Do you, Cooper?"

Bolan blinked and glared at Levesque. "I'm terrified," he told the Frenchman. "You've got me just where you want me."

Levesque sighed. "I thought as much."

To Graybeard, he said, "Do what you will. If you can get something from him, fine. If not, just remember not to drown him to death. Shoot him if you must. We can plant the weapon wherever we dump his body. I do not want to have to arrange some inexplicable drowning scenario only to find some forensics genius has determined the difference between well water and tap water and so on. Or stab him. Carve him up a bit if you choose. That would also work."

"And you, sir?" Skinhead asked. He had returned with the bucket, sloshing water on the floor of the late

Tessier's exercise bench. Bolan could feel water soak his thighs through his pants.

"I am late for a meeting with Gaston. There is much to plan and, I suspect, a bit of overdue celebrating in which to indulge. Carry on. I will leave a detail here to back you up. Although, frankly, if you cannot handle one man strapped to a board, don't come back into the city, for I will kill you myself."

"Yes, sir," Graybeard said.

Levesque turned to leave. "Farewell, Agent Cooper," he said, sounding almost mournful. "I regret that the life of a noble warrior such as yourself should end this way. But I imagine you have never thought your death would be otherwise. Nor do your superiors in the CIA, I should think." He walked out of the room.

"I'll find you, Levesque," Bolan said to his back.

CHAPTER FIFTEEN

Graybeard disappeared for a moment. When he returned he was holding a large butcher knife, clearly taken from Tessier's kitchen. He was also eating a sandwich, also likely taken from Tessier's kitchen. Skinhead looked askance at his partner.

"What?" Graybeard asked, his mouth half full. He closed the door to the rear room, cutting off the sounds of other ES terrorists moving about the house.

"Give me the knife," Skinhead said. "Let's see how brave he is when he's missing a few fingers."

"We should try the water some more."

"All right." Skinhead dropped the knife and picked up the bucket. "Put the cloth on him."

Bolan drew in air and held his breath. The foul, wet T-shirt was again draped over his face. He waited, counting off in his head, while the bucket's contents were emptied over his face. He had read, long ago, about a concentration camp prisoner who had built an elaborate clock in his mind during the long months of his imprisonment. When he was released, that prisoner set about constructing the clock he had imagined. It was an inspirational story, and the kind of thing that could take a man's mind off the torture he was experiencing—

"Look at him!" Skinhead shouted, ripping the T-shirt free and throwing it on the floor. The wet *smack* of cloth against tiles was reminiscent of a gunshot. "He does not care. We could waterboard him all night, and he would continue to lie there. It is time to make him fear for his pieces."

Graybeard smiled. The expression did his face no favors. "Very well. If he will not talk, let us see if we can make him scream."

Bolan, meanwhile, was running the numbers in his head.

He was alone with Skinhead and Graybeard, but in the outer rooms of Tessier's home, there were multiple hostiles. He had no way to know how many, other than the assumption that it was probably a number greater than two and less than a platoon.

There were no assault rifles or submachine guns in evidence. Possibly any weapons of this sort carried by the two men now standing over him had been left in the outer room. He tried to imagine where he would leave his Kalashnikov or MAT-49, were he one of the pair. Such speculation was idle at best. The guns could be leaning on the wall outside the door, or they could be in the trunk of a car outside, or strapped to a motorcycle, or anywhere in the world that might as well be on the moon for all the good it did him.

Graybeard had a pistol in a holster on his belt. It looked like a Makarov. There were enough of those floating around this part of the world, part of a flood of surplus small arms issuing from the former Soviet Union in the wake of its collapse. It wasn't much, especially given the number of enemies he would need to eliminate. But it would have to do.

Time to go back to work.

Bolan drew in a deep breath. Feeling his limbs, his body, his muscles, he concentrated. He could feel every part of himself go tense. To the two ES torturers it had to have looked as if their prey had suddenly gone stiff as a board.

"Look at him now," Graybeard said. "Not so brave now that we're going to carve some pieces off him."

The bench beneath Bolan began to creak and wobble under the strain.

"That's more like it," Skinhead said. He turned to his temporary partner in crime. "Have you ever done this before?"

The weight bench creaked.

"How hard can it be?" Graybeard asked, shrugging. "We start hurting him until it is permanent. When we take out his eyes, when we carve out his tongue, when we chop off his fingers, then maybe he will feel like telling us something useful."

"I want to carve out his eye," Skinhead said. He picked up the butcher knife. "That's a good place to start. He has two."

"And five fingers," Graybeard stated. "Perhaps we start on those next. There is a children's rhyme for fingers, isn't there?"

A piece of the bench beneath Bolan cracked, loudly.

"I do not know it," Skinhead admitted. He turned to the bench. "He is so afraid the bench is shaking apart."

"We'll make it up as we go," Graybeard said. "Why don't you take that knife and—"

The weight bench snapped so loudly that Graybeard started and backed up. Bolan performed what was essentially a sit-up, rearing up at the waist, dragging the pieces of the upper legs where they were taped to his arms. His legs he pulled in at the knees, as if performing a leg press, but so violently that the entire H-frame of the lower legs came with them, tape and all. Graybeard bent, trying to make a grab for Bolan's legs, doing the first thing that came to mind in a situation he clearly had not anticipated.

Bolan smashed Graybeard in the face with the H-frame.

Teeth flew. There was very little blood. Some part of Bolan's mind realized that Graybeard actually wore dentures, and the strike with the weight-bench frame had smashed them while probably dislocating the man's jaw. Graybeard had time to raise one hand above his head as Bolan lifted his legs and brought the H-frame back down. The scream that left the gray-haired man's lips was horrible and brief. His fingers were crushed by the heavy piece of weight bench.

Skinhead cursed loudly. From his position on the bench, Bolan could only swivel and thrust his legs, complete with their H-frame battering ram, at the younger man. The blade of the butcher knife made contact directly in the bundle of tape. Skinhead made the opening bigger when he tried to wrench the knife free, but Bolan swiveled away, taking the weapon with him.

He rolled off the bench.

The floor came up to hit him painfully in the ribs. Curling into a ball, he brought his knees up to his chest and his arms down. The knife was still sticking in the wad of gray duct tape. He brought his hands over it and pulled, ripping free, separating the tape from his wrists. He had just enough time to get his fingers around the butcher knife when Skinhead landed on him.

He saw spots as the air was driven out of his lungs. Skinhead yelled obscenities at him. Bolan, gripping the kitchen knife, brought it up in a tight, vicious arc.

He planted the triangular blade in the terrorist's eye socket.

The death rattle was unmistakable, as was the twitch-

ing of Skinhead's foot against the floor. Bolan wrenched
the knife free of the dead man's skull and cut the tape
around his legs. He moved as quickly as he could. When
the door of the rear room was wrenched open by another of the terrorists just beyond, he was already diving
for the Makarov holstered on the late Graybeard's belt.

The man in the doorway had time to look surprised.
His jaw dropped, and he inhaled sharply to cry out.

Bolan put a round through his open mouth.

The recoil told him the round he was firing was the
9 mm Makarov, which was a little sharper than the .380
ACP or 9 mm Kurz that was another common cham-
bering in this model. He also knew that he likely had
only half a dozen rounds left, possibly less, depending
on how full the weapon's magazine had been kept. He
would just need to make them all count.

Bolan stepped into the adjoining room, which was
one of the home's bedrooms. This one had apparently
been the master; it boasted a large bed and a big-screen
television, on which some lurid movie was still playing with the sound off. One of the terrorists—lying on
the bed, naked to the waist—had apparently been nap-
ping when his partner breached the rear room and died
in the doorway.

The shirtless man, very much awake now, was
scrambling for a Kalashnikov at the foot of the bed.
Bolan beat him to it, clouting him with the heavy steel
Makarov. The terrorist rolled off the bed, unconscious,
and landed in a heap on the hardwood floor.

Gunfire raked the floor at Bolan's feet. He was
forced back, the Kalashnikov just out of reach, and
took cover behind the bed. Bullets punched through
the mattress but, fortunately for Bolan, Tessier had preferred the modern foam kind, not something made of

springs and empty air that would have proven no protection from bullets. The soldier laid flat as the occasional round made its way through to score the plaster wall above and behind him. He was mostly protected.

"I'm hit!" he shouted in French. "I need help." Then he waited.

He hadn't expected them to fall for it. It was an old trick, a stupid trick, one that he would never allow to be used against him. But one of the shooters beyond the opposite door of the bedroom was dumb enough to poke his head in for a look around.

Bolan popped up and put a bullet through his nose.

There were now corpses in both doorways of the master bedroom. Bolan wished he had Bayard's war bag, but unfortunately he had no idea where it or his borrowed pistol might be. These had been taken from him while he was unconscious. His smartphone was also missing. This hindered his communications with the Farm considerably. The phone itself was proof against most intrusions and would destroy itself and any data it carried if tampered with…but it would be a little too much like the bad old days if he had to hunt up a pay phone just to contact Stony Man.

Rolling over the bed, Bolan landed on the opposite side just as yet another ES gunner made the doorway. The man was holding a MAT-49 and, as Bolan turned to bring up the Makarov, the would-be-killer pulled the trigger.

Bolan was showered with plaster and tufts of foam. The submachine gun loosed its volley in a ragged full-auto stream that traveled above his head, through the mattress and into the ceiling. The soldier pointed the Makarov and pulled the trigger, shooting the gunner through the forehead once, twice, pulling the trigger a third time, snapping the man's head and body back, making sure the rise of the weapon continued into the ceiling.

He had felt it on the last trigger pull: the Makarov was empty. He left it on the floor and scooped up the Kalashnikov. The rifle, as familiar to him as breathing, was found on battlefields throughout the world, nearly identical in every incarnation he had encountered. He pulled the bolt back just enough to verify that a round was chambered, set the weapon—which, he had no doubt, was utterly illegal for a civilian to own here in France—to single shot and brought it to his shoulder.

Using the doorway for cover, he peered into the next room, exposing only his eye. He barely pulled back fast enough. Rifle bullets, fired from other assault rifles, began perforating the wall. Again he hit the floor, and again he was pelted with plaster dust and debris as the 7.62 mm rounds wreaked havoc in Tessier's bedroom.

The big-screen television was shot in several places, resulting in crazy whorls on the still-powered plasma screen. A lamp was shattered. A series of shelves bolted to the wall had been brought down, causing a terrible clatter when the various bric-a-brac broke on the floor. Tessier had been something of a hoarder and a slob. There were a million different small personal items piled up in the bedroom, and they were soon in millions more pieces as the ES shooters blazed away.

The violent action was sure to draw law enforcement, too. An isolated shot here or there was one thing. Mysterious comings and goings to Tessier's home could probably be overlooked, even among uniformed men on motorcycles, occasionally wearing masks. Any neighbors in the vicinity would be inclined to look the other way, as men and women all over the world generally tried not to get involved if they could help it.

But a gun battle, an out-and-out indoor war, would prompt someone to panic and call for help. That was a good thing for residents of the neighborhood, provided whichever department responded to the call was not overwhelmed by the violent paramilitary force of ES goons.

But even if the French authorities were equal to the task before them, their presence was bad news for Bolan. They would want to detain him, and when world got back through channels that one Matthew Cooper was in custody, those higher up the chain would want to have him brought in.

Once he was in custody, it was anyone's guess whether Brognola's considerable influence, not to mention the President's, would be sufficient to get Bolan shipped back to U.S. soil.

Given how abruptly uncooperative the French had become—and Bolan would be the first to admit they had plenty of provocation to feel that way—Bolan wasn't looking to put money on that call either way. To say nothing of the headaches it would cause an already harried and stressed Brognola.

Truly the big Fed paid often for his association with Bolan, the currency being in antacid tablets and late-night phone calls with the world's power brokers. The soldier did not envy his longtime friend that responsibility.

Bolan waited for a lull in the gunfire. When it came, he poked his rifle up above the level of the mattress and cut loose several times through the doorway, not knowing or caring if his shots came close to his prey. He just needed to put them back behind cover for a moment. He was already on his feet and moving again.

He reached the doorway, rolled and was almost hit by a burst of submachine-gun fire.

The rounds tore a furrow in the floor at his right. The gunner, another ES man in camouflage fatigues but without his mask, was doing his best to empty a MAT-49 into Bolan. The soldier sidestepped and pumped three shots from the AK into the man's gut, doubling him over. For good measure he punched another round through the top of the enemy's skull.

"Go! Go!" he heard someone shout in the outer room. With the AK at his shoulder he rushed after the voices. No doubt the man hiding behind the couch in the living area was hoping Bolan would miss him as he went through.

The soldier saw the movement and turned as the ES man behind the sofa popped up holding a MAT-49. Bolan fired at him, driving him back behind the dubious cover of the couch, and then flipped his AK's selector switch to full-auto. The *clack* of the switch seemed loud in the living area.

Bolan hosed the sofa.

The scream from behind it and, moments later, a spreading pool of blood told Bolan everything he needed to know. The soldier snapped the magazine out of his rifle, checked it and noted that only two rounds remained.

He snapped the magazine back into the weapon with a practiced movement and hurried through the kitchen to the side door, which still hung open. His jacket—the one Bayard had appropriated for him—was there, hanging on a hook, almost as if he'd put it there himself. He shrugged it on.

There was a chance the enemy was waiting to ambush him outside, but he took that chance, charging through the opening and dropping to one knee when he got outside. When he saw no one, he gambled and ran for the back of the house.

He spotted them then. Two men in camouflage ran from the house through a field adjacent to another property. It was a very long field, close to one hundred yards, he judged. This was the French countryside people talked about.

Trees screened the neighboring home from where Bolan stood. He checked the area, scanning for witnesses and innocents who might get caught in the cross fire. He saw no one. There was nothing moving, for the moment, except the two fleeing terrorists.

He took a step forward, settling into his stance from a standing position, with the AK against his shoulder and the stock pressing against his cheek. Then took a deep breath, let out half and held the rest.

The Kalashnikov was a durable weapon that had generous tolerances and a simple design. The weapon could be kept in working order under conditions that would render a more modern, more ergonomic battle rifle useless. It was not a sniper's weapon.

But any weapon Mack Bolan held *became* a sniper's weapon.

He could feel the wind against his left cheek and made a calculation.

The rifle barked once. A fraction of a moment later, the first of the two men dropped, a ragged exit hole where the center of his head had once been. The Executioner took aim once more, sighted along the second man's lower leg and fired again.

The fleeing terrorist toppled.

Bolan closed the ground between himself and the fallen man at a rough jog. He was hoping to find more magazines for his acquired Kalashnikov, but when he reached the first corpse, he found nothing he could use. There wasn't so much as a folding knife.

Standing, he walked over to where the second man was crawling along the grass. His left calf was soaked in blood, the leg clearly useless to him. The soldier paused long enough to open the back of the Kalashnikov, pull its bolt and throw it as far from him as he could. He dumped the now useless rifle.

The soldier toed the crawling man over onto his back. The man screamed as the movement jarred his leg. Looking up at Bolan, he rattled off a string of invectives in French.

Bolan stared down at him. He bent, patted the man down and found nothing except a square container the size of a sandwich and wrapped in pink antistatic plastic. The fallen terrorist grabbed for it when Bolan took it away from him.

"This," Bolan said in French, "is what you came for, isn't it? What Lemaire's men came to get before you intercepted them. It's Tessier's hard drive."

"Yes," the man replied.

"I'm willing to bet," Bolan said, "that if the evidence implicating Deparmond was manufactured by Tessier, then it's on this drive. That means another expert in the field can verify that Deparmond was framed. That will point the finger of blame to Gaston. And all *that* will ruin Gaston's plans."

"I don't know what you're talking about," the terrorist said. He shook his head and looked away.

"It doesn't matter. Come on. You and I have a long

way to go, and I'm going to have to bandage that leg so you don't bleed out."

"For what purpose?" the terrorist demanded. "So you can leave me in the hands of the police? I will not accept this. You can leave me here to die."

"Not a chance," Bolan said. He reached down, grabbed the man by the collar of his fatigues and yanked him upright. The terrorist got his good leg under himself and glared at Bolan.

"Don't," Bolan warned.

The terrorist's arms snapped up. He wrapped his fingers around Bolan's throat and started to squeeze. It was a desperation play, the kind of thing a man attempted when he left rational thought behind and was operating entirely on emotion. The soldier turned, slashed down with his left arm, then brought his forearm down across the man's elbow joints, breaking his grip. The terrorist flailed and tried to stick his fingers in Bolan's eye sockets.

Bolan speared him in the hollow of this throat with two fingers. Hard.

Choking, the man went down on his back. His hand snaked into his pants, above his crotch. Bolan realized then what he was going for. A weapon hidden next to his groin, where Bolan's cursory pat-down had failed to detect it.

The switchblade that appeared in the man's hand looked rusty and ill-used, but the blade that snapped open was glittery sharp.

Bolan stomped the man's neck.

The effect was immediate. The unrepentant terrorist went limp. The switchblade fell from nerveless fingers. Bolan knelt and, despite his distaste, picked up the weapon, folded it and put it in his pocket. He turned.

He would need to search the house, find any weapons left behind.

While he could pass for a civilian moving through the French countryside, he was unlikely to stay off the radar for long with no adequate means to defend himself. His wallet full of European cash had been taken along with his other things confiscated. He had no phone and thus no means to call the Farm.

The sound of French police horns caught his attention and, suddenly, Bolan realized his day had gone from bad to worse.

French police were moving in on the house, their guns drawn, the lights atop their patrol cars bright and spinning. Bolan hit the dirt, hoping that, prone, he could escape detection. They seemed to take no notice of him. He waited a few minutes to make sure and, when the balance of the officers were inside Tessier's house, he crawled off in the direction of the next property.

Tessier was probably not classifiable as an innocent, but he was dead just the same. There were so many people who had died thanks to the machinations of Gaston and Levesque. Their plot had been a clever one, a complex one, and Bolan had not seen through all of it immediately. He did not fault himself for that. He was, after all, a soldier, not a detective, and his methods were direct more often than not. But as always, he had come to the truth of it.

And now the men behind so many deaths would pay.

CHAPTER SIXTEEN

Outside Marseille

"'I'll find you, Levesque.' Those were his last words to me." The terrorist leader looked up at the lovely young woman in the impossibly small string bikini. She was dark and lovely and had a necklace of tiny purple flowers wreathed in her hair. Her eyes were green and striking.

"Americans and their bravado," Gaston said. He grinned through perfectly capped teeth. "They never seem to tire of it. I am looking forward to making their President bow and scrape and apologize to me for their lack of discretion on French soil.

"The fool will be thinking the whole time that he is simply following the prescribed forms of bureaucracy and diplomacy. He will believe that I am the man he wishes in power. A tractable, useful idiot whom he can push around. It will be such a surprise to him the next time France denies American warplanes travel through French airspace."

Levesque picked out an enormous cigar from the humidor sitting next to him. The patio chairs, padded for comfort, and the woven-topped tables separating them, were of imported rattan. The pool around which the furniture was arranged was not quite Olympic size, but it was suitable enough.

The pool area was full of people, many of them business associates of Gaston's. Quite a few of those were French underworld figures. The rest were some of the loveliest prostitutes the city of Paris and its most exclusive brothels had to offer.

Gaston had spared no expense to make this unofficial party—the celebration of his now-assured victory in the elections over Deparmond—a success with the people who would join him in his march to power. He had carefully chosen his networks; now he was rewarding those fortunate enough and shrewd enough to find themselves within these webs.

He saw them as that, too. They were not interconnections among individuals, but a spiderweb of influence, with himself, the "spider," at its center. The slightest tug on any of the lines radiating outward and Gaston would sense it, could react to it, could control it.

After all, was that not power?

Was that not the *point* of power?

And was not the further point of power the way it erased the distinctions between the elite and the base, the criminal and the enforcer, the haves and the... Well, the "haves" would always have the advantage.

He smiled and, as one of the prostitutes passed by in a bathing suit as skimpy as the one on the young woman Levesque had been admiring, Gaston reached out and groped her, lingering with his hand on her body, knowing that she and any with her were his for the taking.

Paris was one of the most famous and admired cities of the modern world. It had stood for more than two thousand years and was a glittering jewel among the cities of Europe. Known for its contributions to the arts, to education, Paris had been unrivaled in the west until the eighteenth century. Currently the Paris metropolitan area was home to more than twelve million people.

Into such opulence, such history, Henri Gaston had been born to one of the oldest and most profitable chemical dynasties in the country. Gaston Produits Chimiques was a multimillion-dollar corporation, with cumulative assets closer to half a billion U.S. dollars. The fact that he knew the USD figure for it still galled Gaston, but he knew the worm was turning.

American domination of the world's economy was weakening, and it would continue to grow weaker, if he had his way. If he had a new, powerful, aggressive France under his rule, under his *thumb*.

If Paris was proud, France itself was prouder. But its power had been significantly diminished over the past three centuries. Once a world power, it was now that in name only, largely thought of as a joke by the Americans and other Western nations.

Yet Gaston knew that those nations were themselves losing their strength. Years of flagging global economies had taken their toll on all nations concerned, and even the Chinese, seemingly unstoppable on the world stage, were feeling the pressure and deploying various economic acrobatics to combat the downward trend.

None of that would matter if Gaston had his way.

He had made certain the drugs and the women flowed freely at this gathering. All guests had been screened thoroughly for listening devices and recording equipment. Phones and cameras were strictly forbidden. There would be no embarrassing footage recorded here, nothing that could be used to blackmail or to harm politically the futures of Gaston or any of his guests.

And such guests they were! Within the sprawling

estate that was his family's birthright, he counted local law enforcement officials, labor union figures, members of the Parisian criminal syndicates and the bosses of several of Paris's most feared street gangs.

Men—who would lunge across a table or a room without hesitation, desperate to wrap their fingers around the neck of a hated foe—became suddenly docile when told that all around them were here to enjoy the pleasures of the flesh, to indulge in chemical euphoria and, most important of all, to secure their seats in a new France, with Henri Gaston as its chief arbiter of influence.

To avoid the appearance of economic improprieties, Gaston had been forced to set up various shell companies and appoint proxies to handle the business affairs of his family's chemical company. This was not an issue.

Gaston had been keeping a complex set of double books since being initiated to the family business as a young man fresh from university. He had taken to it immediately and easily. Deception was as natural to him as breathing. It had always been so. And it had helped him to build the empire he was now about to bring to fruition.

It was in university that he had first realized something about himself was different. Oh, his parents, now deceased, probably saw something in him. But they had not mentioned it to him. Perhaps they thought his behavior would change as he grew older, that he would stop having the odd impulses that had plagued him during his adolescence.

He had killed three of the family pets. Two were cats, while a third was a dog. Asked by his parents what had happened to the animals, he had told them that he was accident-prone, that he was clumsy. In truth he had killed the pets simply to see what it was like.

By the time he had choked the dog to death, he had decided there was nothing new to be gained by more animal murders. He had never done it again. His parents probably thought it a phase, and, indulgent to their deaths, they had forgiven him and had hoped to forget these unfortunate incidents.

Gaston was manipulative, and while at university, he had put this ability to good use. He had built networks of political allies at all levels of the student body, and among the faculty and administration. He did this by being—for each one of these people—exactly what they had wanted him to be.

He had said what they had wanted to hear; he had expressed opinions they had wished to believe; he had shamelessly flattered all of his targets. Many men would find it difficult to keep up such a charade, but Gaston had learned that he had an endless capacity to change whom he appeared to be when he courted a new member of his spiderweb, as he thought of it.

He felt no pride, no ego, no desire to espouse his true feelings. He knew only that people responded to those who were as those people wished them to be.

He could do that. He could be that.

And so he became popular. Just like that, Henri Gaston was known and liked seemingly by all. In truth, his allies were relatively few, but he picked those in the greatest positions of power and influence: here an administrator whose word was law; there a student admired for his good looks and his acumen at sports; and so on. When word was spread by other scions of popularity that Henri Gaston was one of the most popular people at the school, this was believed. Why would it not be?

And so Henri Gaston got along well at university, and his parents forgot all about the unfortunate behavior he had exhibited as a child. All children had their awkward phases, their difficult developmental times. Surely this was all Henri's difficulties had been.

As he approached his graduation, Gaston realized that he would either have to secure a position of employment outside the family business, or he would be forced to work as a subordinate to his father within the company. Neither possibility appealed to him.

He had been learning about his family's chemical business all his life. He felt he belonged there. No other career felt right, and he did not think he would react well to starting from the bottom of the corporate ladder at some external firm.

His parents would likely approve of him setting out on his own, knowing that they could rescue him from his folly if it did not work out…but he was not interested in pleasing them one way or another. The concept meant nothing to him. Their approval, their feelings, were irrelevant.

Henri Gaston was aware, of course, that he was an utter sociopath. He was not stupid; he possessed, if not eidetic memory, an advanced degree of recall that pushed his IQ scores to stellar heights. All he had required was a basic psychology class to teach him what his feelings, or his lack thereof, meant to his mental makeup. He felt as little about being a sociopath, however, as he did about having murdered his parents.

He had been careful; there had never been any suspicion that he was involved. But for Gaston to have what he wanted, his parents would have to go. They were in the way. He, their only child and heir to the family fortune, stood to inherit everything and to have sole control over it, when they passed on.

Fortunately his parents were also creatures of habit. He had simply waited until they had prepared to take their annual summer holiday through Europe. Then he had snuck into the garage where his father's touring car was kept. Considerable calculations went into the adjustments he made to the brakes.

His father kept to a fairly consistent route during his summer trips away from home. It was not easy, considering that multiple routes might be taken, but Gaston sabotaged his parents' brakes in such a way that the brakes failed while his father was negotiating a particularly dangerous turn.

The accident had left him an orphan…and a millionaire many times over. He had never regretted his actions for a moment. He was not capable of regret.

With money came pleas for the giving of that money. Beggars and shirttail relatives crawled out of the woodwork in droves. Overtures were made by local criminal syndicates. Government figures made it known that their pockets were deep and ready for the lining.

Henri Gaston obliged them all.

Well, not all. He picked and chose his victims as carefully as he had his allies in school. He bribed those whose loyalties could be bought most firmly with cash. He befriended hoodlums whom he thought could form the backbone of street muscle for his business ventures. He used his underworld contacts to do everything from manipulate labor disputes to influencing elections.

And it was there that he determined his real passion was to be. He would work his way up in the government, taking his power and influence with him, gathering his elaborate network of allegiances bought and bribed and otherwise bargained for, and he would build a dynasty that would last well past his own life.

Not that he cared about what came after him. But to enjoy true power in this world, that power had to be so great that it outlasted a single individual. The words of a particularly self-indulgent French monarch came to him. "After that, the deluge!" It didn't matter what became of Gaston's empire after he was gone.

In the meantime, he would live a fine life, taking whatever he wanted. Making the acquaintance of ES had been an especially good move. Levesque and his people were not simply effective muscle—they were the key to influencing public opinion and thus shaping the political narrative Gaston sought to build. For what greater lever was there in today's world than the threat of terrorism to shape voter behavior? He could think of none.

As Machiavelli had said, it was better to be feared than loved if one of the two had to be lacking. Gaston thought the idea a bit sentimental. Why rely on the vagaries, the mercurial loyalties, of love, when fear was so predictable? Self-interest, and fear of harm, was the greatest motivator in the world. It had always been so.

Gaston had been a man of thirty-one when he had committed his first murder of a human being.

The victim was a homeless man. Gaston had left his home, dressed in plain clothes and wearing a hat low over his head to prevent his recognition by camera or human witness. He had chosen a homeless man from among those in the vicinity of one of Paris's poorer neighborhoods. He had stalked and followed that homeless man for the greater part of the night, enjoying the game, especially when his quarry realized something was wrong and began actively trying to evade him.

The indigent, the marginalized among Paris's street denizens, were accustomed to abuse and mistreatment. They were cunning and suspicious, like feral animals, Gaston thought. He took real pleasure in staying with his prey, running the man down until the poor fellow was exhausted and frantic. By the time their race was over, the homeless man was dead.

Gaston had attacked the man from behind. He had held one hand over the poor man's mouth as he had shoved the blade into the man's kidney.

Something went wrong during that initial foray into the night. Gaston had difficulty recalling exactly what. His memories were glazed with the excitement of the kill. Somehow it had been necessary to stab the victim repeatedly, over and over again, watching the blade go in and out, studying the blood flow, staring down at the red on his hands and on his clothes and on the paving stones at his feet....

The memory aroused him. He reached for the humidor and selected a cigar for himself. With a snap of his fingers, he summoned one of the prostitutes, who took a box of matches from the table next to the humidor, bent before him to give him a spectacular view of her assets and struck the match for him. She pursed her lips as she lighted his cigar for him.

He smiled at her and pictured her lying on the floor at his feet with a knife in her ribs.

A scientist or psychologist or someone, somewhere, had published a study not all that long ago declaring that psychopaths, or those with psychopathic personality traits, made the most effective politicians, lawyers and people in positions of power.

Gaston had never understood why anyone could or would believe anything else might be true of power and those who wielded it. He supposed, however, that not all people were prepared to be as honest about the world as Henri Gaston.

He looked over at Levesque, who looked exceptionally pleased with himself. Nearby, in proximity to the pool, one of the lieutenants attending the party with a local gang leader had perhaps consumed a bit too much alcohol or a few too many lines of cocaine. He was arguing loudly with a uniformed member of the ES, who were providing security for the party.

Levesque had chosen to clothe his men in striking urban camouflage, without their masks, for the event. It marked them as security forces and made them look exotic. This was the type of attention to detail that Gaston liked in Levesque, and he approved. But as he watched, the gang lieutenant—a dark-skinned man with long dreadlocks, dressed in leather pants and vest with no shirt—began pushing the ES man.

"His name is Guilo," Levesque said, following Gaston's gaze. "He reports to a new coalition within Paris's underworld calling itself the Red Spiders. They are a response to the power vacuum created by the violent incursions of the American CIA man."

"It would seem the Red Spiders need a lesson in manners," Gaston said. "I do not know what started the dispute, but we cannot tolerate any challenge to our authority, even at an event such as this one."

"No," Levesque agreed. He stood and took off the T-shirt he wore. His upper body, while pale, was surprisingly well developed. Levesque also bore several prominent scars, possibly the result of his previous work as mercenary and terrorist.

"And what will you do with the American exactly?" Gaston asked, as Levesque began stretching his arms and legs, shaking his hands as if to improve his circulation.

"At this point," Levesque replied, carefully placing his cigar on the edge of the table by his chair, "I would say it is a question of what to do with his *body*. We will of course place it wherever it is most embarrassing for the Americans. You will need to decide precisely what story you wish to tell them."

"That should not be difficult. We will have time. And there is much work to be done. There will be some delays while our government determines precisely how best to give me my victory without making it seem they are trampling on Deparmond's corpse."

"Poor Deparmond." Levesque arched his back, stretching it. On the other side of the pool, Guilo was now engaged in a shouting match with the uniformed ES man.

"There will be hearings, of course," Gaston said. "Tessier's digital evidence will be required to establish beyond doubt that Deparmond was guilty of conspiring with the ES. We will have to begin purging the backgrounds of your top men. And finding and applying a new identity for you, my friend, if you and your upper tier of ES leadership are to join me in the halls of legitimate power."

"Of course. My men have secured the hard drive. There will be nothing to refute the official records already sent to the authorities. Tessier will be written off as a victim of Deparmond's thuggery. Or perhaps they will become especially unimaginative and simply declare him a suicide."

Both men laughed. Gaston looked to Guilo and then to Levesque. "What is it you intend to do?"

"One moment, please." Levesque sauntered to Guilo, tapped the gang member on the shoulder and waited for the man to turn. When Guilo instead swiveled with force and tried to throw a wide hook punch, Levesque avoided the blow, backed off a pace and threw a high kick that snapped Guilo's head back and dropped him to the deck.

Then Levesque shoved the man into the pool, where he sputtered and splashed weakly. The poolside drama was greeted with applause by the other partygoers and more than a few admiring looks from the working girls.

"What on earth was that all about?" Gaston asked as Levesque returned to his chair. The terror leader retrieved his cigar and puffed deeply on it, blowing smoke rings.

"I like to keep my hand in."

"You mean your feet," Gaston said.

"Those, too." Levesque looked down at his cigar, then stared at the behind of a passing woman. "Lemaire was good at savate when he met me. But I taught him much more."

"But not everything you know?"

"No," Levesque said. "Not everything."

CHAPTER SEVENTEEN

Paris, France

So far Bolan's only weapon—the switchblade taken from the ES operative in the field—had broken when Bolan had tried to use it pry open the collar of the steering column on his stolen car. While enough of the blade had remained to allow him to strip the wires, the knife was useless for anything else. He had discarded it when he got the car running and ditched the car several blocks from his destination.

The soldier at least had some money. Among the account numbers he had memorized was a wire-transfer number that he could use to have funds sent. He had availed himself of that and was now in possession of a wad of euros. He had also purchased a change of clothes and a canvas messenger bag from a shop down the block. The jacket he had gotten from Bayard was still serviceable, so he had hung on to it.

The hotel he had checked in to was an emergency safehouse, where rooms were kept on hand for CIA or other U.S. operatives who needed unexpected accommodations. Bolan had used another memorized account number for just such an occasion. The account was nominally traceable to a global internet marketing firm that specialized in providing motivational speakers for different business gatherings.

It had been necessary to explain to the hotel desk that his passport and other documents had been lost with his luggage en route to Paris. No doubt he had looked like the sort of harried traveler who had been forced to sleep in the same set of clothes on a plane or in an airport.

Bolan was an expert in role camouflage, in pretending to belong where he was and in making those around him believe it. The harried traveler was not a theme that was unfamiliar to him. He did not even really have to work at it. As the hotel was somewhat seedy, the desk clerk did not bat an eye. He'd probably heard the story many times.

The hotel had an internet kiosk. Bolan had gone on-line right after checking in, to search for bazaars and markets in the city, looking for references in the popular press and "alternative" newspapers to the sorts of markets that might have illicit weapons for sale. There was a feel for that sort of thing, a flavor that the black markets of all cultures seemed to share to varying degrees.

The only exceptions were, for example, the truly lawless areas. There were parts of Pakistan, for example, where any firearm could be had by anyone for a price, including handmade counterfeits of famous designs. Such places in the world were rare but were as close to anarchy as any human being would truly experience.

Unsurprisingly anarchy was always ruled by the willingness and the power to do violence.

Bolan was now armed with a mental list of the sites he would visit. He would have to use caution and discretion.

Mack Bolan stood under the shower, which was turned nearly to full-blast hot, and let the water sluice over his body, washing away the grime of the field in which he'd dragged himself, the engine grease from the car he had hot-wired and stolen, and the aches and pains of what had already been a demanding and less-than-ideal mission.

The precarious nature of his position in France, however, was brought home to him when he picked up the hotel room's phone and dialed a series of numbers. That numerical sequence eventually got him a scrambled line to the Farm, although there was the possibility that someone, even just staff on the hotel switchboard, could be listening on Bolan's end.

"Party line," Bolan said, when Barbara Price answered him. This would warn her that he was calling from an insecure location and not from his secure satellite phone, although this last information would be evident on the display boards at Stony Man Farm.

"Cooper," Price replied, using his code name. "I take it you've had some setbacks."

What Price was really saying to Bolan was *Striker, we're aware that you've lost ground and are operating without a full complement of equipment.*

"You could say that. Thanks for wiring me the cash I needed. The airlines lost my luggage. I have a change of clothes now, but otherwise I'm pretty much empty-handed."

Bolan's message was thus interpretable as *I've got money, but I'm unarmed.*

"I can see how that would be inconvenient," Price said. "I take it you've lost your company phone?"

How badly are you compromised? was the question Price was really asking. *Why aren't you using your secure smartphone?*

"Unfortunately," Bolan said. "Also my passport and my driver's license."

"I'm sure we can make arrangements to get you replacements," Price told him. "But it might take a little while."

"Why's that?"

"It looks like import restrictions have been tightened," Price said. "Something about the threat of terrorism. The authorities in France have proved very difficult. They're looking for the people responsible and they seem very angry to have been taken advantage of."

The meaning of that was very clear. The French authorities were irate about the behavior of Agent Cooper and could be presumed to be hunting Bolan. That he had already known, but Price's confirmation meant that no amount of diplomatic hand-holding from Brognola himself had managed to improve the mood among the Powers that Were in Paris.

"I'm aware," Bolan said. "As you know, I'm on an aggressive schedule. I'm going to have to move forward before my new stuff arrives."

Despite whatever complications you're dealing with, Bolan was telling her, *I'm going to pursue my mission my way, on my timetable.*

"Understood, Cooper. Just be advised that our travel agent is getting a lot of resistance to that idea."

Bolan could just imagine. She was most likely referring to Brognola, but Bolan already knew that his actions would have consequences across the ocean. It could not be helped.

Gaston had duped the people of France and rigged the elections. He had secured his ill-gotten gains not just by manipulating the people, but by murdering Deparmond and making sure of his victory.

Deparmond might have been a xenophobe, and his election was not desired by the Man back home, but a free and fair election by the French people was far pref-

erable to some rigged game perpetrated by a power-
broker pushing an agenda.

"Cooper?" Barbara spoke after his long silence.

Bolan had wasted very little time wondering why
Gaston had perpetrated such a widespread, complicated
fraud. The plan was an ambitious one, even by international political standards, after all. The extensive, even
exhausting effort to portray himself as a moderate had
to be convincing to any and all who examined Henri
Gaston and the man's political aspirations.

No doubt he had been vetted by intelligence agencies
around the world, at least on a cursory basis. No world
leader, or prospective world leader, took the global stage
without inspiring at least a perfunctory interest among
the other industrialized nations and their intelligence
mechanisms.

The implication—given Levesque's admission of cooperation with Gaston—was that Gaston was capable
of playing a complex and long game, manipulating both
the public and the political machine in France, building
multiple allegiances and sculpting a public image and
message…all while cultivating his "relationships" with
criminals and terrorists, using that underworld muscle
to build power behind the scenes and then murdering
and framing his political rival.

Gaston was a powerful man indeed.

"Cooper, are you there?"

Brognola's original briefing on Gaston and Deparmond had contained nothing to indicate that Gaston was
capable of any of this. Bolan summoned to mind what
he recalled of the file. Gaston was the child of wealthy
parents and heir to a chemical-company fortune. That
explained how he had financed his ambitions. Rich men

were as common in politics as celebrities were common on the French Riviera.

"I'll get in touch with you again as soon as I'm able to," Bolan told Price. "Maybe then we can make arrangements for getting my identification and a new company phone."

"All right, Cooper. If you check your corporate email on the web, we may have some suggestions for you, some tourist areas to check out. Be careful. You're one man in a foreign city. It could be dangerous."

"I will," he said. "I'll talk to you soon." He replaced the hotel phone in its cradle.

If anyone had been listening to or recording his end of the call, they would have heard nothing that could compromise the Farm. Bolan looked at the neatly made hotel bed and realized he could not remember when he had last slept. Freshly showered, he climbed between the sheets and put his head on the pillow.

Darkness took him quickly.

WHEN HIS EYES snapped open again, his internal clock told him that it was early morning, perhaps three or four. Someone was tampering with the door to his hotel room.

He rolled out of bed and padded to the wall beside the door, but not before ripping the digital alarm clock out of the wall. The clock trailed its electrical cord as he held it in his right hand. The door opened. From what Bolan could hear, there were two of them.

They stood in the doorway for a long moment, trying to determine if Bolan was in there and asleep, but the room was dark and the light from the door only illuminated the area at the base of the bed. The first of the two intruders took a step inside.

Bolan smashed him in the back of the head with the alarm clock.

The intruder grunted and went down. Bolan flew into action, driving his knee into the gut of the second man, knocking him to the floor. He went after the second man, straddling him and punching him repeatedly, fully aware that there was still a semiconscious hostile in the room who might choose to reenter the fray.

When the second man was groaning and moving slowly, Bolan rose, swiveled and teed off on the first man, kicking him in the jaw. He felt the man's head snap back, scraping the intruder's beard stubble along the top of Bolan's bare foot.

One of the men on the floor groaned, then said in English, "One day I'm going to get the best of you, Cooper." Bolan recognized that voice. He went to wall switch and hit the light.

The two men on the floor were Musson and Flagel of the DCRI.

Bolan grimaced.

Musson was already going for his gun. Bolan dived for him, collided with him, and the slim Walther PPK went flying from the inspector's hand. Bolan kicked it farther and Musson growled. The soldier smashed one fist into Musson's face, rocking him back, but not scoring a knockout blow. Musson crashed into the wall of the hotel room and did not try to rise again. His chest rose and fell heavily.

"I really do not like you, Cooper," Musson stated.

Bolan turned, remembering Flagel. The other DCRI inspector was on his hands and knees, trying to push himself to his feet. He wore a bandage over the bridge of his nose, evidence of Bolan's previous handiwork. The soldier pushed him over, causing him to grunt again, and then patted down the battered inspector. He took the Browning Hi Power and the backup revolver Flagel carried.

"Stop," Musson ordered.

Bolan looked back at Musson over his shoulder. The inspector was holding an NAA mini-revolver in his fist. The weapon was tiny, almost like a toy, but the business end was no joke. Bolan had once known a man who carried a miniature revolver in his prosthetic limb. It was a deadly weapon.

"That's right," Musson said. "I have five rounds of .22 Magnum here. I will put a round in you if you do not stop. Or five rounds. Give Flagel his guns back."

Bolan very nearly sighed. He put the guns on the carpet and pushed them back toward Flagel.

"Sit on the bed. Hands behind your head."

Bolan did as he had been ordered. "How did you find me?" he asked. "Did you distribute my description to all the area hotels?"

Flagel and Musson exchanged glances. Now in the light and with the time to look at him more closely, Bolan could see that Flagel really did look worse for wear. He had deep, dark circles under both eyes, the result of the blow to his nose. Clearly they were not eager to give up any of their secrets.

"We should bring him in like this," Flagel said. "Let us cuff him and be on our way."

"You are under arrest," Musson stated. "As you were informed before, your behavior here in France is subject to strict oversight. You have stepped outside your authority, Cooper, and frankly it would give me pleasure to gun you down for the killer you are. But I won't do that. That is not how the DCRI operates."

"It's not how I operate, either," Bolan said. "Or you two would be dead by now. A few times over."

Flagel and Musson once more looked at each other. Flagel spit on the carpet. "I have had enough of you," he said angrily. Then he punched Bolan in the gut. The blow was not an especially bad one, but Bolan gave the Frenchman what he wanted. The soldier bent at the waist and made a show of catching his breath. If he brazened it out, pretended like it hadn't happened, Flagel would only become more agitated. There was no point in getting killed over a point of pride.

"Stop it!" Musson ordered Flagel. "What is wrong with you? Shall we beat him to death before we get him back to headquarters?"

"It is the type of thing he would do to a suspect," Flagel growled.

"Not really," Bolan said.

Flagel stepped in to take another shot. Musson got in between them. "I said stop it!" Then Musson realized he was in striking range and whirled, his gun at the ready. "Don't move, Cooper! Do not make me kill you!"

Bolan had expected that reaction, which was why he hadn't bothered to try. Musson was convinced he was dealing with a rattlesnake, at this point, and he was not incorrect. But Bolan had not lived as long as he had, fought in as many battles as he had waged, by underestimating the reflexes that fear gave a man.

Musson was jumpy, worried he would end up embarrassed and humiliated again. He was also determined to bring in the dangerous mad dog that was Matthew Cooper. Bolan could see it in his eyes and hear it in his voice.

"We will have him dress," Musson said. "We will then cuff him and bring him in. We are not animals.

We are agents of the DCRI. We will conduct ourselves accordingly."

"He will try something!" Flagel insisted. He put his guns back in their holsters. His movements were reluctant, grudging, as if he wanted to pistol-whip Bolan for good measure...or simply put a bullet into the big American who had caused so much trouble.

"What would you have me do?" Musson asked. "Cuff him first? How will he put on his clothes? Stand over there, across the room, and train your gun on him. If he makes even the slightest of suspicious moves, shoot him dead. Is that clear to you, Agent Cooper?"

"It is," Bolan said. "I would like to point out again, though, that if I was the rabid animal you think I am, neither one of you would be talking about it right now."

Musson jerked his head toward the chair on which Bolan had draped his clothes and jacket. Bolan began pulling on his clothes.

"Flagel, check his boots."

Flagel nodded. Bolan's combat boots were near the door to the room. The inspector checked them to make sure they contained no weapons or obvious hidden compartments. He tossed the boots across the room, within Bolan's reach.

"You're awfully up in arms over a bunch of gang scum," Bolan said.

"Gang scum," Musson repeated. "Yes. The men you eliminated were bad people. You accomplished a great deal of 'police work' in a short amount of time, Cooper. But have you considered what we will have to live with in the coming weeks and months? The gangs are scrambling for control of the territory now. Out of fear, they are cooperating.

"A new coalition has arisen under the name of the

Red Spiders. They are not as powerful, nor as well equipped, but they are compensating by employing greater patience and stealth. You have simply driven some of the overt crime underground. The Red Spiders are now on the move, consolidating their grip on the neighborhoods they claim."

"And it was better when it was aboveground?" Bolan asked. "When gang leaders walked your streets with impunity, convinced of their own safety in the middle of Paris's no-go zones? Just what do you think happens when power like that goes unchecked? Your society's predators grow out of control until they're the ones in charge. That's the framework you're trying to protect, Musson. You're a lawman. You should know better."

"I know the difference between law enforcement and murder!" Musson insisted. He produced a pair of plastic zip-tie cuffs from his pocket.

Bolan knew that once those cuffs were on his wrists, it would be nearly impossible to get out of them. He would need to find a blade of some kind to cut the plastic. He could strip the flesh from his own wrists before he managed to work the ties loose otherwise. He couldn't afford to let them tie him.

Flagel was a hothead, sure, but Bolan understood where he was coming from. He had felt such feelings of righteous indignation himself. He finished dressing and pulled on his jacket. The door behind Musson, the door to Bolan's hotel room, had not been shut completely. The soldier could see the line of light from the hallway behind. As Flagel started to move in, his Browning at the ready, Musson brandished the zip-cuffs.

Bolan held out his hands. "I just want you to know something," he said. "Well, two things, Musson."

"And what is that?" Musson reached out to place the loop of the cuffs over Bolan's wrists.

"I'm sorry."

Bolan struck.

Extending his hands, he struck with his palms, up and forward, as if holding a ball in his hands. The double-hand strike took Musson under his neck, and whipped his head back and down. The blow staggered the inspector and dropped him to the floor, dazed. Bolan was already moving, using the momentum of his attack to propel him over Musson's body.

The detonation of Flagel's pistol shook the room with sudden thunder, pummeling Bolan's eardrums. He kept going, not looking back, not giving Flagel the pause the man would need to target Bolan properly.

The soldier barreled down the hotel corridor.

"Cooper!" Flagel roared. "Stop!"

Bolan reached the end of the corridor and yanked open the fire door. Once inside he descended rapidly, sliding down the railings when he needed to shorten the distance. Above him, he heard the fire door open again, and at least twice the stairwell echoed with shots from Flagel's gun, but Bolan was outpacing the inspector, and Flagel knew it.

When Bolan reached street level, he forced himself to walk at a normal pace.

The streets were still dark, but even now in the pre-dawn, there were people moving about, going to and from their jobs. Bolan strode purposefully down the street, taking the first corner he found, then ducking into an adjacent alley.

He set a brisk pace but never broke from a walk, switching back and changing his pattern until he was certain he had lost Flagel and had picked up no other

DCRI tails. It was possible, after all, that someone was watching the building at street level, ready to acquire or even kill Bolan should he escape custody.

He wasn't sure how they had found him, but there were a number of possible ways. That was irrelevant now. He had rested as much as he could permit himself. It was time to continue the war, bring the battle to Gaston. He knew the address of Gaston's estate; it had been in the original intelligence briefing. He made a practice of memorizing critical mission data. You never knew when the technology on which you depended might stop working.

For the moment Bolan had no weapons, no equipment, except the boots on his feet, the clothes on his back and the brain in his head. Fortunately for the Executioner, the human brain was the most effective weapon yet evolved. And his was exceptional.

Mack Bolan disappeared into the crowds on the streets of Paris.

CHAPTER EIGHTEEN

"Are you all insane?" Alfred Bayard shouted. "He is an operative of the United States government, a nation with which we are allied, and his targets have been the most dangerous and violent of our criminal element! He has actively fought terrorists on French soil and saved the lives of French citizens!"

Director Jean Vigneau of the DCRI peered at Bayard over his half spectacles. His suit was two decades out of fashion, and his tie was thicker than good sense or the decade prescribed. Two tufts of gray hair hung on for dear life to either side of his otherwise bald head. His face was a road map of lines and wrinkles, wrought from years of responsibility and sour moods. A disapproving look from Vigneau was enough to back Bayard up a pace.

"Inspector Bayard," Vigneau said, never once raising his voice, "I will thank you to calm yourself and retake your seat."

Bayard realized then that he was standing. Somewhat sheepishly he sat again. In the wooden chairs to either side of him, Musson and Flagel sat nursing their fresh wounds. Both men were bruised and battered. Fortunately for them, nothing had been broken. The two kept looking at each other and to Bayard.

"What you are suggesting," Bayard said, trying to calm himself, "is ludicrous. It is a betrayal of everything we stand for. If you give these Red Spiders the information they need to hunt and kill Cooper, you are giving the criminals of this city the means they need to eliminate the man who has put them on their heels.

"The Red Spiders will be emboldened. And you can bet they will trumpet their victory on the street. They might put Cooper's head on a pike and parade it through the streets. Are you prepared for such a spectacle? The ethnic enclaves will become worse than ever, more hostile to our people than ever."

"Hostile?" Vigneau repeated, glaring at Bayard. "I am led to understand that you have found ways to work with the powers in the enclaves before. That you were able to secure certain arrangements, certain considerations."

Bayard could feel heat rushing to his face. He tried to continue. "But it is one thing to make certain arrangements of convenience with street trash," he said, "when one's goal is to try to keep peace. What you are suggesting is empowering the new gang. If they find and kill Cooper, they will use this as a badge of their power. It will become the thing that 'makes' them, so to speak. Their power will be assumed, and we will find it even harder to oppose them in the future. To say nothing of the damage that could be done to international relations, especially with the Americans—"

"The Americans?" Vigneau interrupted. "Did the President of the United States show any great concern for his relationship with France when he inflicted this, this *cowboy,* this Agent Cooper, on us?" He opened the center drawer of his desk. From within it he took a digital sound recorder. He placed it on the desk before pressing the Play button.

"As you know, I'm on an aggressive schedule," Bolan's

voice said. "I'm going to have to move forward before my new stuff arrives."

"That means nothing," Bayard stated. "The intelligence provided by our eavesdropping device is not conclusive."

"Now who is insane?" Vigneau shot back. "Given what this man has done in the time he has been here, do you believe anything less will follow? Especially as he 'moves forward' with whatever violent agenda he is pursuing?"

"What really frightens you?" Bayard demanded. "That this Cooper might kill still more of France's most wanted criminals? That the streets might be that much safer? Why are we not simply getting out of his way?"

"Now I know you are insane. Not so many days ago you believed as I do. You would sneer at the methods of a man like Cooper. You would want him brought to justice. What has changed, Alfred? How has he gotten to you?"

"It isn't that," Bayard said. "But I saw the results he got. I saw the good he did. I did not like how he did it, especially at first. But, Jean, consider how many years we lived with the threat of—"

"You forget yourself, Inspector Bayard," Vigneau interrupted again. "I am your superior officer. You have already put yourself in a precarious position by facilitating Cooper's mad rampage through the city. Do you have any idea of the collateral damage that could have been done? The innocent lives lost? Do you really want to be party to that again?"

"What innocent lives?" Bayard asked. His voice was rising again, but he could not help it. Musson and Flagel looked nervous. "I have never met a man who worked harder to avoid the loss of innocent life. To say nothing of how he had protected law enforcement officers. Look at these two."

Vigneau made a disgusted face. "Yes, look at these two," he said. "Respected, trusted operatives of the DCRI, who twice now have been beaten and humiliated by your American cowboy."

"Do you not see that is the point?" Bayard demanded. "He could have killed either or both of them. He did not. Even given another opportunity to do so, alone in a hotel room where you sent them to arrest him in the dead of night, he did not do so. And a man like Cooper, accustomed to dealing with his enemies with such finality, could easily and with all consideration have killed these fools—"

"Now wait a moment," Musson began.

"Fools?" Flagel said.

"Could have killed these fools," Bayard repeated, "because they attacked him while he slept. How many armed men, do you suppose, could have walked into that room with guns on their persons and walked out alive again? But Cooper let them live because he operates by a code. He does not kill law enforcement officers."

"How noble!" Vigneau said, his voice dripping with sarcasm. "How very cinematic! Perhaps we can make a television movie about Cooper. We shall have to budget a great deal for *explosives*."

Bayard decided to try a different approach. "Director," he said, "I understand completely the position in which you find yourself."

"Do you?" Vigneau asked.

"I do. Cooper has proved to be a wild element. Uncontrollable. But I propose to use him to do what we have been unable to do. I say we get out of his way. We let him operate. And when he is done we pick up behind him, perform damage control. The benefits will be great. I trust Cooper, Director. I would trust him with my life."

Vigneau brought his palms together in a slow clap. "We shall have to include that speech in the movie," he said, "because that is fantasy, not reality. You, Inspector Bayard, will immediately arrange for a special tactics team to accompany you. You will, using the asset we have placed on Cooper, track this man down and bring him in. You will kill him if he refuses. Is that clear?"

"No," Bayard said.

"No, it is not clear?" Vigneau looked at him, confused.

"I will not do it. I will not hunt Cooper."

"Your career will suffer accordingly for this insubordination," Vigneau told him. "Consider yourself censured. I will be placing a letter in your file. Only your seniority, Alfred, prevents me from taking your credentials from you. Musson, it falls to you."

Musson paused. Finally, he opened his mouth, closed it and then opened it to say, "No, Director. I cannot."

"What?" Vigneau demanded. "Why not?"

"Alfred is right. Cooper had the means and the reason, more than once, to end my life. If he was the animal you say, he would have. Instead he chose to spare me and Flagel. His methods are not ours, no, but he is an honorable man. He chose not to do serious injury even though we may well have killed him in the attempt to apprehend him. I will not do it. I cannot do it."

"Then get out of my sight!" Vigneau told him. "I am suspending you with pay. You need to think about where your career is going, Musson."

Musson walked out of the office. Bayard glared at Flagel. "Well?" he said.

Flagel shook his head. "I will do what is asked of me."

"You could take a lesson from Inspector Flagel, Alfred," Vigneau stated. "Now get out of my office. *Your* suspension is one month, *without* pay."

Bayard felt his temper flare. He reached into his jacket, produced his .38 and jammed it, butt first, into Flagel's stomach. "Here," he said. "Take my gun."

Flagel looked confused but took the weapon, rubbing at his gut.

"What is the meaning of this?" Vigneau asked.

"I quit." Bayard took out his badge and placed it on Vigneau's desk. "I won't be party to this…this lynch mob."

"Stop this," Vigneau said. "Let us not get carried away. Alfred, you have always been a reasonable man. A man who understands practical realities."

"Lynch mob!" Bayard repeated.

"And who gave us the concept of the lynch mob?" Vigneau asked. "I would say it was the Americans, was it not?"

"And we gave the world the glorious guillotine," Bayard replied. "I would say we have no position from which to throw stones. Certainly you do not, Director. Hunt Cooper if you must. I won't be part of it. And I won't be part of the DCRI if this is how it conducts its affairs."

"Get out," Vigneau spit.

Bayard left.

He went immediately to his desk, not knowing what else to do. Once he was there, staring at the workspace that had been his for more years than he wanted to think about, he realized that he kept almost nothing at work. There were no mementos, no family photos. Bayard had no living family and was not particularly sentimental.

He had served in the French military briefly before a knee injury—since rehabilitated—but that had necessitated finding another career. His keen mind and his sense of justice had led him to law enforcement. He had toiled there, looking for that justice, hoping to make a difference, ever since.

It was true that Cooper was dangerous. Bayard thought perhaps he had never met a more dangerous man. But Cooper was also a *good* man. It had taken him time to see that. He had benefited from seeing the direct way Cooper fought for others. He still had reservations. But he would not condemn Matthew Cooper. And he would not participate in any organization that would hunt him down like a dog.

How strange, to have reached this point. To have changed his mind so radically.

From an adjacent office he took an empty file box that he placed on his desk and, without thought, he began scooping up the contents of his desk that were not official files or issued supplies. He had much room left over when the task was completed. He stared at the box. It included several plaques, commendations he had received for his performance as an inspector.

He wondered if the authorities issuing those awards would feel differently, knowing the corners he had cut, the times he had agreed to look the other way, the occasional payouts he had received.

Bayard was not corrupt in the sense that he would allow evil to be done with his sanction. He would never allow that. But he had indeed accepted the lesser of available evils, in the past. He had embraced pragmatism in order to create peace. He had permitted wrong-doing, illegal conduct, criminal enterprise, to fester in the enclaves as long as little blood was spilled, as long as all involved did their best to conform to the framework and the power structure that was the status quo.

Where did that leave him? What was Bayard to do with his life?

The specter of a retaliatory investigation loomed. Vigneau, if he were feeling spiteful, could choose to make Bayard's life very difficult. But it was a two-way street. Bayard had been with the DCRI long enough to know where many bodies were buried, most of them figurative. He did not think Vigneau would risk reprisals.

It was only when he reached the street with his pitiful box of belongings that he realized he had no car. Not after the damage done to the Peugeot during his adventure with Cooper. He shook his head. The man was a force of nature, indeed.

A Mercedes pulled up alongside him. He peered in. It was Flagel.

"Alfred," he said, "get in, quickly. I will explain as we go."

"What is this?" Bayard asked.

"Please, Alfred. Trust me."

"Very well." Bayard threw his box into the backseat, then climbed into the passenger seat. Flagel pulled away from the curb. On the seat next to him was an electronic tracking device. Bayard's eyes widened. "I thought I said I would take no part in this."

"It is not what you think," Flagel said, negotiating traffic. "Musson is at his flat, but he says to telephone if we require him. I agreed to head the mission because I thought I could then control it, see to it that Cooper was not injured too badly."

Bayard eyed Flagel's bruised face and the bandage on his nose. "Why would you, of all people, care about that?"

"Because what you said was true," Flagel told him. "I don't like Cooper. I think he is dangerous. But he is not the enemy. And if we treat him, and the Americans, like the enemy, what do we gain? Nothing but more destruction in Paris."

"Cooper is arguably the greater destructive force," Bayard said.

"Not destruction like that. You know what I mean. The destruction of our culture. The destruction of our people. The creep of criminal gangs and the establishment of more enclaves where the police cannot go. Do we need another month of riots, of burning cars, of protests, before we see that?"

"So you will lead the investigation? The hunt for Cooper?"

"No," Flagel said. "I stole the backup tracking device from the evidence locker. Vigneau has hatched a scheme that I cannot pretend to be part of. He saw it in my face and ordered me from his office after he told me. He also instructed me to share it with no one at the DCRI."

"Then you are breaking your word."

"Am I?" Flagel asked. "I thought you resigned."

Bayard's mouth widened in a tight smile. "So I have," he said. "So I have indeed. What is this plan you could not be part of?"

"I think it must be what he wished all along," Flagel stated. "I think he was counting on our objections to justify it. Why bother asking us, otherwise? Vigneau has given the tracking device and the bug frequency to the Red Spiders. Using his contacts in Paris's underworld, Vigneau has made it known that Cooper is a wanted man. The price on his head is a small fortune. The exact number varies with each telling."

"We hardly have the budget for that," Bayard scoffed.

"You resigned," Flagel reminded him.

Bayard made a rude noise. "You know what I mean."

"It doesn't matter because no bounty will be paid. Anyone attempting to claim it will be used as a scapegoat. That scapegoat will be presented to the Americans as the reason for the loss of their agent."

"Are you telling me—"

"It is as bad as you think, Alfred," Flagel said. "Vigneau has given the criminal element the means to track the American agent. Vigneau has told them they will be rewarded handsomely for killing that American operative. And Vigneau intends to use this to mask what is essentially the assassination of Agent Cooper on French soil."

"My God," Bayard said. "We must stop this. How much time do we have?"

"Very little. With any luck, nobody saw me leave with the tracking device, and thus our interference will not be anticipated. But already the Red Spiders will be closing in on Cooper."

"Where is he?" Bayard asked. He picked up the tracking device and examined its illuminated face. "Hmm. It looks like he is approaching the street bazaar nearby," he said, pointing. "That is several blocks away through heavy traffic. Hurry. But we must detour here."

"Musson's flat?"

"Yes," Bayard said, nodding. He took out his wireless phone and placed a call to Musson. When his fellow inspector answered, Bayard explained to him what they were after.

"Of course," Musson agreed. "I will meet you on the street."

Musson was as good as his word. The three inspectors rode in silence as Musson checked his Walther PPK and Flagel reached into his jacket. When Flagel's hand reappeared, it held not one of his own pistols, but Bayard's .38.

"I thought you'd need this, so I brought it along."

"You do realize what this means," Musson said.

"What is that?" Bayard asked.

"We are all much closer to Cooper's way of thinking than we would like to believe."

"Good," Flagel replied. "Perhaps he will stop hitting me."

"I do not know what you are complaining about," Musson said. "My neck *still* hurts."

"And yet but for some bruises you *look* fine," Flagel stated. "I look like I lost a fight to an entire tavern's worth of miscreants."

"You never looked that good to begin with," Musson said.

"I still do not like him."

Bayard looked in the rearview mirror. "Flagel, how much longer to the bazaar?"

"A few minutes. Why?"

"We do not have a few minutes," Bayard said. "Faster. Faster now."

But the sirens started behind them. The unmarked vehicles bore magnetic lights on their roofs. These were DCRI cars, not regular French police.

"Vigneau, or someone working for him," Flagel said. "He must have realized what we are trying to do. Probably sent someone to follow me."

"Or the tracking device is itself bugged for counter-espionage purposes," Musson stated.

"Get your weapons ready," Bayard told them. "They are closing. I see weapons out."

"But we are men of the DCRI." Musson turned to look out the rear windshield. "Surely they wouldn't—"

Whatever Musson thought they surely wouldn't, it appeared their pursuers surely would, for the bullet that punched through the rear windshield continued on to bore a tunnel through Musson's head. The exit wound sprayed the interior of the Mercedes with blood, splashing Bayard and Flagel, causing Flagel to lose control and overcompensate. The Mercedes crashed into a parked car, left a broad swath of paint alongside it and rammed a concrete post used for handbills. There were people on the street who screamed and scattered as the Mercedes crashed to a halt.

Two of the cars continued past the accident site, but the third and last one stopped just short of the crash scene. Three men, whom Bayard recognized as DCRI operatives with whom Vigneau was close, climbed out of the car. They aimed their weapons at the Mercedes.

"Go, Alfred!" Flagel shouted. "Get to the bazaar! Warn Cooper!"

"I will not leave you here," Bayard said.

"I am not offering you that option." His forehead was bloody from the crash. "You must find Cooper and see to it Vigneau is brought to justice." He looked back at his former partner. "Musson's murderers must not go free."

Bayard nodded. "I will do it. But—"

"Go!" Flagel yelled. With his Browning Hi Power in one hand and his revolver in the other, he ran from the car, firing both weapons into the DCRI men who had killed Musson. The bullets from Flagel's guns shattered the windshield of the pursuers' vehicle and dropped at least one of the enemy gunmen.

Bayard fled.

He knew which direction he needed to go. The bazaar was directly ahead. Behind him, as he ducked and dodged through alleys and in between parked cars, past frightened shoppers and curious street people, away from pedestrians and commuters, he heard the sounds of a furious gun battle.

Flagel, whom he had always dismissed as perhaps the lesser of the men with whom he had worked, had proven at the end to be an honorable man, a man who believed in justice. A man who was now selling his life dearly in order to preserve both Bayard's life and Cooper's chances.

Vigneau's corruption could not be allowed to stand. This was surely granting sanction to evil. The murder of Musson could not go unpunished. Vigneau would be made to face what he had done. Prison or death. Those were the only options fitting for such a man, a person who would sacrifice both the ideals of the rule of law and the lives of good men.

He reached the outskirts of the bazaar. Cooper was here somewhere. The inspector prayed that the American had not already moved on, had not already left the area. Bayard had to find Cooper and undo the damage already done.

If anyone could help Bayard bring Vigneau to justice, it would be the American.

CHAPTER NINETEEN

Mack Bolan made his way through the busy street bazaar. He was at the edge of one of the ethnic enclaves, which was why he had chosen this particular site. It would see traffic from both sides of the street, as the saying went. Customers from within the enclave and from outside of it would come here to meet certain specific consumer needs. It was in the sometimes-awkward mesh of legitimate and otherwise that the most opportunities for illicit goods were created.

During their phone call Price had hinted that information would be forthcoming to his "corporate email." What she was in fact referring to was a secure webmail site, the login credentials he knew by memory, that allowed the Farm to pass coded data. Early that morning when Paris's shops and cafés had begun to open again, he had stopped at an internet café. He had checked the account and found a series of numbers. Each was a pairing of a two-digit letter-number combination, such as E3, J6.

Knowing Stony Man's protocols, Bolan had memorized the combinations and then found a shop that sold maps. He selected the most popular of the Paris street maps and discovered, to his lack of surprise, that it was divided into letter-number grid squares. Then he simply correlated the grid squares with the addresses he had learned the previous day, all of which were markets where, he hoped, he might find illegal goods for sale.

The fact that the system worked at all was a little amazing, given how many different ways there were for something to go wrong, but the Farm and its personnel were firm believers in maintaining contingency plans. Bolan was, as well. He could not complain.

Ultimately he had chosen this bazaar as much for its relative location as for its size. It was the largest of the possibilities and thus had the most potential. Now he made his way through tables that were set up on top of each other and in close proximity to one another. They were sheltered by tarps and tents and other awnings, to provide shade and as a hedge against rain. The result was a spotty maze full of shafts of sunlight and caverns of shadow, where space to walk was sometimes at a premium amid the crowd of fellow customers.

A complete cross section of Paris's citizens seemed to be represented by the shoppers here. He saw street people, dressed in worn clothing; he saw merchants at every point on the spectrum of affluence; he saw tourists and Paris locals alike, notable mostly because the tourists were obvious in the same way the locals were not. There were wealthy business people, too, dressed in designer suits and, in some cases, accompanied by burly giants who could only be private security.

Strangely absent were any uniformed police officers.

Some of the tents were so dark, so cut off from the sunlight without, that there were lanterns hanging inside. In one of them, connected to a row of smaller awnings with tables stacked end to end, Bolan found himself looking at an array of duffel bags and purpose-built packs.

The old man behind the table was a Sikh—

recognizable by his turban and wide bracelet. Bolan knew that it represented Sikh warrior culture. A chain around the man's neck disappeared under his tunic, but very likely bore a ceremonial knife or knifelike pendant.

The old man looked up at Bolan from where he sat at the table. He looked across his array of bags and shook his head sourly.

"I'm sorry?" Bolan asked.

"Not these," the old man said. "These are for the tourists. You are not a tourist."

Bolan stared hard at him. "You know me?"

"I do not know you, but I know what you are. I see it. I see it in the way you move. I see it in the way you watch these others." He spread his hands to indicate the throngs at the market. "A wolf among sheep. Mine is a warrior people, American."

"How did—"

"Your accent," the Sikh replied. "A moment." He bent and rummaged around under the table. When he came up again he had produced a heavy brown canvas musette bag. It had a long, wide shoulder strap.

"I could use that," Bolan said.

"I know." The old man pushed it across the table. Bolan peeled off some bills from his wad of cash and handed it to the man.

"You are very generous. You wish to bargain? I could accept less."

"No," Bolan said. "I'm satisfied."

"My people are a warrior people," the old man told him. "We recognize our brothers. And we see a battle for what it is. Behind you and to your left, American. Fight well."

Bolan turned. He saw the group of hard cases moving through the stalls and pushing aside awning stakes as they walked. While they wore a variety of punk and civilian clothing, they all had a red bandanna tied around their biceps, their necks or on their heads. Gang colors, unmistakably.

"They are called the Red Spiders," the old man said. "A new gang, born of the remnants of the Suffering and the Red Death gangs, so I hear. I can see recognition in your eyes. These men are known to you."

"Suffering and the Red Death, yes," Bolan said.

The old man looked at him with what might have been renewed respect. Bolan wondered if the merchant suspected something. How connected was he with what went on in the enclaves...or the battles that Bolan had already fought there?

"The Red Death became the Red Spiders," the old man told him. "The new gang has subsumed the old, merged with Suffering, become once again a dominant force, if perhaps not as fearsome as either gang was before their recent difficulties."

"Difficulties," Bolan repeated.

"You look like a difficult man." The old man smiled through crooked teeth. "And here, in this place, you have one advantage."

"What advantage is that?"

"They will be reluctant to use guns. Many things are ignored in this place, to the benefit of all. Gunfire is one thing that cannot be ignored. Gunfire is bad for everyone. Gunfire brings the police, who begin looking where many would prefer they not." He paused, still watching the activity beyond Bolan. His smile turned into a frown. "They are coming, American."

"I thank you," Bolan said, pulling the empty musette bag over his shoulder and across his body and hurried away.

He was reaping what he had sown on French soil, that much was true. It didn't explain why the Red Spiders were here now, though, nor how they had known to target Bolan specifically. Had he walked past an unseen spotter, someone who had notified the gang to come looking? He was a big man and, despite his skills in blending in, identifiable enough if one knew what to search for. Something about this just didn't feel right, though. He felt like he had crosshairs painted on his back, and he wanted to know why.

He wondered briefly if some kind of satellite tracking, or a technology he was yet unfamiliar with, might be at play. That seemed unlikely. There had been no indication of that kind of hardware in use in the region. Could the DCRI be using a tracking web of some sort? That had greater promise. The simplest solution, however, was that he was carrying some kind of tracking device—

His musings were cut short by the gang member who plunged from between two tables that were laden with rusty animal traps. Bolan managed to sidestep danger just as the gang member, who wore a red bandanna over long black dreadlocks, shoved a giant recurve-bladed folding knife through the air. The tip of the knife narrowly missed Bolan's arm, cutting away a piece of his jacket.

Bolan snatched a heavy animal trap from the table. The spring-loaded mechanism was as long as his forearm, designed to catch a fox or a wolf in its iron jaws. He smashed the trap across the gang member's face. The *crunch* as the man's cheekbone gave way was a sound Bolan had heard before.

He smashed the man one more time before dropping the bloody trap and continuing on. The knife had fallen somewhere among the tables, and he could not see it. He passed a table bearing a radial-arm saw and several blades. As the vendor shouted something at him, he tossed a wad of euros on the tabletop, snatched up the blades and then broke left, running between awnings.

"There!" someone shouted in French. Bolan looked back to see more gang members, dressed in leathers and military castoffs. They could only be more Red Spiders; they wore red bandannas on their arms. One of the pair started to reach inside the load-bearing vest that he wore. His partner, who wore mismatched BDUs and a backward-facing baseball cap, stopped him. The man in the cap pulled a switchblade from his pocket and snapped it open.

He took a step toward Bolan.

The Executioner hurled a circular saw blade at him.

It was a good throw—a powerful, vertical throw that allowed Bolan to use gravity and the fall of his arm to impart spin to the blade. The whirling disk's teeth bit deep in the gang member's face. He screamed and dropped his knife, clutching at his cheek and eye, as blood gushed from both. The saw blade had not stuck in him. It had instead rolled and fallen, leaving a flap of his scalp hanging, as it clattered on the ground beyond him.

The man in the vest yanked a sturdy Glock combat field knife from his belt. Bolan didn't give him time to close the distance. He hurled the remaining saw blades he held. None scored as decisive a blow as the strike he had managed against the other gang member, but Bolan's enemy was forced to protect his face and took a pair of blades across the arm. Blood sprayed everywhere.

Bolan continued ducking and dodging through the

tables. He upended one accidentally, smashing several glass bottles. There was no one tending that stand. He crawled on hands and knees beneath another, side-stepped between two of the darker tents and found himself in a larger vendor tent that boasted a number of sporting goods. There was a collapsible minibilliards table, a pair of lacrosse sticks, a catcher's mitt and soccer balls of every conceivable color and pattern.

Two more Red Spiders hard cases were closing from the opposite end of the tent.

Bolan reached into a bin full of billiard balls and began hurling the heavy spheres. He smacked the lead man in the face, causing him to hit the deck on his knees and grab at his bloody nose. The second man dodged a second ball, then a third, and Bolan switched to lacrosse. He grabbed the larger of the two sticks and, wielding it like a sword, leaped through the air and slashed at the second man's head.

The stick cracked against the side of his opponent's skull. The gang member bleated like a goat before the air rushed from his lungs. He collapsed in a heap, as still as any man Bolan had seen, and the Executioner knew he'd managed a killing blow with one shot. It was rare to kill a man with a single blow to the head with a relatively light tool like the lacrosse stick, but it was not unheard of.

Bolan knelt, searched both gang members and came up with a pair of pistols. One was a Tokarev. The other was an FÉG, a copy of the Browning Hi Power. This particular FÉG had seen a very rough life. Its finish was almost completely worn away to bare steel. He tucked the FÉG in his waistband and held the Tokarev low next to his thigh, but not before checking the gun to make sure a round was chambered.

It felt good to be armed again, but it was not exactly the weapons-free rule the old man spoke of. Bolan could not afford to have the police descend on the bazaar any more than could the market's denizens. So far his isolated acts of violence did not seem to have triggered a panic…but then, they wouldn't. Everyone around the danger zones would be trying very hard not to get involved. The worse the environment, the greater the survival instinct.

There would be no shopping for armament here, not with the Red Spiders combing the bazaar and hoping to assassinate Bolan. He would withdraw, find another location and count himself lucky for acquiring the two handguns he had already obtained.

He nearly tripped over a trio of Red Spiders blocking the path to exit the bazaar. They collided and crashed in one three-headed mass, blundering through a pen full of live chickens and then smashing a table carrying recording equipment that was decades old. Bolan picked up a wood-paneled hi-fi turntable and smashed it down on the head of one of the gang members, flattening him. The man went limp.

The second man had a long Japanese-style knife with a traditionally wrapped handle. Bolan slapped the man's forearm, passing the blade, and smashed the gang member across the bridge of the nose with his recently acquired Tokarev. The blow staggered the man but did not stop him. The third man was pulling an expandable baton from his belt. He snapped it open and raised it to smash Bolan's skull.

The Executioner had no choice. He pointed the Tokarev and shot his attacker through the neck.

The gunshot had immediate consequences. People screamed and began fleeing the bazaar. That was good;

it would get innocents out of the line of fire. The soldier was close enough to the perimeter of the market that he would draw other gang members away from the center of the bazaar, closer to the outside. Having already crossed the point of no return, Bolan pumped a second round into the man he had pistol-whipped. The gang member had fallen to one knee and was struggling to stand. The round entered through the top of his head. Bolan plucked the long knife from the corpse's fingers.

Bolan reversed the knife in his hand so that the blade projected downward. With the Tokarev in one hand and the knife in the other, he backed up to the very edge of the bazaar. Scanning the running, screaming people, he picked out of the crowd several knots of Red Spiders gang members. When Bolan was sure he was not standing between them and any civilians who would be caught in the line of fire, he stood at his full height and waved his arms.

"Hey, you! Over here!" he shouted at them.

The gang members pointed and yelled. One of them drew a pistol and took a shot. Bolan crouched, resting on one knee, the Tokarev braced on his left forearm and the knife at the ready in his left hand. The approaching hostiles continued to close. The man with the pistol kept shooting, but his aim was poor. The bullets struck tables nearby but came nowhere close to injuring the soldier.

"Stop!" one of the hard cases shouted.

Bolan simply waited, moving to his left to put another table between him and the pistol-shooter, making sure he did not simply take a bullet as the enemy got near.

The trio of gang members was on top of him. Bolan popped up, on his feet, and slashed out with the knife, opening the gunner's neck. Blood sprayed, and the pistol fell to the pavement under the awnings. Bolan kicked it away, as he couldn't risk bending to pick it up and didn't want the other two hard cases to grab it.

He shoved his Tokarev into the belly of the closest hostile and pulled the trigger until the weapon was empty. Then he pushed the dead body of the gut-shot man to the side and smashed the Russian-made pistol barrel-first into the eyeball of the third gang member.

The man screamed.

Bolan released the Tokarev, its slide now embedded in the man's eye socket, and watched him fall. He drew the FÉG from his waistband and checked it. There was no time to find the fallen pistol. He was armed, but still far outgunned, and he needed to get out of there before more Red Spiders reinforcements showed up.

The activity in the market hadn't died down, and that was a bad sign. He bent and peered through the maze of awnings and half-wrecked stalls as best he could. There were at least two dozen men, all of them wearing mismatched and outlandish clothing, and here and there he saw a flash of red from one of the gang's bandannas. They were closing on his position fast.

He knew he had value as a target. If the Red Spiders truly were the combination of the gang he had faced before, taking him down would go a long way toward establishing their power, "making their bones" on the street. "You mess with us, you kill some of us," they would probably say, "and we find you and make you pay for challenging our power."

It was the way things worked all over the world, in wretched neighborhoods, ethnic enclaves and entire impoverished nations. There weren't too many differences among people, really, for all that their cultures might differ in the small things.

Human beings, and the predators among them, were a constant.

He did not have enough rounds to take on all of the Red Spiders that were coming at him. Much as he hated to withdraw, that was the only option. He turned, made for the exit of the bazaar and fled.

Except that he couldn't.

The soldier faced three cars full of the gangsters. The doors of the late-model BMWs had been spray-painted sloppily with red. Across this canvas, stencils had been used to paint, in black, a crude spider logo. There was no mistaking what Bolan faced: these were "troop vehicles" of the Red Spiders, a gang strong enough, at least, that they did not fear identification by any law enforcement they encountered. Then, too, Bolan was in one of the no-go ethnic enclaves on this side of the bazaar. There was every reason to think that these hostiles were the law in this part of Paris.

The car doors opened one after another and the gang members stepped out. If they had a leader, it was not apparent. What they had, however, was enough firepower to level the bazaar. Bolan saw three Kalashnikovs, a short-barreled AR-pattern rifle with a massive twin-drum magazine and at least one man wielding dual single-action revolvers with pearl grips, of all things. Their dress was as outlandish, and as street-trash typical, as that of the other gang members in the bazaar had been. At the very least they were consistent.

Bolan got off one shot then a second and a third, taking down two of the gunners and managing to wound a man who ducked behind the cover of his vehicle. Then the return fusillade came, and it was all Bolan could do to avoid getting his head shot off. He hugged the pavement as bullets tore through the now mostly empty bazaar behind him.

Mostly empty except for the Red Spiders gunners approaching him.

He was caught in a cross fire, but for the moment, so were the gunmen climbing up his six. The heavy rain of automatic gunfire from the men at the BMWs tore through the unsuspecting gang members in the bazaar. In seconds they were mostly dead or dying, their moans and cries like something from a horror movie.

Bolan ejected the magazine in his FÉG as he lay prone. He had four rounds left.

He had no other options.

The Executioner considered that. He was outnumbered, outgunned. If he tried to run he would be shot. The words came, unbidden, to his mind.

Forward. Toward the danger.

He rose and, shouting bloody murder in an attempt to confuse the enemy, ran at them as fast as he could, all the while shooting his FÉG.

The gunners standing at the BMWs saw him but did not know what to do. A couple took cover. Still another started shooting, too wide, too late. Bolan was closing the distance before they had assessed what threat Bolan truly represented. If he could just get to the cars, put the vehicles between him and the main body of his adversaries, he would have the cover he needed to fight at close quarters.

It was a desperation play, a wild play, the sort of charge that used to be preceded by the fixing of bayonets. Bolan reached the BMWs and planted the long Japanese-style knife in the throat of the gunner he came to first. The knife stuck, held fast in the gunner's flesh, and, as the body fell away, the weight of the corpse jerked the knife from his hand. There the knife stayed, lodged in the dead gang member's neck at Bolan's feet.

It was the man with the double-drum AR, a cut-down weapon whose selector read only Safe or Auto.

In Bolan's hands, its shells fall like rain.

The muzzle-blast of the short-barreled weapon was tremendous. A gout of flame leaped from the gun, and with it came a withering spray of 5.56 mm rounds that shredded the adjacent BMW's hood and roof while scattering its auto glass in a snowstorm of pebbled debris. The Red Spiders hard cases were cut down, their blood splashed across their vehicles.

Bolan still had plenty of ammunition left when he saw a taxi speeding toward him. It was headed directly at him; there was no mistaking the driver's course.

Settling into his shooter's stance, he leaned into the weapon, lining up the sights for the longer shot, prepared to work the trigger to milk from it only a short burst. The taxi grew ever closer, closer still and Bolan took a deep breath.

The taxi skidded to a halt on squealing brakes. The driver's window was down.

"Get in!" Alfred Bayard shouted.

CHAPTER TWENTY

They had not gone more than two blocks deeper into the enclave when another group of Red Spiders vehicles, two Jaguars and a Mercedes, met them. Bolan rolled down his window, swiveled in his seat until his back was against the dashboard and knelt in place. The chopped barrel of the AR-15 was now leaning on the open window. He was using the car door to steady the assault rifle.

"Inspector," Bolan said over the rushing wind. "It's good to see you."

"Despite myself," Bayard replied, "I must admit that it is good to see you, as well, Cooper. Shall we commence with the rampage?"

Bolan grinned at the Frenchman. "Let's."

He pulled the trigger of his assault rifle.

Empty shells sprayed the side of the car and trickled through the window to pool in the floorboard beneath Bolan's seat. The weapon was deafening, and Bayard shouted in exhilaration. The Mercedes's hood was pocked in thirty places in less time than it took for Bolan to estimate the damage. He shot out the windshield and sprayed the blood of the driver and his front-seat passenger all over what was left of the car's interior.

One of the Jaguar sedans pushed past the Mercedes, nudging it out of the way. The collision left a long streak of black paint down the flank of the white Jaguar. Both

Jaguars, in fact, were white, with their black spider logos stenciled on the doors.

"The gangs wasted no time consolidating," Bayard observed.

"We can discuss that later," Bolan said, "when we're not trying to not get shot."

"With you, Cooper. I question whether there is ever a period of your life long enough without gunfire to qualify."

Bolan had nothing to say to that.

The first of the Jaguars came up alongside them. Bolan hammered away at the front end of the car, destroying the tire on that side and raking the engine. Smoke began to pour from the grille and from the seams around the hood. Bolan raised his point of aim and shot out the driver, who was trying to level a MAC-10 machine pistol through his open window. The weapon discharged when it hit the pavement, spraying Bayard's taxi in the right rear and destroying the taillights.

"Were we just shot by a falling weapon?" Bayard asked, incredulous.

"Yeah. That happens."

"Your world is insane, Cooper."

Bolan's endless drum magazines finally ran dry. He looked down at the AR regretfully and then tossed it into the backseat. "Do you have a couple hundred rounds of 5.56 mm in the trunk?" he asked.

"No," Bayard replied. "But now I know what to buy for you at Christmas."

Bolan shook his head. "That alley up there. Take the right. They'll follow us in. We'll use the same tactic as before."

"That tactic resulted in a great deal of destruction, as I recall," Bayard stated.

"If it's stupid and it works, it isn't stupid."

"I have a better idea." Bayard guided the taxi to the alley, hit the brakes and the parking brake lever and brought the taxi screaming around. Then he pointed the nose at the second Jaguar and tromped the gas, sending them straight toward the oncoming vehicle.

"Okay," Bolan said, looking at the inspector.

"Yes. Okay." He put the accelerator to the floor.

Bolan reached up and grabbed the roof handle on his side. If he was going to go out, at least he would go out with a bang.

"Tell me something, Cooper," Bayard said, as the two cars closed on each other. "We are about to die. Who are you, really?"

"I'm just an American," Bolan replied.

"A concerned citizen, no doubt."

"Yeah," Bolan agreed. "That's me."

"You are a liar," Bayard said, smiling. "And now I die without ever knowing the truth."

Just before the vehicles collided on the narrow Paris street, the Jaguar swerved.

The violent maneuver rammed the vehicle into the side of a building. There was no doubt that the men in front were instantly killed, had to have been dead the moment the car stopped. Bayard halted the taxi and Bolan got out.

The soldier inspected the rear of the wrecked Jaguar. In the distance, he could hear police sirens. There was no one alive in the rear of the vehicle, either. The weapons he could see were coated with blood. He thought for a moment about climbing in and retrieving them, but the sirens were coming closer. There was no time.

"Cooper!" Bayard said, exiting the vehicle. "A moment!"

Bolan looked at the inspector as if the man had lost his mind, but he did not move when Bayard came over, grabbed the bottom of Bolan's jacket near the zipper and tore the seam out of the jacket's lining. A small device the size and shape of a quarter fell out. Bayard took this and tossed it into the back of the Jaguar.

"Is that what I think it is?" Bolan asked.

"I will explain on the way," Bayard replied. "Let us go now!"

The two men got back into the taxi and Bayard pushed the vehicle for all it was worth, shooting up alleys and down side streets. When both men were satisfied that they weren't being followed, Bayard slowed the vehicle and pulled over. The neighborhood in which they now sat was one of the worst in Paris.

Garbage was strewed in the streets. The only cars parked here were burned out. The windows were all either boarded up, barred or broken out. No one moved outside, but Bolan saw flashes of movement here and there through the windows that weren't sealed.

"When I gave you the jacket," Bayard said, "and earlier, before you lost your own coat, I planted a bug on you. It is standard DCRI procedure. We have been listening to you and following you around the city."

Bolan considered that. He would have to speak with the Farm about possible countermeasures for such possibilities in the future. Reviewing in his head, he concluded that nothing he had said out loud would compromise the Farm. The security of the Stony Man counterterror mission was still viable. But he did not like what this had to mean for his position in Paris.

"You said the DCRI has been tracking me," Bolan said. "That explains how Musson and Flagel found me."

"Yes," Bayard admitted. He looked down. Bolan caught the Frenchman's expression.

"What is it?" he asked. "What's wrong?"

"Musson and Flagel have been killed. It is why I am here. The director of my agency, Jean Vigneau, is corrupt. He has always been, as one might imagine, one to take a payoff, *n'est-ce pas?*"

"He's in bed with the Red Spiders?"

"No, not in the way you are thinking," Bayard said. "He is ruthless. If something gets in his way, he will do whatever is required. The law, our mission, what is right and what is wrong, these things do not matter to him. And he does not care about relations between our country and yours. When my men and I would not head the detail tasked with bringing you in, when we would not treat you like an enemy of the state, he communicated the frequency of the tracking device to the Red Spiders. He even concocted a lie, telling them that a reward would be paid if you were killed."

"So he contracted out my assassination, gangland style," Bolan said.

"Just so. I would not have believed it possible. But I have seen the results. Musson and Flagel stood with me. They remembered that even when pressed, you did not kill them, as you surely were capable of doing. And I think some part of them, the idealistic part, was moved by the deeds you have done on French soil. As I have been."

Bolan frowned. "What happened to them?"

"Flagel gave his life so that I could escape," Bayard said. "The DCRI knew where you were, just as the gangs knew. Vigneau rightly assumed that I would try to help you when I learned of his plans to have you, as you would say, 'taken out.' He sent DCRI agents loyal to him, men who I assume are being paid by him, to intercept us on the way to you. Musson was killed outright. He did not believe Vigneau or our fellow agents could be capable of this. And Flagel was a better man than I knew him to be. He stood between the DCRI and me. That is why I am here."

"And the taxi?"

"I stole it off the street," Bayard said. "I could not bring myself to acquire a private car. The taxicab is at least a fleet vehicle, insured for theft. It seemed the least of the possible evils."

"You're all heart, Inspector."

"So what is your plan?"

"What makes you think I have one?"

"If you do not, then we die."

"I need weapons," Bolan told him. "The AR back there might do, but we have no ammunition for it."

"I have my revolver."

"A single .38 Special won't get us very far. I was here looking to shop for some heavy artillery."

Bayard nodded. "I see. You are looking for an arms dealer. And he can be found in a place much like this but at the other end of the enclave."

"You know who I'm looking for?"

"I do," Bayard said. "He is called Levi on the street. A very ugly fellow."

"Tough customer, eh?"

"That, too. But I mean this as I said it. He is quite horribly ugly. Disfigured by some childhood ailment. His face is deeply pocked and scarred, and he is blind in one eye from it. But Levi can get anything you require."

"Then let's move," Bolan suggested. "I don't want to be a static target if we can help it."

They drove in silence for a time. Bayard, who knew

the enclave well, guided them skillfully along poorly maintained streets and through the narrowest of alleys. He explained as he went that he was avoiding those thoroughfares most likely to have Red Spiders gunmen stationed on them. This task was complicated by the fact that the new gang was not following all the old patterns of the two gangs that had been absorbed to create it.

"These Red Spiders," Bolan said. "Who's leading them? What's the new head of the snake?"

"You think you will chop this off and all will be well, yes?" Bayard asked. "How do you think the new gang came to be so quickly? The Red Spiders movement has been here for a long time. 'Red' in this case does not come from the Red Death. They are Communists, true believers in the paths of Marxism and government by all."

"A Communist movement from within the gangs?"

"Yes. When you dealt your damage to their power structure, it allowed the movement behind the scenes to come out, to seize power. There were Red Spiders sympathizers in both gangs. Killing those villains brought this about. It is neither better nor worse. It is not as if you have done harm.

"There are no central leaders in the Red Spiders. Each component of the gang is like an independent terrorist cell. They have limited information of each other except for the couriers and prepaid cell phones they use to communicate among the gang members. This is why they identify themselves by symbol and color publicly. It is as much for their fellow members as for any other—"

"Stop the car," Bolan ordered.

Bolan stepped out of the taxicab.

"Where are you going?" Bayard asked.

"Hang on." Bolan entered the small market, not unlike a bodega back in the States, and found what he was looking for. When he returned to the car, he was carrying a pair of red bandannas and a can of red spray paint.

"Put this on," he said to Bayard, handing the inspector one of the squares of cloth. Bayard leaned out his open window as Bolan began hastily spray-painting the door. It was a messy job, but at a distance, it would make the taxi look like one of the Red Spiders vehicles. The taxi sign wouldn't give them away from a certain distance.

"Let us hope we do not run into a gang task force," Bayard said with a straight face.

Bolan looked at him through the open driver's window. "Seriously?"

Bayard's mouth split in a toothy grin. "Aha. I had you fooled, Cooper. I did not think you were so gullible."

"Being a fugitive agrees with you, Inspector."

As they pulled away, Bayard began nodding. "You are right. I hate to admit it, but I have not felt this young in a long time. Up close, even at a distance, we will never pass for members of the gang, you know."

"That's not the point," Bolan replied. "The point is to prevent them from unloading on us the moment they see us. This camouflage job may help us do that. Get us across the enclave and to your very ugly arms dealer."

"And then?"

"Then I'm taking the fight to Gaston," Bolan explained.

Bayard looked aghast. "But you cannot mean to harm a national—"

"It's not what you think," Bolan said, interrupting. "It's actually worse." He removed the hard drive from his jacket. "I need to get this out of the country. It contains proof that Gaston, not Deparmond, is in league with ES. The video evidence implicating Deparmond is a hoax. And it was the ES, led by Levesque, who murdered Deparmond."

As they drove, Bolan filled Bayard in on the details. It took a while. They saw two Red Spiders-tagged vehicles but were not stopped or harassed. Either the camouflage was working or they were lucky. The travel was slow going, as roads in the enclave were poorly maintained and often blocked by debris or other vehicles.

When those vehicles were still mobile they were double- and triple-parked, blocking off entire sections of the town. Within the impromptu squares thus delineated, everything from hanging laundry to sleeping babies in improvised cribs were visible.

The sight of children reminded Bolan just how many innocent lives were at stake. He could not rid Paris of crimes or gangs or corruption. That was simply impossible, as the population naturally and inexorably produced predators with each generation. What he could do, however, was smash the power structures that propped up those predators, as he had done with Roelle, and as he was planning to do now.

Brognola wouldn't like it. Once Bolan had a chance to explain the situation, to get the data out of the country, to see to it that Gaston's reputation was ruined, the fact that Bolan had removed Gaston from the picture would be something Brognola and the Man could live with.

After all, the goal of sending Bolan in was to help ensure a French government that was agreeable to domestic interests and was not run by a xenophobic, terrorist-sympathetic madman. But in the past, Bolan had figured in the collapse of more than one foreign power. He knew that it made Wonderland nervous. This wasn't just because of the stability issues that were always created when one dictator or another fell out of power.

No. Deep down, no politician no matter how good his intentions was entirely comfortable with the idea of an armed insurrection destroying the status quo. It was just a little too close to the mark, and Bolan could respect that.

Not that he would hesitate to wipe Gaston off the map of France.

"Merde," Bayard said.

"What is it?" Bolan asked. Then he, too, saw what Bayard had noticed, far up ahead. Police vehicles blocking the road.

"We can't face them down," Bolan told him. "I'm not going to draw on French police."

"I would lose all faith in you if you did. But those sedans there, parked next to the police vehicles. Those are DCRI, I would bet my life. Unmarked, but I recognize them. We have few enough vehicles at our disposal."

"Better take a side street," Bolan directed. "Try to move casually."

"Too late." Bayard pointed to the rearview mirror. Bolan looked back. Two more dark sedans, which the soldier assumed were also DCRI in pursuit, were coming up from behind. As if to verify his suspicions, the drivers of the rear cars placed magnetic lights on their roofs. The colored lights came to life.

"They mean to arrest us," Bayard stated.

"We can't let them."

"No, we cannot, Agent Cooper," Bayard said, stomping the accelerator.

CHAPTER TWENTY-ONE

The taxicab plunged straight for the barricades. It took the police and the DCRI men—who Bolan assumed were either unaware of the facts or bought and paid for by Vigneau—a moment to react. When they did, their weapons came out.

"Down!" Bolan ordered.

They managed to crouch behind the dash as bullets perforated the windshields fore and aft. They were now caught in a cross fire between the barricade at the front and the DCRI men behind them…and they could not shoot back, not without killing law enforcement officers.

Bayard cut it close. He slammed on the brakes so hard that Bolan thought the discs would crack. The taxicab laid down so much rubber that the cloying, burning smell was thick inside the vehicle. The nose of the taxi stopped short of the barricade, scattering the men gathered there. They dived to the ground on either side in anticipation of the spectacular collision that never occurred.

"Back now, back, back," Bolan urged. Bayard was well ahead of him. With one arm hooked over the seats, looking over his shoulder and again flooring the car, he swung the wheel wide as he pushed the taxi in Reverse. Something in the front wheel on the passenger side began scraping loudly against the wheel well. At this rate their ride wasn't going to last them for long, Bolan thought.

The vehicle rolled back and around, side-swiping the grilles of the DCRI vehicles, drawing more fire from the men stationed there. Bayard simply kept his foot on the gas, causing the taxi to leap and buck. Something heavy and metallic began to bang against the under-carriage of the car. Bolan assumed it was something important that had broken loose in all the collisions.

"Brace yourself, Cooper," Bayard said.

The taxicab, now pointing in the opposite direction, smashed between the DCRI cars in a shriek of metal, glass and tortured plastic. Bolan risked a look back through what was left of the taxi's rear windshield and saw several side-mounted rearview mirrors lying in the street in a pool of broken safety glass. The scene rapidly diminished as Bayard urged the battered taxi down the road. He began taking side streets and other random turns in order to lose any pursuit that might be mounted from the roadblock.

"We will need to work our way around," Bayard said. "Like a sailboat tacking into the wind. The DCRI has taken the rare step of mounting roadblocks in the enclave, probably with permission and bribe money spread around to and from the Red Spiders. I could not tell you in which direction the money goes, but possibly Vigneau is again using the promise of a reward to gain the Red Spiders' cooperation in hunting us down."

"Is there any chance they're still tracking us?"

"I have my wireless," Bayard said. "I had better discard it."

"Not a bad idea." Bolan took the phone from Bayard, pulled the battery and tossed both phone and battery out the window.

They went a few more blocks. Bayard turned seemingly at random but insisted that he knew precisely where he was going. Bolan saw no reason not to believe him. Eventually they came to a section of street where another Red Spiders vehicle was parked. This one was a Toyota Camry. Bayard parked behind it.

"A step down from some of the cars we've seen so far," Bolan commented.

"We all make do in these difficult times," Bayard said. Bolan shot him a look. He wasn't certain if Bayard was making a joke or simply offering a deadpan observation.

The structure in front of which the car was parked looked like a three-level block of flats. Club-style music pumped from it, causing the panes in the windows to vibrate. Bolan glanced at his watch. It was a little early in the morning for that sort of thing, unless the partyers inside had been at it all night. If that was the case, it was a little late.

"Feel like crashing a party?" Bolan asked. He looked at the Toyota and then back at their taxicab. "I think I'd feel better traveling the enclave in their car over ours. Wouldn't you?"

"We have only my .38," Bayard pointed out. "Do we dare beard them in their den?"

"There's an old saying. 'If you've got a knife, you can get a pistol. If you can get a pistol, you can get a rifle.'" Bolan climbed out of the car. "Pop the trunk."

"The switch is broken."

Bolan tapped at the trunk experimentally. He tried pulling at it with his fingers. Finally he chose a spot and hammered it with his fist.

The trunk popped open.

Bayard opened his mouth to speak, thought better

of it and took out his revolver to check its loads. Bolan, meanwhile, took a tire iron from the trunk of the car.

"Let's do this," the soldier said.

"Let us do this," Bayard agreed. The two men took up positions on either side of the door to the flat.

"I'll make an outlaw of you yet, Inspector," Bolan said.

"As if you have not already." Bayard held his revolver low, in a two-handed grip, ready to breach the door. It was only in the movies and on television that men prepared to breach doorways with their guns held by their ears.

Bolan rapped on the door with his tire iron.

"Who is it?" a voice called in French. "What do you want?"

"Housekeeping," Bolan said. He motioned for Bayard to back away slightly from the door. With one hand he made an exploding gesture.

"Boom," he mouthed to Bayard.

The oh-so-predictable burst of automatic gunfire that ripped through the door almost made Bolan smile. He did not stand in front of doorways after knocking on them. It was good to know that some habits paid off.

"You knew that was going to happen," Bayard said. "Tell me you did not."

"It's kind of a running joke," Bolan said, over the sound of the rounds ripping through the door. "Wait for it…"

Bayard nodded.

The lull, when it came, was spaced correctly to be the emptying of a magazine. Bolan knew there was a calculated risk involved, but everything they were doing now was fraught with risk. They would have to be bold if they were going to carry the day. He kicked in the splintered door and dived low with his tire iron, allowing Bayard to go in high.

The .38 barked once, then again, dropping a man who was struggling to reload a cut-down Kalashnikov with a folding stock. Bolan had time to move to the adjoining doorway, which connected to a small kitchen area and a hallway, before another man holding a 1911-pattern pistol came rushing through.

Bolan rapped him in the face with the tire iron, dropping him in his tracks.

There was screaming from a room at the end of the corridor past the kitchen. That would be the living area, and it was from here that the party music was loudest.

"Do you hear that?" Bayard asked.

Bolan made a face. "Yeah, I do, oddly enough. 'Soul Finger,' by the Bar-Kays. There's no accounting for taste."

"Not the music, smart guy. A whirring, mechanical sound."

The soldier turned to look back the way they'd come. A device mounted above the door caught his eye. It was connected to a mechanism of moving gears, all of this connected to a trigger cord of some kind that had been wired to the door.

"Down!" Bolan shouted. He threw himself across the room and tackled Bayard.

The explosion that followed shook dust from the ceiling and set off a series of alarms from outside, probably car and security systems on adjacent blocks. The explosive package above the doorway had apparently been a shaped charge. The wall, and even the doorway itself, was largely untouched.

The entryway room, by contrast, had been shredded. The explosive was an improvised device packed with nails and screws. Bolan rose slowly, helping Bayard to his feet, and looked around, assessing the danger and searching for new targets. Bayard still had his revolver in his hand, but he was looking closely at the wall near him. Embedded in its surface were hundreds of wood screws and roofing nails.

"A vicious device," he said finally.

"That door charge was on a delay," Bolan stated. "That's what the gearing mechanism was for. It's totally mechanical, independent of any power source. Probably had a mechanical trigger, too. Maybe something as simple as the strike wheel from a butane lighter. Something flammable to touch off the main charge."

"The police break down the door," Bayard said. "And after they do, naturally they assess the situation, perhaps cuff suspects. And then this explodes and kills them."

"Or leaves them maimed for life." Bolan reached down and picked up a twisted piece of metal shaped like a cooking pot. "This was a pressure container. The Boston bombers in the United States used something similar. Only the lowest sort of scum use sharp shrapnel like this. They load up the bombs with anything they can find that fits the description, knowing these pieces of hardware will rip through the air and tear up anybody who stands in the way."

"Do you think there is a link to terrorism here?" Bayard asked.

"No. Just like minds. Predators are predators, and they don't care who gets killed." He gestured. The man with the 1911, whom Bolan had laid out with the tire iron, had apparently come to and stood just about the time Bolan was tackling Bayard. That man was riddled with shrapnel. Half a dozen wood screws jutted from his forehead. Blood was everywhere, and with it the coppery smell of death.

In the far corner of the room, the man Bayard had shot was slumped over, his corpse desecrated by the bomb. Bayard tucked his revolver in his waistband and picked up the Krinkov-style AK-47 assault rifle the gang member had used. He found an extra magazine on the dead man and swapped out the one already in the gun, which was nearly empty.

"Trade you," Bolan said.

"I am an old man," Bayard said, hefting the AK-47. "I need all the help I can get."

Bolan almost smiled at that. He checked his newly acquired 1911. The .45-caliber handgun was badly rusted and pitted, but the rounds in its magazine looked new, and it was reasonably clean. He discovered that it had no round in the chamber, which spoke volumes about his dead enemy's level of preparedness.

Bolan racked the slide to chamber the first round, made sure the safety was off and positioned himself in the kitchen ahead of the connecting corridor.

Whimpers and voices could be heard in the living area beyond. The music had been shut off. Bolan was very aware that he did not know how many hostiles were in the living room. He also did not know to what degree the women, either gang members or prostitutes, were part of the threat. He had raided safehouses and other places before to find seeming innocents who, at the first opportunity, turned guns on him. He was not about to take anything for granted.

Bayard crept along the wall, backing him up. Once again they stationed themselves on either side of a doorway.

"Give up," Bolan said in French.

"Go away!" a man replied, his reply punctuated by several shotgun blasts. Bolan could hear a pump gun being operated furiously between each shot. He waited. The shots stopped.

"I didn't catch that," Bolan called, goading the man.

Another furious salvo erupted from the living area. The shotgunner was loading slugs, Bolan noted. A cluster of holes, each the size of a quarter, was being punched through the facing wall of the kitchen. Bolan and Bayard, pressed against either side of the corridor opening, were in no danger.

"You do not think he is that stupid?" Bayard asked.

"I figure they've been partying," Bolan said quietly. He paused as a renewed series of shotgun blasts echoed through the flat. Between each blast, he managed to continue speaking to the inspector. "He's probably high or half out of his mind from lack of sleep."

"I'm going to toss a grenade in there, pal," Bolan called. "You better get ready. They're going to be scraping you off the walls by lunch."

"But we have no grenades," Bayard said quietly.

"Sure we do. Bolan reached out and snatched a heavy wooden salt shaker from the kitchen counter. "I'm pulling the pin now. Three! Two! One! Fire in the hole!"

Bolan tossed the salt shaker into the living area.

A woman screamed. Bolan heard a sharp *snap* from the room beyond. That was a striker falling on an empty chamber. Then he heard the pump of the shotgun being worked, followed by the same snapping noise. The shotgun was empty.

"You go high again," Bolan said to Bayard. "I'll go low."

"Lead the way, Cooper."

They went for it. Bolan was able to place two men

in the room as well as three women. The women were
in various stages of undress. Two were cowering behind a sofa while a third was hiding behind a chair. The
shotgunner was kneeling in the middle of the room, his
weapon braced on his hip. The second man was lying
on the floor at an odd angle, not moving.

Bolan aimed his 1911. "Stay where you are. Don't
move."

The shotgunner stood.

"I'll put you down," the soldier warned. "Drop the
shotgun, put your hands behind your head and don't
make any sudden movements."

The shotgunner growled and took a step forward.
He raised the shotgun like a club.

A burst from Bayard's AK-47 ripped through the
floor. Bolan risked a glance and saw that that the man
on the floor had been faking it. He had a kitchen knife
behind his arm and rose to strike with it when Bayard
stitched him. The assault rifle had done its work as ef-
ficiently as ever. The man with the knife would now
stay on the floor.

All that happened in a fraction of a second, but the
distraction was all the shotgunner needed. He crashed
into Bolan, using his empty weapon as a riot stick, trying to press the shotgun against his adversary's throat.
Bolan shoved his pistol under the man's chin, ready to
blow his head off. He pulled the trigger.

The weapon made a burning, fizzing sound. Mis-
fire, possibly a critical mechanical failure. The rusted
weapon was not sound.

The shotgunner pressed harder.

Bolan let the useless gun fall to the floor and grabbed
the barrel and the stock of the shotgun. He levered it up
and out of the man's hands, twisting it, putting the man

off balance. The man had no choice but to let go or be put in a painful wristlock. He chose to release the empty weapon, at which point Bolan reversed it and smashed him in the face with the buttstock.

The shotgunner collapsed. One of the scantily clad women crawled out from her hiding spot and, instead of going for the door, grabbed for the fallen man. Bolan tried to stop her, but she was quick. She snatched something from the fallen shotgunner's pocket and held it out for Bolan to see.

Her slim finger pushed a lever in the handle of a front-opening switchblade. A serrated tanto-type, black-coated blade shot into position on powerful springs. She positioned herself in front of the other two women.

"Whoa," Bolan said. "Nobody wants to hurt your friends."

"Cooper," Bayard shouted. "Look out!"

The woman slashed at him, hard and fast. Bolan brought up his forearm just in time. The secondary point of the knife's modernized tanto tip cut a long stripe down his forearm, leaving a bright red weal of blood.

Bolan grabbed her by the arm and the shoulder, applied leverage and managed to get her in an armlock as he turned her. She squealed. He applied pressure and brought her, gently, to the floor. Once there he plucked the knife from her hand, put his knee in the small of her back and looked at Bayard.

"You wouldn't have any flex cuffs, would you?"

"As it happens, I do." Bayard reached into his pocket and came out with one of the thick zip-tie strips. Bolan took these and secured the woman, while Bayard, AK in hand, checked the other two women. He exchanged a few words in French with them, received an answer and nodded. At his urging they left the room, hurrying out of the flat.

"Local talent," Bayard said. "No one of consequence, or so they said. Just in case, we should leave here as quickly as we can. What do you propose we do with her?"

"Normally," Bolan replied, "I'd see to it the proper authorities took custody of her. Unfortunately, given our status, I don't know if that's practical." He zip-cuffed the unconscious shotgunner, too. "To say nothing of this guy."

"We are somewhat 'extralegal,' as you might say," Bayard admitted.

"Yeah, that's how I see it. I suppose we could just leave them here. Eventually their people will find them. And once we're gone, there's nothing to stop them from getting up and walking out of here, even with their hands secured."

"You could execute them."

Bolan shook his head. "Not like this. I don't kill the helpless. And she's just probably defending herself against some guy she thinks just broke in here."

"For a killer of men you have many rules."

"That's right," Bolan said. "I do."

"Then it is settled. Benign neglect is the order of the day. Come here. That is a nasty slash."

"It's not that bad."

"And she could have been snorting coke laced with drain cleaner off that blade last night. You have no idea how bad it is. We should clean it at the very least."

"Inspector, I had no idea you had this parental streak in you."

"I do not. Tell no one of this." Bayard had a small medical kit in the inside pocket of his overcoat. He motioned for Bolan to sit on one of the wooden chairs in the kitchen. The prostitute they left to sulk on the floor. Bolan pocketed her knife.

Bayard cleaned the wound first, making sure to use plenty of disinfectant, then set to dressing Bolan's wound. Bayard had just enough bandage material in his kit.

"Let me see the knife," Bayard said.

Bolan handed him the weapon. It had a switch that extended or retracted the black-coated blade automatically. Bayard flicked it open, examined it, sniffed at it and then flicked it closed. He returned it to Bolan.

"A quality blade," Bayard said. "Surprising in one so dissolute. Probably only recently stolen, given how clean it looks. I would say you will be fine, unless it was used to stab someone just today who carried a blood-borne disease. And the blade looks very clean."

"You're a ray of sunshine," Bolan told him.

"What was your plan?" Bayard asked. "Hit them and take their heavy weaponry?"

"Yeah. Unfortunately they don't seem to have much. An AK with a partial magazine, a 1911 that doesn't work and a switchblade.".

"Do not forget the empty shotgun," Bayard reminded him.

"That, too," Bolan said. "I…" He trailed off, then looked directly at Bayard as the Frenchman finished bandaging Bolan's arm. "I just realized something. Check the bedroom. Grab a bag or a duffel or a blanket or something. We'll take all the weapons we have here and put them with the empty AR. Then we'll take our friends' car. They won't need it."

"I will look for car keys then," Bayard said. "You mean to use the weapons for barter?"

"Yeah. I have cash, but these will supplement it. Gives us a chance to put together something truly memorable."

"Memorable. That is a loaded term. It implies that what happens to us will be worthy of note but makes no promises regarding our survival of such an event."

"You know the old Chinese curse," Bolan said.

"May you live in interesting times? Yes, I have heard of this."

"It's like that."

"Indeed it is. You are an interesting man, Cooper. And I do not mean that in a positive way."

"I get that a lot."

CHAPTER TWENTY-TWO

The shantytown was as rank as any in a third-world nation. Bolan had seen his share all over the world. This one was not as large as some others; it was crammed into a plot of space defined by the intersection of four different Paris neighborhoods.

At the edges of each of those zones, which decayed as one moved farther to the junction of the neighboring areas, heavy concrete barricades had been erected. These had been heavily spray-painted with racist and antigovernment slogans during the previous riots that had raged through Paris.

In many cases, stacks of burned-out automobiles—each one little more than a blackened, stripped chassis—were still piled atop each other. In the cleanup following the riots, during which the delineation between the neighborhoods of Paris was reinforced, many stacks of cars had been dumped near the enclaves suspected of causing the damage. There they rusted, as if they had been deposited in punishment for the locals' misdeeds.

Bolan and Bayard parked their newest transport at the edge of the enclave. Flagged with Red Spiders tags, it was probably safe. Bolan thought it likely other residents of the shantytown would simply give it a wide berth, rather than run afoul of any gang warfare that might be associated with the vehicle's occupants.

The independent-cell structure of the Red Spiders was working for them, in this case. As no member of the gang could be certain that he knew every other member of the gang, even in smaller areas, traveling in a Red Spiders vehicle was good camouflage.

The shantytown was not an enclave so much as it was an armed camp. They saw the Red Spiders logo spray-painted everywhere. It was on the sides of the shacks, built from plywood and corrugated tin and tarps and anything else that was at hand. It was painted on cloth hung as banners and suspended as flags. It was even painted on the bodies of some of the people moving around within the shantytown, in the form of Red Spiders body paint and a tattoo or two.

Guards were posted everywhere. Bolan did not like the look of that. It portended a high degree of resistance if anything went wrong. And if he were any judge of these things, there was a great probability that something *could* go wrong.

The posted sentries wore red bandannas, plus a riot of different clothing. They resembled modern-day Somali pirates. Donning all their stolen goods must be de rigueur, given the military gear and mismatched, but often expensive, civilian clothing they wore layered under their gear.

Each carried a dizzying array of personal weapons. At least one man Bolan spotted had a Soviet World War II–era Mosin-Nagant rifle over his shoulder with the bayonet affixed to its barrel. The bolt-action rifle was as tall as the man toting it.

"Too bad," Bolan said. "No floor mats."

"Whatever are you talking about?" Bayard asked. The two men made their way through the aisles and walkways of the shantytown, their red bandannas tied around their arms. Bolan wondered if they were fooling anybody, but hopefully they would be standing in front of the arms dealer soon. Money and trade items would smooth over any other possible misunderstandings, or so he hoped.

"Cooper?" Bayard prompted.

"Floor mats," Bolan told him. "In the United States a lot of businesses have floor mats that are regularly changed, sent away to be cleaned, with new mats left in their place. It's a whole industry."

"I am vaguely aware of that," Bayard said. "How is this relevant?"

"In the typical delivery, a driver in a box truck shows up at your door. He carries a floor mat rolled up over his shoulder. When he walks into the place, nobody gives him a second look. As long as his truck and his uniform look right, they just assume he's the floor-mat guy. Nobody looks at the floor-mat guy."

"Meaning that if this man were to carry a weapon in the rolled-up mat…"

"Yeah," Bolan said. "Instant terrorist attack or office shooting."

"Why are you even thinking of that?"

"It's what I do," Bolan replied. "I think of these scenarios so I can anticipate the tactics my enemies will use. And a long time ago I realized that nobody looks at the floor-mat guy."

"We are going to die, and that will be the last ridiculous thing I remember," Bayard said sourly.

"Like I said, a ray of sunshine."

They reached a plywood shack that was much larger than the others. They were in roughly the center of the French shantytown. Looking around, Bolan wondered how few people in the world knew this place existed, or even suspected that a festering pit like this lay on the face of Paris like so much blight. So many things were out of sight, out of mind.

Two guards, each armed with FAMAS assault rifles —expensive, high-end military hardware—stood at either side of the rickety door to the large shack. They moved aside slightly to let Bolan and Bayard pass, but they were in no hurry about it. Bayard had been leading to this point, but when they cleared the threshold, he stepped aside, allowing Bolan to step in front.

The arms dealer, Levi, was certainly ugly. He was, in fact, repulsive. Weighing well over four hundred pounds, Levi sat pooled in an overstuffed recliner behind a makeshift desk of three different tables. The tables had been arrayed in front of him, forming a display area. On them was an array of military-grade hardware, pistols and explosives. Bolan saw battle rifles, machine pistols, and a stack of grenades and RPGs. There was also an RPG launcher and several attachments for launching grenades from the barrels of rifles.

Levi, for his part, grinned at them. He wore a grill of diamonds over his front teeth, which made his mouth look like he had just eaten a handful of precious gems. He was bald except for some ragged dreadlocklike wisps that trailed from the sides of his scarred, melon-shaped head. His skin had been ravaged by whatever childhood ailment had marked him.

Levi wore a caftan of fine, brightly colored cloth that looked to Bolan like silk. His sausage-thick fingers were festooned with gold rings, and he wore what had to have been half pound of gold chains around his thick neck.

When the massive arms dealer leaned forward in his chair, fixed Bolan with a baleful glare and put an ivory, bell-mouthed pipe up to his lips, Bolan knew he was dealing with a truly dangerous man. Levi had the look. He might be fat, he might be scarred and he might look silly, but Levi was a killer who would not hesitate to order Bolan and Bayard slaughtered.

"What you want, man?" Levi asked. His accent was a curious mixture of American and Jamaican, without a hint of French influence. The patois was hard to define. It appeared to be an affected accent.

"I'm told," Bolan said, "that Levi can get me anything. That Levi is the man to see. And that Levi is not a man to fuck around with."

Levi stared for a moment longer. Then he closed his eyes, tilted back his head and laughed. Bolan had never heard anything quite like it.

It was deep and sonorous, but it was also edged with a higher pitch, as if Levi's vocal cords were distending from the strain of the air being propelled through and past them. When Levi finally stopped guffawing, he held his massive stomach, and rocked forward and back, silently, his mouth open as if he were still laughing. No sound escaped him for at least a full minute.

Finally he opened his eyes again.

"You make me laugh. I like that. Yes. You give Levi trouble, Levi gives you more trouble than you ever want, ever need, ever live through."

"My name is Belasko," Bolan said, deliberately avoiding the use of his cover identity. There was no telling what kind of law enforcement notices about Agent Cooper had made their way into Red Spiders territory.

"Belasko," Levi repeated, rolling the name around in his mouth. "Belasko. Belasko. What you want, Belasko?"

"Military-grade weaponry. An M16/M203, preferably. A supply of 40 mm grenades, including frag, incendiary and antipersonnel buckshot if you have it. That .44 Magnum Desert Eagle I see on the table there, provided it's in good shape. Extra magazines for it, loaded. A Beretta 93R machine pistol and a supply of 20-round box magazines, loaded. As many loaded 5.56 mm 30-round magazines as I can carry. A small tactical flashlight if you have one, no less than 60 lumens minimum. And something for my friend. Maybe a MAC-10, plus ammo for it."

Levi blinked. "No knife?"

"I have one," Bolan said.

Levi's curious laughter broke across the room, shaking the massive arms dealer so hard that he nearly lost his delicate perch on his upholstered chair. Finally with much coughing and wheezing, he managed to calm himself. He snapped his fingers and one of the door guards brought him a can of beer from a cooler hidden behind Levi's three-table desk.

"I have one," Levi repeated, as if it were the punch line to a hilarious joke. He sipped his beer. Bolan did not recognize the brand.

Bayard looked from Bolan to Levi and back again. The guards at the door were fidgeting around quite a bit. Bolan had noticed it, too. This did not bode well for their chances.

"And what you offer me?" Levi asked. "That quite an order, Belasko. Quite an order. But I can do this. If you can pay me."

Bolan pulled out his wad of euros. He put it on the table in front of Levi and then backed up a pace. Levi took the money, smelled it. Then he put it in his mouth and mashed it with his lips, as if he were trying to make sure it was real. Then he counted it, very carefully. Twice.

"Not enough," he pronounced.

"That's why I brought some trade items," Bolan said. He hefted the duffel bag he and Bayard had dragged through the shantytown. He placed it as respectfully on the table as he could. Levi shoved weapons aside to make room for it, impatient to unzip it. Then he looked inside. The chopped AR with its double-drum magazine seemed to be the only thing he really noticed.

"Oh," he said. "Oh, my, Belasko. This here. I like this. Okay. I take this and these other things." He snapped his fingers again. One of the guards disappeared and, when he returned in a few minutes, he was carrying a heavy canvas bag of his own. The bag was placed at Bolan's feet.

"Open it," Levi ordered imperiously. "Everything be there."

Bolan glanced at Bayard, not quite believing that was possible. When he looked, though, Levi had been true to his word. Bolan began arming himself, placing loaded magazines in his musette bag, shoving the Desert Eagle—a brand new and very gaudy chromed model—in his waistband and the Beretta 93R opposite it. He hadn't been kidding about having a knife. The switchblade was still in his pants pocket. He handed the MAC-10 and its magazines to Bayard and watched as the inspector loaded the weapon.

Bolan slung his new M16/M203 assault rifle–grenade launcher combo and filled his shoulder bag with grenades.

Levi watched, seemingly pleased. He was absently munching a snack cake of some kind, one of a pile next to his upholstered chair, when he started as if someone had poked him. Fishing around inside his caftan, he produced a wireless phone. The tiny slimline device looked comically small in his thick hand.

"This here Levi," the arms dealer said, after snapping the phone open. His eyes widened in surprise. Then he pressed a button on the phone and stared at the device. A moment later, it chimed. He pressed another button.

"A pleasure doing business with you," Bolan said. "We'll be on our way now."

Levi held up a fat finger. "Hold up now. Here. Look this." He thrust the phone at Bolan. There was a picture displayed on the phone's screen.

It was Bolan.

The image appeared to be from a traffic camera. Levi closed the phone and tucked it away again.

"Problem?" Bolan asked.

"Problem," Levi replied. "Red Spiders in charge now. I sell to them. I sell to you. I don't care. But I live with the Red Spiders. They say I'm in the gang, I'm in the gang. Business. But I can't let you go. Spiders business. Gotta stop you. Sorry. Keeping your money."

Bolan made a show of hitching his thumbs in his waistband and sighing. "That's going to be a problem, Levi."

"You said yourself. You don't mess with me. I'm a bad man."

"I don't care if you're the baddest man in the whole damn town, Levi," the Executioner said. His tone turned darkly serious. "We're stepping out of here under our own power. If you *don't* let us walk out of here, when we do leave, we're going to be leaving footprints in your blood."

Levi's hideous face fell. His brow furrowed. He was thinking about it.

Bolan's hands edged closer to the butts of his weapons.

"The DCRI has access to the traffic camera feeds," Bayard said. "This is systemic corruption, Cooper."

"He is Cooper," Levi stated. "Not Belasko. I know it."

"Corruption is a way of life here," Bayard said. "It sickens me."

"You can't leave," Levi told them. He glared suddenly.

Bolan took a step backward. "Like I said, big man," he warned. "We're leaving." The words were meaningless. Levi had been given his orders by the Red Spiders, to whom he was beholden no matter what might be his personal thoughts on underworld politics in Paris. No doubt the man was kept well fed by a steady stream of gun sales to the local gangs. He would not endanger that.

Bolan backed up until he was standing between the two sentries. They began to unsling their rifles. He looked at them. They looked nervously back at him.

"I would run," Bolan advised them.

The two sentries exchanged worried glances.

"Kill them!" Levi roared.

Bolan yanked the guns from his waistband, extended his arms and pulled both triggers.

The Beretta loosed a 3-round burst. Two hollowpoint rounds from the .44 Magnum Desert Eagle cracked liked thunder. The heads of the two sentries practically exploded, painting the walls of the shack with blood and gore.

Bolan charged the fat man's desk. He plowed through the triple table setup, upending the platforms, throwing them aside, until he was face-to-face with Levi. The arms dealer was not helpless, however. He ripped open his caftan to reveal a suicide vest ringed with cylinders of plastic explosive.

"You can't touch Levi!" he shouted. He raised a trigger switch connected to his vest by a wire. One big thumb was poised over the button. "This a dead-man's switch, and when I press—"

Bolan shot him in the face.

The Desert Eagle blew whatever Levi had been about to say through the back of his head and out the wall of the shack.

"Let us make like a stand of trees and depart quickly," Bayard said.

Bolan shot him a look. "What?"

"Did I say it wrong, Cooper?"

"Remind me to ask you later if you were just screwing with me," Bolan replied. He checked the doorway. There were armed Red Spiders guards moving along the walkway leading from Levi's shack and more on the way in response to the gunfire.

"What is that?" Bayard asked.

Bolan listened. It was a bell of some kind, being rung repeatedly, perhaps hit by a mallet. "Local alarm, I'm guessing. And we just triggered it. Come on."

The big soldier tucked away his guns and brought the M16 to his shoulder. It felt good to be behind a powerful, properly configured battle rifle again. The flat-top M16 boasted an expensive holographic sight. He crept along the walkway in a half crouch with Bayard bringing up the rear. The Frenchman's MAC-10 was good support, capable of throwing a lot of lead very fast in close quarters.

"Above! Above!" Bayard shouted. He aimed the machine pistol upward and, with the wire stock braced against his shoulder, sprayed the corrugated roof of Levi's shack, dislodging a Red Spiders guard with a revolver. The dead man crashed into an adjacent shanty and caused it to collapse in a heap. There was a lot of yelling and cursing from underneath the wreckage.

"Cooper, which way?" Bayard asked.

"Follow me." Bolan ramped up to a run and poured on the speed. Gunfire crackled all around him. He raised the M16 and began firing in long, measured bursts, first to the left, then to the right, hammering away as more guards boiled out of the shanties.

Something was wrong. What was it? He could not quite put his finger on it. Then it hit him.

The shanties were all wrong. In the third world a settlement like this one betrayed all aspects of human life. There were lines of drying laundry. There were children playing in the muck. There were men and women going about the business that men and women have gone about for thousands of years, ranging from love to politics to simply making a living. He had seen no shops. He had seen no real activity of any kind except for guards, sealed shacks and Levi's centralized lair.

He had expected there to be innocents. He had expected that he would need to choose his shots very carefully to avoid catching any civilians, any bystanders, in the line of fire. It quickly became apparent that Levi and the Red Spiders had turned this little settlement into some kind of headquarters for the gang, centered around the arms dealer's commercial activities.

Bolan stopped. Bayard nearly crashed into him from behind. He put one hand on Bolan's shoulder and half-turned him.

"Cooper! Are you all right? What is it?"

"Levi's shack. It's full of weapons and explosives. And this whole settlement is a Red Spiders safehouse. There are no kids here. No other people. Just gang members. That's all we've seen."

"You're right," Bayard said. "What are you going to do?"

"Cover me."

Bayard took up a position on Bolan's flank. He immediately began firing measured bursts from his MAC-10 as more Red Spiders gang members closed in from all sides. They were trying to squeeze between the shacks, crawl along the roofs and sneak from one side through to the other in those shacks that had small window holes or pairs of doors. Bayard swapped magazines, pulled the bolt back and renewed his efforts.

Bolan snapped open the M203 grenade launcher. He inserted a 40 mm incendiary grenade, closed the launcher and took careful aim as he shouldered the weapon.

The launcher chuffed as he triggered the round.

The grenade sailed down the walkway, threading the needle between the closest shacks and entered the open doorway of Levi's shanty. Bolan turned, grabbed Bayard and shoved him forward.

"Run for the exit," Bolan instructed. "We'll steal a car once we get there. Make distance, Inspector."

The explosion that erupted at their backs was not a single burst. It was a staggered, layered series of detonations, a staccato rhythm of thunderclaps that built to a crescendo as the heat from each new reaction added to the bloom of flame and light that incinerated the pitiful shanty. Whatever explosives had been stockpiled within burned a crater deep into the ground, shredding the nearby shacks and sending wooden and metal debris dozens of feet into the air. Around Bolan and Bayard, it began to rain pieces of shanties...and pieces of men.

It was the distraction they needed. The two men made the perimeter of the settlement, and then put another two blocks between themselves and the networks of shanties. Bolan located a Peugeot that looked relatively new and had commercial courier tags, much to Bayard's relief. Using the switchblade, Bolan cut his way into the wires under the dash, made the necessary connections and switched on the interior lights. Then he struck the ignition and got the car going. They were soon on their way.

Behind them a pall of black smoke marked the destruction of Levi the arms dealer and the Red Spiders gangsters who had been guarding him.

"Cooper," Bayard said.

"Yeah?"

"You enjoy doing things the hard way."

Bolan rolled down his window. As the car sped on through the streets of Paris, headed out of the city, the Executioner allowed himself a smile.

"Sometimes," he admitted.

CHAPTER TWENTY-THREE

Outside the Gaston Estate, Marseille

The idyllic countryside outside Marseille sped by. With the window of the stolen Peugeot down, Bolan thought he could smell the Mediterranean Sea in the air. The two men had traveled in silence, for the most part, but it had been a comfortable silence. Bayard had come a long way since his earlier suspicion of Bolan. Seeing the elephant, as the saying went—getting into the thick of it and facing down the war from the inside—was enough to convert a lot of men. Bayard was a decent man at heart.

They were discussing that fact as they neared the Gaston estate.

"I told you," Bayard said. "I have not always behaved as a police officer should. I have accepted certain bribes. Spread others. Used these as leverage to create a practical condition, one that I thought benefited the people in my charge. I am not a good man."

"Yes, you are," Bolan said. "You're putting it on the line to do the right thing now. Risking your life. I don't know if that's absolution, Inspector, but it's as close to it as any of us get. I know a certain pilot who used to take money to look the other way. He worked for criminal syndicates for years. But when it came down to it, he realized he could do the right thing, realized he had a choice. He decided to start fighting for what's right, and he's been doing that ever since. He's one of my oldest friends in the world, and I wouldn't believe anybody who tried to tell me he's not a good person…despite his previous failings, despite the times he looked the other way."

"I do not know."

"I do," Bolan said. "That's how these things work."

They had acquired a prepaid cell phone at a shop outside Paris. Bolan had used it to communicate with the Farm, updating them on his mission. Using a commercial express courier, Bolan had shipped Tessier's hard drive to a drop point that the Farm's intelligence network would access to recover it.

The information on that hard drive would go a long way toward putting things right on the political scene, especially with Franco-American relations roiled as they were. But until that data could be processed, the Man did not want Gaston harmed in any way.

Yet Price, Brognola, the President and Bolan all knew that rooting out Gaston, dealing him the Executioner's brand of justice, was exactly what Mack Bolan was going to do.

"Roadblock," Bayard said suddenly. "Cooper, roadblock!"

Bolan hit the brakes. The Peugeot slowed, but the police had chosen their ambush point carefully. The checkpoint was visible just around a blind curve and, behind them, another police car was moving into position to stop them. These were two uniformed policemen before them. Two cars had been parked in a V-formation, permitting only the most careful access between them.

Bolan could not shoot the policemen any more than he could fly over them.

"Better stop," Bayard said. "Perhaps I can talk our way out of this."

"Worth a try."

They pulled up to the checkpoint. The uniformed men were young and nervous. The lead cop, a blond who looked like he'd never had to shave, approached the passenger side of the vehicle. Bolan worked up his most pleasant smile.

"Good day, Officer," Bolan said in French.

"Step out of the vehicle, sir," the policeman replied. "You and your traveling companion match the description of wanted fugitives. We are calling for more men. You would be wise simply to—"

Bolan hit him in the throat.

There was no time to argue, and they were going to be boxed in if he didn't do something drastic. He was very careful to pull his blow, rapping the man on the side of the neck, knocking him sprawling to the pavement. A strike there at full power could have serious consequences. As it was, the policeman was stunned, and he'd likely have a hell of a headache caused by the edge-of-hand blow to the area of the carotid artery.

Bolan threw himself over the hood of the car. He used both feet to crash into the legs of the other cop, bringing him down to the pavement. Once he had the man there he applied a rear naked choke, folding his arms around the man's neck and pressing the back of the policeman's head into Bolan's hold. It did not take long to put the cop to sleep. The soldier set him down gently.

The third car hit its lights and a peculiar-sounding siren and began to burn pavement toward them. Bolan reached into the Peugeot, pulled out the M16 and blasted away. He managed to get two of the car's four tires and then burned away several pieces of the car's engine as the grille came around to face him.

"He can do us no real harm," Bayard said. "You will not hurt him?"

"Of course not. I didn't hurt them, either." He jerked his chin to the two men on the ground. "Not that much. They'll be fine. I can't speak to their wounded pride."

Bayard moved over to the driver's seat. "Come on, Cooper," he said. "Let us—"

"Make like a stand of trees?" Bolan interrupted. "I'm all for that."

They were very close to the Gaston estate when they heard the helicopter. Bolan leaned out the window and looked up. "I was afraid of that," he said. "They must have radioed for air support. We're going to have to deal with that helicopter somehow."

"Can the grenade launcher knock it down?" Bayard asked.

"No, not even if they weren't cops."

"But they are not cops," Bayard said. "That is a civilian helicopter. It is not a law enforcement aircraft."

"Then we have bigger problems, because it's trailing us, and it's coming down for a run."

"A run?"

"A strafing run," Bolan explained.

Just then, automatic gunfire raked the road on either side of them, ripping the mirror from the passenger side of the Peugeot. Bayard did his best to chart a random course, swaying left and right, but the helicopter stuck to them.

A man with a red bandanna tied around his neck was leaning out the side door of the chopper, held in place by a harness anchored to the helicopter's crew area. He had an FN Minimi on a second harness around his body. It was a fearsome weapon, fielded by the United States military as the Squad Automatic Weapon, the SAW. The chopper passed them and began making a wide circle. The pilot was looking for a better angle, while keeping the gunner out of range.

"Corruption is a way of life, Cooper," Bayard said. "The police must have orders to communicate our position to elements within the Red Spiders. Vigneau is still using them to eliminate us."

"Do you think he's trying to protect Gaston?"

"Doubtful. You said yourself that what is left of Levesque and his ES is guarding Gaston at the estate. Vigneau does not care much for politics as long as he controls the streets. He will be prepared to work with Gaston as readily as anyone else, but the elections are already chaos. Vigneau will not care about that. This is about his control. His ability to eliminate us."

"My people won't be happy about what I'm going to do to Gaston," Bolan said. "But it's what's best for the country and, more important, it's what's best for the French people. Gaston's a power-mad, corrupt lunatic. Not to mention a murderer who consorts with and uses terrorists. He can't be allowed to ascend to power. Just the appearance of legitimacy will make him that much harder to dislodge, like an engorged tick."

"That is colorful," Bayard said. "I agree with you. We should—"

Whatever Bayard was going to say was cut off by the violent maneuver he was forced to make. The Frenchman turned the wheel so hard that Bolan felt the passenger-side wheels come off the ground. The helicopter was back, strafing them again. The SAW's bullets chewed up the road on the driver's side, tearing into and through the Peugeot, doing serious damage to the engine compartment. Black smoke began to pour from the engine. The vehicle slowed.

There was blood all over the seats.

"Bayard!" Bolan shouted. He had the M16 in his lap and was trying to find an angle from which to return fire on the chopper. The pilot was good, though; he was using his height advantage to keep the craft to the rear and sides of the Peugeot, putting the car's roof struts between the chopper and Bolan, using the ground vehicle's natural blind spots.

"I am all right," Bayard said. He was clenching the wheel with white knuckles. "A scratch. Much blood, but nothing serious. We must get off the road or he is going to get alongside us and kill us at his leisure. Stop looking at me that way. I am all right, I tell you."

But Bayard was not all right. He was gravely wounded, perhaps mortally so. He had taken shrapnel to the face and blood was freely flowing down the side of his head. He was steering with one arm, clutching at himself. Bolan wanted to stop and look him over, but there simply wasn't time to argue with him. Then the idea hit the soldier.

We must get off the road or he is going to get alongside us, Bayard had said.

That was it.

"Bayard," Bolan instructed, "slow down. Get over, put lots of room between you and the opposite side of the road. I want you to look as juicy as bait can look."

Gaston's estate loomed ahead. The road they traveled was a winding one, but it led to the large building. A low wall encircled the estate, most likely providing cover for multiple gunmen. Bolan relished the thought of getting into the thick of battle with the ES once more. It was time to smash those terrorists for good.

"Trust me," Bolan said. "We can do this."

Bayard nodded. He slowed the car, and, just as the soldier had hoped, the chopper dipped low. The SAW gunner was probably urging his pilot on, too. He wanted the delicious target that was the Peugeot directly in his sights, broadside, like a tiny sailing vessel bracketed by a mighty galleon, helpless under the onslaught of the larger vessel's guns.

"That's right," Bolan said softly. "You want it. Come get it."

Blossoms of gunfire began to glitter along the wall surrounding the estate.

"They are shooting at us from the house," Bayard stated. "They must be in contact with the helicopter."

The chopper crept up, low and slow, on the passenger side of the Peugeot. The skids were scant feet from the ground now. The SAW gunner lined up his shot and savored the thought of it. He began to lean into the butt of his weapon on its harness.

"Bayard," Bolan shouted. "Make a hard left, now!" He brought up the M16 and shoved it out the window.

The SAW gunner saw it, but too late. Bolan triggered the grenade launcher as Bayard pulled the damaged Peugeot away from the chopper. The grenade struck the aluminum skin of the helicopter and detonated.

Bolan would always remember the expression on the face of the gunner when his world turned to fire.

The grenade tore open the chopper and spilled it and its contents across the vast field next to the estate's approach road. The SAW landed in the dirt. The tail of the chopper ripped through the rear of the Peugeot, spinning the car, pushing it over on its side. Bolan tasted blood as something smacked him in the side of the head. His ears rang with the force of the blast.

Then the vehicle stopped moving.

Bolan crawled out of the Peugeot, dragging the wounded Bayard with him. Their stolen car was now standing on its side with part of a helicopter sticking out of its trunk. The car was good cover as bullets began to rattle around and past it. Bolan risked a look past the chassis. A delegation, of sorts, was driving out along the estate road. It was a pickup truck full of men in camouflage fatigues and black face masks.

Some portion of what was left of ES was coming to meet him.

Bolan made sure Bayard was sitting up and resting as comfortably as he was able. There was a lot of blood. The Frenchman looked at Bolan, dazed, but the soldier shook his head. "Stay here," he said. "Don't try to move too much."

Bolan was going to give the ES what they came for.

He found the M16 on the ground. It had been thrown from the vehicle, but it did not look damaged. He checked it, made sure a round was chambered and loaded a fresh 40 mm grenade into the M203. Then, using the Peugeot to shelter his body, he waited for the truck to come just close enough.

"American!" someone from the back of the pickup truck shouted through a bullhorn. "Surrender and you will not be killed."

"That's fine for me," Bolan said, "but what are you going to do about not getting killed?" He stepped away from the damaged car, flicked the M16's selector switch to 3-round-burst setting and stroked a symphony of death from the trigger, laying into the oncoming vehicle with precise trios of 5.56 mm NATO rounds.

He shattered the headlights and the mirrors. He perforated the radiator and spiderwebbed the windshield.

He watched as blood coated the interior of the truck, and the dead driver, slumping against the wheel, turned it too sharply in his death throes. The pickup truck tried to make a ninety-degree turn and failed, flipping over, crushing several of the ES troops beneath its spinning, hurtling chassis.

Bolan emptied his magazine into the ES gunmen.

There were some who were still alive and some who were wounded. All were still a threat. This was no time for mercy.

When he was certain no resistance remained, he set his sights on Gaston's estate. He judged the distance; it was not too far. He gauged the angle; it was not too severe. Then, with his M16/M203 combination, he advanced on the estate and began firing high-explosive and incendiary grenades at the wall around the estate perimeter, targeting the muzzle flashes of enemy guns.

The gunfire sometimes reached out for him, came close to him, grazed the dirt at his feet. Bolan ignored it. He was intent only on unleashing his lethal payload on the men trying to protect Gaston. Finally when he ran out of grenades, he began firing the M16, using the holographic site, emptying magazine after magazine, reloading automatically, using aimed bursts to bring down all who dared to mount that perimeter and oppose him.

It was not enough; it was never going to be enough to take and hold the building. For that the Executioner would have to enter. He would have to bring the fight right up under the enemies' noses. He was fueled by a desire to once and for all bring his mission to a close.

He was spurred by righteous anger about all the innocents who had died at the hands of the ES, at the hands of the gang leaders and the corrupt officials, at the hands and through the machinations of corrupt men like Jean Vigneau. It was these conditions that the Executioner had set out to correct, to put right, to eliminate with the force of his guns and his fists and his fury.

The immediate threat was nullified, and the next step was to proceed to the main house. But first he had to see to Alfred Bayard, who he knew was dying.

Stinking of war, Bolan went back to the Peugeot and knelt next to Bayard, who leaned against the upended car and stared at the blue sky. Tears were running down his right cheek. His left cheek was covered in blood. He was smiling.

"Inspector?"

"It is beautiful," Bayard said. "It is beautiful because it is the last thing I shall see. The blue sky of Marseille. The clouds. A flock of birds. And the black smoke of your revenge, Cooper. I am not going to survive, am I?"

Bolan paused. He checked once more, to be sure. He had been right; when Bayard was wounded in the attack, it had been mortal. His condition was not the result of the crash.

The soldier had seen enough wounded men to know. It was a miracle that Bayard had hung on this long, in fact. How he had continued to drive like that, Bolan could only chalk up to an iron will. Bayard's shirt was completely soaked through with blood. He had one arm wrapped around his abdomen, and it was holding in his intestines. A piece of shrapnel had blinded him in one eye, but he did not seem to notice.

"Can you do one thing for me, Cooper?"

"I will."

"Please," the inspector said. "It is going to drive me crazy for not knowing. Who are you, Cooper? What are you?"

"I'm a member of a counterterrorist organization,"

Bolan told him. "The Sensitive Operations Group. I was sent here specifically because of the threat to American interests represented by ES's interference in the elections…and because of the people I could help. The lives I could save. Using methods that…well, that you didn't approve of when we met."

Bayard smiled again. "Of course. Of course I did not. Who are you, Cooper?"

"I'm just an American," the Executioner said.

"You are a liar. But I thank you. It…it felt good, Cooper, to do the right thing. To fight…to fight for… what was right…"

"Inspector, I want you to know that you're a good man. And it was an honor fighting beside you."

"You can tell me your name," Bayard said. "I will not have time to tell anyone before I die."

"My name," the soldier told him, "is Mack Bolan."

"I…know that…name…" Bayard whispered. He was struggling now. "I remember. I *remember*."

"So do I," Bolan said to the dead man. Bayard now stared at the sky without seeing it. A look of peace had come over his features.

Mack Bolan stood and looked down at Bayard, offering a quick prayer to the universe. Then he checked his M16/M203. He had emptied its grenades and most of its ammunition. It had served its purpose. He discarded it. The fallen SAW appeared undamaged. He picked it up, slung its heavy weight over his shoulder and made sure it was ready to fire.

The Executioner walked toward the house, ready to take on everyone inside. He did not look back at Bayard.

He did not look back at his friend.

CHAPTER TWENTY-FOUR

Mack Bolan stalked through the halls of Gaston's main house. The resistance he had encountered outside had been the majority of the forces arrayed against him. Once inside the lavish home, he had found relatively few enemies. Those he did, he cut down unceremoniously with the SAW. The weapon's heavy rounds and high rate of fire enabled the Executioner to scythe through his opponents.

Bolan prowled through the halls, checking every room he came across, searching for Gaston. He rounded a corner and gut-shot an ES terrorist who almost ran into him. The SAW blew the man onto his back, and Bolan stepped over him.

He found himself facing an ornate wooden door. The French word for "library" was carved into its frame. He tried the doorknob, which turned at his touch.

Gerard Levesque stood there. "You!"

"Me," Bolan said, dropping his chin, peering at Levesque with death in his eyes. "I hope you're ready for that trip to the other side we talked about, because I'm going to send you there screaming, Levesque."

Levesque actually paled. "My men are dead," he said. "There is no one left but Gaston, hiding at the pool. He is through these doors behind me." He pointed to the set of doors at the other end of the library. "We dismissed all the girls, all the hangers-on. We were prepared to fight you tooth and nail…but yours were the sharper teeth, yours the stronger nails. So. You can kill me. Or you can bring me in."

"I'm not bringing you in."

"Think of the information I have at my disposal," Levesque pleaded. "My knowledge of international terrorism, my connections."

"I'm prepared to live without that," Bolan said. "Seeing as how I was going to let you do the honorable thing and blow your brains out."

"But I can be of so much help to you and your organization, Cooper!"

"I don't want your help." The soldier leveled the SAW. "I'm going to cut you in two now. Although if you'd like to blow your brains out before I do, be my guest. I figure you've got one coming."

Levesque held up his hands. "Please! Please! Do not kill me, Cooper."

Bolan's jaw worked. Finally he said, "You're right. Shooting you in cold blood like this, while you're begging. I can't do it."

Levesque looked relieved.

"Do you have a gun?"

"I do," Levesque replied.

"Drop it."

Levesque removed the item from his coat and threw it far across the library.

Bolan unslung the SAW. His shoulders ached from its weight. He fixed Levesque with a glare.

"You have a knife?"

"Yes. Shall I lose that, as well?"

"No," Bolan said. "I want you to *use* it."

Bolan dropped the SAW to the floor. The switchblade snapped open in his hand. He charged Levesque, and the Frenchman, operating on instinct, reacted, slipping back, dodging the blade. His own fighting knife came out in his hand. It was a bayonet of some kind, an old M7, Bolan thought. Levesque's expression changed when, suddenly, he thought he might have a fighting chance.

"A duel?" he said. "You actually want to *duel* me, Cooper? I'm flattered that anyone could be so foolish. You thought Lemaire was good with a knife? I'm better."

"You talk too much."

Levesque tried a series of savate kicks. Bolan easily dodged them. Levesque was fast, but he lacked practical experience against a man who wasn't fooled by his tricks and refused to fight at Levesque's preferred range. With each kick, Bolan would step in, smashing away with hammer-fist blows to Levesque's thighs, until finally Levesque gave up on the technique. His movements were less agile now. He was feeling the beating.

Their knives flashed. Bolan surged forward, direct, unafraid. He slashed and stabbed, working an angle pattern, pressing his attack. Levesque proved adept at staying out of the "barrel," the zone in which the knife was dangerous to the opponent.

The Frenchman used very precise footwork to turn back and away at forty-five-degree angles, staying out of the range of a counterattack. But he was trying to pass Bolan's blade and step in for a thrust or a slash of his own, and he was finding this difficult. That was because Levesque knew knife fighting, savate and close-quarters combat very well.

But Mack Bolan was more adept.

"I have always wanted to have a grand, climactic battle like this with a worthy adversary," Levesque said as they moved back and forth. He seemed to have no lack of wind with which to jaw while he fought Bolan. The pair fought for a few minutes more until Bolan decided he was tired of toying with the French terror leader.

Then Bolan poured on the power.

The knife was not a weapon that required strength behind it. This was what made the blade so effective. It merely had to be fast, clever, to get past an opponent's defenses and cut deep. Combine those attributes with good footwork, good structure to one's techniques, and you had a "knife fighter," a man who was very deadly with his chosen weapon.

Combine all of that with real strength, with raw power, and you had a warrior. You had a special operations soldier.

You had an executioner.

With a grunt, Bolan stepped in, and now when Levesque tried to deploy his techniques, the soldier slapped the man's arms away with such power that the blows were dealing damage by themselves. The pain began to register on his adversary's face. Bolan was hammering away at him with a ferocity he had not expected and had not previously encountered.

Levesque came in again. Bolan let the strike come.

He lowered his knife and smashed Levesque's forearm between his right elbow and his left hand, snapping the bone. The terrorist leader screamed as his knife fell to the floor.

"Cooper—"

"This isn't a grand, climactic battle, Levesque. This is a rabid dog being put down."

As Levesque tried to retrieve his blade, Bolan slammed his switchblade into the hollow of Levesque's throat, jerked it left then right and then turned it as he yanked it out.

The terror leader collapsed in a gurgling, bleeding, dying mess.

Bolan stepped over him and walked away without a second glance. He pushed through the doors leading from the library and headed for the pool area.

He found the man who would be France's next president hiding under one of the pieces of pool furniture. But he was not alone. He was flanked by two more uniformed ES terrorists.

"Now that's masculine imagery," Bolan said. He drew the Desert Eagle from his belt and shot the first armed man through the face. The second tried to raise his Makarov, but Bolan simply moved the triangular muzzle of his chromed .44 Magnum hogleg two inches to the right. The bullet dug a crater through the man's skull.

Now Gaston was cowering underneath a table while a pool of blood closed in on him from both sides.

"Gaston, I'm going to have to ask you to come out from hiding."

Gaston looked up at him. "You're going to murder me."

"That's not what I do."

"You murdered all of *them*," he said. "What of Levesque?"

"He was alive when I last saw him," Bolan said, which was true.

"Alive?"

"A little. Let's go, Gaston, we're done here." He reached down, grabbed the man by the collar of his button-down shirt and dragged him bodily from behind the table.

"What are you going to do with me?"

"You're going to write a letter of resignation," Bolan said. "Or whatever you call it. You're going to hand-write it. Say you've changed your mind. You've given up on politics. The cost is too great and all that. Come on. Let's go find you some stationery in the library."

The sight of Levesque's staring corpse galvanized Gaston. He wrote the letter Bolan asked him to write and left it on the writing table in the library. Then, as if this had lifted a weight off him, he turned to Bolan.

"I kill people, you know. I'm just like you."

Bolan stared. "What?"

"It's just something we do. We're alike. You killed Levesque. I've killed people like that before. Well, not quite like that. But I have. We don't have to be enemies. We could work something out. I can pay you a great deal of money."

"You're going to prison for what you've done," Bolan said. "Complicity in terrorism. Murder of your rival. A host of lesser crimes. You won't see the sun for a long time."

"But I will," Gaston told him.

Bolan stopped and looked at him.

Gaston, encouraged, grinned widely. "I have the best lawyers and plenty of money. They will let me out soon enough. And when they do, I will kill again. I will devote my next victim to you and to America. And every time I kill again after that, it will be because you couldn't stop me."

Bolan grabbed the Frenchman and dragged him back to the pool.

"Wait!" Gaston cried. "What are you doing! Stop!"

The big American said nothing. He was thinking of innocent lives. Innocent lives that would be taken by a damaged soul like Gaston's, a man who had just told Bolan that he would murder other people in the name of shaming whomever let Gaston live.

He walked into the pool at the shallow end, dragging Gaston. In a desperation play, the Frenchman tried to ram his elbow into Bolan's throat, but it was no go.

The soldier wrenched away his arm and hip-rolled the man into the edge of the pool. As Gaston recovered and tried to head butt his adversary, Bolan grabbed him by the neck and the top of the head, pushed him down into the water. He held Gaston there until he stopped moving.

And that was all there was.

EPILOGUE

Washington, D.C.

Hal Brognola watched the waters of the Potomac, leaning on the railing running along the edge of West Potomac Park. In the distance the Lincoln Memorial was visible. Around him a few civilians walked or ran. It was a warm day in Wonderland, and Brognola was feeling the heat under his suit jacket. He reached up and loosened his tie.

"Isn't this the park where we almost got mugged that time?" Mack Bolan asked, walking up to join his old friend at the railing.

"*You* almost got mugged," Brognola stated. "You draw trouble like a magnet draws metal."

"Seriously, Hal," Bolan said, turning to him. "I know what this had to have cost you in political capital. You know I wouldn't have put you through that needlessly. It had to be done."

Brognola sighed. "I do. And so does the Man. But he isn't thrilled about where we ended up, if only because of how we got there."

"Do we have a problem?"

"No. He's a pragmatist, just like every man before him who's held that office. He won't interfere with SOG. You saved the French elections, Striker. Although...I have to be honest. You're putting an awful strain on the Cooper identity."

"Another legend is born," Bolan said. "So what's the word from the French government?"

"The DCRI is cleaning house. They've appointed an up-and-comer to head up the investigation, and apparently he's taking scalps. Fellow by the name of Flagel."

"Flagel?" Bolan asked. "Seriously? Bayard thought he'd been killed."

"He was wounded by compromised elements from within the DCRI. I think that's one of the reasons they picked him. They have a flair for the dramatic. It's a real Eliot Ness kind of scenario."

"I wish him luck," Bolan said. "And Jean Vigneau?"

"Corrupt as they come. He has ties to the gangs currently operating in Paris, or what's left of them. Apparently the issue was building for a while. We've uncovered evidence of some pretty serious financial traffic between the gang leader, Roelle, and Vigneau's office. It explains why the situation on the ground in Paris was allowed to get as bad as it did.

"When you upset the balance of power on the street, you hurt Vigneau financially. He pulled out all the stops to nail you and forgot to cover his trail in the computer. Not to mention giving up any pretense of using the DCRI for anything but his personal hit squad. You beat him mentally, Striker. You broke him. He did the rest of the work for us."

"He's in custody?"

"In the worst prison they have," Brognola replied. "The French aren't thrilled about a glorified criminal holding such a high position of power. I think if they still had the Bastille, they'd throw him in it."

"And Alfred Bayard?"

"Per your recommendation, and thanks to our renewed relationship with the French government, Inspector Alfred Bayard will be awarded posthumously with membership in the Ordre national de la Légion d'honneur."

"The National Legion of Honor?" Bolan said. "Yeah. I think that works. He was a good man, Hal. Maybe he took some shortcuts to get there, maybe he forgot what he was supposed to be doing along the way…but, when it came down to it, when it counted, he was there. He was on it. And he died doing the right thing, fighting against the corruption and the evil that Vigneau, Levesque and all of their cohorts represented."

"I know," said Brognola. "You don't have to sell me."

"What about the elections?"

"As you probably know from the news," said the big Fed, "it's been a mess. The proof you provided to the Farm has been vetted and already made the news over there. Deparmond—for all the good it does the poor dead bigot—has been cleared of any wrongdoing. Gaston's connections to the ES and to the terror attacks on French soil have come out.

"Apparently a few very imaginative conspiracy theories are becoming popular, at least one of which holds that Gaston was all a patsy to some shadowy organization bent on running France from the confines of a proxy government. His very convenient suicide by drowning just encourages these rumors."

"He left a note and everything, resigning from the elections," Bolan said.

"Striker, don't whiz on my leg and tell me it's raining."

"I looked up conspiracy theories on the internet once. Apparently reptiloid aliens from the center of the earth control everything."

"I've heard that, too," Brognola deadpanned. "The French have scheduled new elections. The candidates are boring and a lot more moderate. Neither really strikes a chord with the Man, so however things work out, we'll be better off, most likely. But with international politics, you just never can tell."

"No, you can't."

"I know what you're thinking," Brognola said. "You're thinking if their government turns bad on us, you'll just go in and topple it."

"Was not."

"Were so." Brognola stood at the railing, looked around and took a deep breath. "You know something, Striker? It really is a wonderful day." He took off his suit jacket, folded it across his arm and checked to make sure nobody had noticed him transfer the clip-on holster from his waistband to under the bundle made by his jacket.

"Glock?" Bolan asked.

"Yeah. The .45. I was feeling nervous when I got up this morning."

"I know the feeling," Bolan said.

"Speaking of nervous, how is your arm healing? Your debrief said you took a pretty bad slash."

"It wasn't deep. Healing fine. I didn't even need stitches."

"I'd hate to pay your medical bills," Brognola said.

"Don't you?" Bolan asked. "I submit for reimbursement, you know."

It took Brognola a moment to realize Bolan was joking. Or at least he thought the soldier was joking. "At any rate," he said, "with the French voters rejecting extremists on both ends of the spectrum, it looks like the White House won't be displeased with the eventual outcome. You saved the French from a colossal blunder, Striker."

"How are we on the interagency front?"

"Nothing succeeds so much as success," said Brognola. "INTERPOL, the DCRI and some other elements within France have got religion about police corruption. Everybody's conducting investigations, and the status of the no-go enclaves in Paris and other major urban centers is being reevaluated."

"You think anything will change?"

"Hard to say," Brognola replied. "Stranger things have occurred."

"Yeah." Bolan turned. "I guess I'll leave you to your stroll then."

"All right, Striker. You're taking your downtime at the Farm, I assume?"

"Yeah," Bolan said. "I'm overdue. I tell you, Hal. I wish this victory felt more like a win. A lot of good people have died. We managed to blunt the impact on the innocent, but Bayard wasn't the only decent guy who bought it this time out."

"You think the cost is too high?" Brognola asked.

"No, I think the fight is worth it. I always have. I just don't want to get complacent. As long as people need me, I'm going to fight for them."

"I know that you will."

"Yeah," Mack Bolan said, leaving his longtime friend to walk back to his parked rental car. Over his shoulder, he said, "Watch yourself on the street, Hal. You never know what sort of people you're going to meet."

Brognola watched the Executioner disappear into the crowd. He shook his head, looked back out over the waters of the Potomac and thought of all the criminals, terrorists and predators who were still alive and free.

"Good hunting, Striker," he said quietly to no one. "And thank you for your service."

* * * * *

DEATH METAL

Extremists play for hidden nuclear weapons in Scandinavia...

When a Scandinavian heavy-metal band claims to possess the ordnance to wage a war, no one takes them seriously. But then a band member is murdered, and the weapons stash proves authentic. With news of the cache spreading, rabid political and paramilitary groups vie to seize the weaponry. The U.S. has just one good move: send in Mack Bolan. The frigid North is about to be blown off the map unless Bolan can force the warmongers to face the music. And the Executioner's tune is almost always deadly.

Available April wherever books and ebooks are sold.

GSB165

The Executioner
Don Pendleton's ®
PATRIOT STRIKE

Superpatriots decide Texas should secede with a bang

After the murder of a Texas Ranger, Mack Bolan is called in to investigate. Working under the radar with the dead Ranger's sister, he quickly learns that rumors of missing fissile material falling into the wrong hands are true. The terrorists, die-hard Americans, are plotting to use the dirty bomb to remove Texas from the Union. As the countdown to D-day begins, the only option is to take the bait of the superpatriots and shut them down from the inside. You don't mess with Texas. Unless you're the Executioner.

GOLD EAGLE ®

Available April wherever books and ebooks are sold.

GEX425

JAMES AXLER

DEATH LANDS®

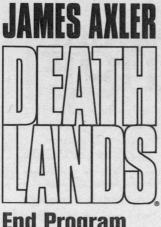

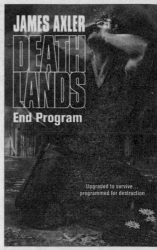

End Program

Newfound hope quickly deteriorates into a fight to save mankind

Built upon a predark military installation, Progress, California, could be the utopia Ryan Cawdor and companions have been seeking. Compared to the Deathlands, the tortured remains of a nuke-altered civilization, Progress represents a fresh start. The successful replacement of Ryan's missing eye nearly convinces the group that their days of hell are over—until they discover the high tech in Progress is actually designed to destroy, not enhance, civilization. The companions must find a way to stop Ryan from becoming a willing pawn in the eradication of mankind....

Available May wherever books and ebooks are sold.

AleX Archer
GRENDEL'S CURSE

A politically ordered excavation unearths more than expected

Skalunda Barrow, rumored to be the final resting place of the legendary Nordic hero Beowulf, is being excavated, thanks to charismatic—and right-wing extremist—politician Karl Thorssen, and archaeologist Annja Creed can't wait. But with the potential to uncover Hrunting and Nægling, two mythical swords the politician would kill to possess, the dig rapidly becomes heated. As Thorssen realizes the power of possessing Nægling, he is quick to show how far he will go to achieve his rabid ambitions. And when Thorssen marks Annja for death, the only way she can survive is to find a sword of her own.

Available May wherever books and ebooks are sold.

The legend of Beowulf could tear a country apart...

GOLD EAGLE®

GRA48

··· James Axler
Outlanders®

NECROPOLIS

When an all-consuming darkness enters Africa, even the fittest may not survive

As immortal god-kings continue to lay claim to the planet as their own, the epic fight to repossess Earth continues. Although the Cerberus rebels exist to protect mankind, nothing can prepare them for what lurks in vampire hell. From her hidden city beneath the African continent, Neekra, the vampire queen, emerges to stake her claim to blood power. As her minions swarm to outmaneuver her rival, the taint of the undead descends across Africa. The rebels race to contain an unfurling horror and escape a dreadful destiny as tortured ambassadors for the vampire kingdom.

Available in May, wherever books and ebooks are sold.